PRAISE FOR THE NOVELS

"Gripping

—Lifeofanavidmc

C000082416

"Freak

—Ron.

"It Blew me away."

—Melena's Reviews

"The plot is sheer poetry."

—Readers' Favorite

"A riveting crime thriller packed with
mind-blowing twists and turns."

—NetGalley Reviewer

"A sassy, edgy page-turner."

—Wall to Wall Books

"A brilliant read."

—NaturalBri Reviews

"A spellbinding thriller."

—The Long and Short of it Reviews

"The suspense keeps you on the edge, while
the emotions tug at your heart."

—Reviewing Shelf

"This is one Wild ride. A very good psychological thriller that
will keep you up until the wee hours of the morning."

—The Cubicle Escapee

"An intense psychological thriller…haunting and complex."

—NetGalley Reviewer

ALSO BY GLEDÉ BROWNE KABONGO

Winds of Fear
Autumn of Fear
Game of Fear
Swan Deception
Conspiracy of Silence

Available in Audio
Conspiracy of Silence
Swan Deception

OUR WICKED LIES

GLEDÉ BROWNE KABONGO

BrowneStar

Media

BrowneStar

Media

www.brownestarmedia.com

OUR WICKED LIES

Copyright © 2021 Gledé Browne Kabongo

All rights reserved. Unauthorized reproduction or distribution of this book is illegal. With the exception of brief quotations embodied in critical articles and reviews, no part of this book may be reproduced in any form by electronic, mechanical or any other device existing or invented hereafter without written permission from the author. These forms include but are not limited to xerography, photocopying, scanning, recording, distribution via internet means or information storage or retrieval systems.

Notice: This book is a work of fiction. The names, characters, places, and incidents are products of the author's imagination or have been used fictitiously. Any resemblance to actual events, locales or persons, living or dead is purely coincidental.

Cover and Interior Design by Qamber Designs & Media

ISBN: 978-1-7333253-9-4

*"The human heart is the most deceitful of all things,
and desperately wicked. Who really knows how bad it is?*
— Jeremiah 17:9 NLT

CHAPTER 1

ALICIA GRAY COULD still taste the acidic bile that had climbed up her throat during the cocktail party last night. The nausea tainted the beauty of the serene suburban morning outside the kitchen window.

If she didn't immediately address what she saw last night, she would lose her nerve. Her emotions had been too raw to confront him on the ride home. Shock and confusion had swallowed her whole as she prepared for bed, so she'd decided to wait until morning, hoping that by then she would have gained some perspective and the answers she craved.

Eliot was finishing his breakfast and would leave for work soon. As he drained the last of his coffee, pushed back from the kitchen table and stood, the idea of dealing with this tension the entire day filled her with dread.

It was now or never. A chill snaked up and down her spine, however. Doubt circled her consciousness. Was she mistaken? Did her eyes deceive her? She closed her eyes and summoned a last-minute dose of courage.

"You got a minute, Eliot?" She turned around to face her husband while fidgeting with a button on her blouse.

Eliot cast an anxious glance at his watch and then back at her. "Can't it wait until tonight?"

Her fingernails dug into her palms. She said, "No, it can't. Have a seat. I'll keep it short."

He adjusted the pocket square in his suit jacket and sat. He blinked twice—his *Am I in trouble?* expression. "Is everything okay?"

Alicia took another deep breath. She couldn't believe she was asking this. "Why did you let her touch you like that?"

He swallowed hard and leaned in, his hands clasped together. "What are you talking about?"

"You know. You and Kat. I saw you."

His breath hitched a little. He reached for his coffee mug and put it back down upon realizing it was empty.

"What did you see?"

She bit her bottom lip. A sob gained momentum. She bit down harder—the inside of her cheeks this time. She wouldn't cry. It would be silly, especially since she didn't have his side of the story yet.

"Kat with her hands all over you. Your crotch, to be exact."

Jealousy curdled in Alicia's stomach once more as she conjured up the image. It happened a mere eight hours ago—Kat and Eliot in a dimly lit alcove of Arnie Tillerson's lavish Beacon Hill townhouse to the tune of Bach's *Brandenburg Concerto No. 3*, the perfect backdrop to the laughter and socializing of the wealthy and influential guests. Attentive servers had kept the champagne flowing and delectable appetizers replenished.

Eliot squeezed his eyes shut. When he opened them, he wouldn't meet her accusing gaze.

"Babe, I'm so sorry. It's not what it looked like. I'd hoped nobody saw. Especially you."

She said nothing, just stared at him. Her words snagged on something deep inside her chest. It was worse than she thought. Not only did he confirm what she'd seen, he'd hoped nobody had caught them.

After a moment of stunned silence, she asked, "You wanted to keep it a secret?"

"I didn't want to upset you or draw attention to the situation. It was embarrassing. Katalina was drunk, out of control. I tried to handle it tactfully."

"You still haven't answered my question," she pressed. "Were you going to tell me that my best friend brazenly felt you up at a cocktail party hosted by your boss, in his home?"

"She caught me off guard, too. I'd never seen her lose it like that."

"I watched the two of you. I wanted to say something, but the shock made me speechless." Alicia finally left the sink and joined him at the table. "Her behavior didn't seem to bother you at all, though, Eliot. Did you enjoy the attention?" She spat the words at him.

"Don't be ridiculous. What do you take me for? I was as shocked by her behavior as you were. It was surreal. Came out of nowhere."

She should be used to it by now, but she wasn't. Women constantly flirted with Eliot. She never thought, however, that her best friend would be counted among those who did. Eliot was long and lean, immaculately clean-shaven with sharp

3

features and a magnetic personality that made it hard to say no to him. She should know; it was what drew her to him in the first place. At forty-six, he was in better shape than most men half his age, thanks to a disciplined exercise regimen and no smoking, drugs, or alcohol.

Alicia, on the other hand, was no great beauty. She was okay with that, though. The only distinguishing physical feature she possessed was a single dimple on her left cheek that went so deep Eliot joked he could crawl into it and hibernate for months. As a stay-at-home mom, she worked overtime to convince herself that it was enough that she kept an impeccable home, was an amazing mother to their two daughters—Eliot's words, not hers—and the perfect corporate wife. That *she* was enough.

Apparently, she wasn't enough. The image flashed before her eyes once more. Eliot hadn't removed Kat's hand right away. Why not? Why wasn't he angry or offended? Maybe it was as he'd said, that he was in shock, just as Alicia had been.

"What if Arnie had rounded the corner and caught you and Kat?" she insisted. "What if Richard had stumbled onto your little display?"

He went slack-jawed, as if the idea of being busted by someone other than his wife never occurred to him. Four years ago, Eliot made partner at Tillerson Brenner, an elite law firm where he specialized in project finance, a highly lucrative sub-specialty of corporate law. He was the only Africa-American to attain that position in the firm's seventy-five-year history. Tillerson Brenner advised some of the largest corporations in the world, and Eliot worked hard to make a name for himself within the firm and with clients in an industry where reputation was everything. He couldn't afford to make careless mistakes. Yet he had.

Eliot stood. "I have to go," he said. "I'm really sorry about last night. I'm sorry it upset you so much. There was no enjoyment or encouragement on my part. I would never disrespect you that way. You're the only woman for me. Nothing and nobody will ever change that."

He came over to her, planted a kiss on her forehead, and told her he loved her. As he grabbed his Bottega briefcase off the kitchen island, he added, "I hope we can put this ugly incident behind us. It was a strange encounter and will never happen again."

After he left, Alicia poured herself another cup of coffee and returned to leaning against the kitchen sink. Her gaze wandered over the scenic backyard, with its expansive views, lush trees, and manicured grass—a stark contrast to the chaotic thoughts bouncing around in her head like rogue tennis balls. She had no reason to doubt Eliot's version of the events from last night. Next week would mark their twentieth wedding anniversary. At no time during their marriage did he ever give her reason to doubt his commitment or fidelity. Not once. However, she couldn't let Kat get away with what she had done. She owed Alicia an explanation.

CHAPTER 2

A LICIA NEARLY SLICED off her index finger as she chopped vegetables for a salad. She slammed the knife down on the kitchen counter and took a minute to compose herself. *It was just a drunken mistake. Don't make a big fuss about it.*

Her best friend had been avoiding her all day. Alicia had left numerous voice messages, texts, and had even emailed her. No response. Kat and Richard DeLuca lived on the same street as Alicia and her family. It would have been easy to march herself over there and demand an explanation, but Alicia neither wanted nor needed a defensive Kat who would put up walls and make extracting the truth ten times harder.

She shoved her irritation aside and went to check on the lasagna in the oven, even though the timer would have alerted her it was ready.

Marston, her oldest daughter, and almost eighteen, sauntered into the kitchen, her long braids cascading down her face. "Hmm. Smells amazing, Mom. Do you need help with anything?"

"Yes, can you finish the salad, then set the table for dinner?

6

I'll get the garlic bread from the oven."

Though she would never admit it to anyone, not even on a whispered breath, Marston was Alicia's favorite child. Marston preferred the simple approach to life in everything from her wardrobe choices to her small social circle and volunteer work. But her firstborn's true love was writing. She had talent, and it wasn't just Alicia's motherly pride talking. Marston had the prizes, and a college acceptance from Hamilton College—a small but elite liberal arts school in upstate New York where she planned to study creative writing.

Her younger daughter, Lily, was the opposite of "no fuss Marston", as the family had nicknamed her. Lily loved fashion and socializing. During the summer months, she altered her makeup and wardrobe choices based on her deepened skin tone. At sixteen, she'd already decided on a legal career, to follow in her father's footsteps. Lily adored children and wanted to spend her career advocating for them, but she would do so with the backing and resources of a top law firm. Practical Lily didn't see any reason that she couldn't rake in the big bucks and still do good in the world.

Alicia was proud of both her girls, their strong sense of self, ambition, and independence. They made her see the possibilities in life. The idea of returning to school to finish the degree she had abandoned, due to a personal tragedy, had been weighing on her mind lately. With Marston heading off to college in the fall and Lily not far behind, Alicia's girls wouldn't need her as much. It was time to finish what she'd started all those years ago. Her abandoned career didn't matter financially—they were well off, thanks to Eliot's jaw-dropping salary and astronomical bonuses. Alicia just wanted to accomplish something on her own.

As Alicia and Marston were putting the finishing touches on the lasagna dinner, Eliot strolled into the kitchen, a few minutes before six—a miracle. He worked grueling hours, usually barely ever home in time for dinner, but she never complained. That was the norm at top firms like Tillerson Brenner.

"Hi, Dad," Marston greeted him as she placed the large bowl of salad on the table.

"Hey, kiddo. How's it going?"

"Great."

He circled Alicia, then kissed her on the mouth. "Guess what I have?"

"What?" She breathed a sigh of relief, glad the tension from this morning's confrontation had faded, though her annoyance with Kat for dodging her calls lingered stubbornly.

He whipped one hand from behind his back and presented Alicia with a bouquet of stunning blood-red roses.

"Thank you, baby," she crooned. "They're beautiful."

"The flowers will shrivel in a few days, but your beauty is eternal," he said.

"Don't make me barf before dinner," Lily declared. She barged into the kitchen with her smartphone in hand and sporting a white Balmain T-shirt with black leggings. She plopped down at the table. "Dad, aren't you a little too old to be using cheesy pickup lines on your own wife? Mom, you're not falling for this drivel, are you?"

"Mind your own business," Alicia quipped. "I think it's romantic."

Eliot kissed her once more, flaunting his wholehearted agreement.

Lily rolled her eyes and turned her attention back to scrolling through her phone. Marston took the flowers from her mother, found a vase for them, and placed the display on the kitchen island next to her father's briefcase.

"It is romantic," she said. "Don't listen to Lily, Mom. She's just jealous that Dad's got game, and Jeff, her so-called 'boyfriend', has the romantic finesse of a cheese sandwich."

All four burst out laughing as they took seats at the dinner table. Alicia relished these precious family moments. She had longed for stability and a family of her own after her miserable childhood. Her father, Reginald Thomas, an MBTA bus driver, had left Alicia and her mother poor and destitute when he abandoned them for another woman. Over the years, Alicia had tried to erase the image of him leaving, with mixed results. His belongings packed in a red, vintage suitcase with brass snaps, a young Alicia clutching her favorite Cabbage Patch Doll, begging him not to leave while tears streamed down her face. He had not acknowledged her cries or her mother's stoic expression. Years later, Alicia lost her mother to a rare form of cancer.

Alicia shook off the depressing memory and focused on her blessings. She turned to her daughter as they began to eat. "How's the new short story coming along, Marston? Did you get over your writer's block?"

"No. I'm moving in a different direction instead."

"What's that?" Eliot asked.

"I've started writing my first novel," she revealed. She tucked a loose braid behind her ear and flashed an animated grin.

"That's wonderful, Marston. Congratulations," her father said. She beamed at him.

"What made you change your mind?" Alicia asked. "You're

quite the short-story expert."

"I wanted to challenge myself. Besides, becoming a novelist is my dream."

"What's the story about? I bet it's sassy, chick-lit," Lily teased.

"No! I've not worked it all out yet, but all the books I've read on writing fiction say I should condense my story into one sentence—an elevator pitch or premise."

"Okay. Go for it," Lily encouraged.

Marston cleared her throat, put down her fork, and straightened up in her chair.

"Dark secrets and the shocking murder of a neighbor's son lead to the destruction of a happy family."

Silence fell over the table. Eliot frowned. Alicia bit her lip. Lily cut into her lasagna and popped a piece into her mouth.

Alicia spoke up. "Um, that's a little bleak, isn't it, honey?" How did her sweet, sensitive Marston come up with something so twisted? Was that how the mind of a writer worked?

"It's a psychological thriller," she explained. "They deal with the dark side of human nature, what ordinary people are capable of when pushed beyond their limits."

"Oh, that's not what you normally read, is it?" her father asked.

"No, not usually, but I was browsing the bookstore and found this cover that drew me in. After I read the blurb, I was hooked. I finished reading it in two days. Aunt Summer says psychological thrillers are hot right now. Lots of movies and TV series are being made based on the books."

Summer Gray, Eliot's younger sister, worked as an acquisition editor at Webster & Crawford, a major New York publisher. The fact that Marston reached out to her aunt worried Alicia. Of course, Summer had helped Marston with her writing ever since she was little, but Alicia didn't want her daughter getting her hopes up of literary success simply because she had a relative inside the publishing world. Summer had cautioned Marston about the fickle nature of the industry, but when she got an idea in her head, it was hard to keep her grounded in reality.

What if Summer read the finished manuscript and thought it was no good? Sure, Alicia and Eliot thought Marston had talent, but she had never tackled a full-length novel before. If her aunt gave negative feedback, it could crush her.

"Writing a novel is a huge undertaking. But you can do it. Your dad and I support you, one hundred percent."

Eliot agreed. "Yes, totally, honey."

"You can bounce ideas off me," Lily volunteered. "Just don't come up with horrible characters that no one likes, or unrealistic plot lines. Those are the worst. I mean there's this show on Netflix…"

The conversation soon shifted to the upcoming combined junior and senior prom. Lily had already purchased three dresses but said that, although they were 'nice' choices, none of them had the dazzle factor.

Marston remained silent.

Alicia looked over at her eldest daughter as Lily prattled on about the difference between varying shades of pink tulle. Lily let it slip that Marston had pinned her hopes on Brandon Carr—a fellow senior she had been spending time with—asking her to prom, but that he'd asked someone else instead. As a result, she had decided to skip the most important social event of her high school life and refused to discuss the matter any further.

"I have an announcement, too," Eliot said.

Alicia looked at her husband, grateful that he'd changed the subject for Marston's sake but confused by his statement. He met her gaze and smiled.

"What is it, Dad?" Lily asked.

"I'm taking your mother to Paris to celebrate our twentieth wedding anniversary. If she'll agree, that is."

Alicia's eyes popped wide and her pulse quickened. "Eliot, are you serious? You're not just teasing me?"

"No, baby. I'm dead serious. I know how upset you were that the meeting had been scheduled on our special day. So, if I can't get out of going to Europe, we might as well turn a boring old business trip into a romantic getaway."

She hadn't accompanied him on a business trip in eons. Tillerson Brenner had multiple European offices: Paris, Brussels, London, and Frankfurt. Because the firm represented large, multi-national companies, strategic meetings between U.S.-based attorneys and their international counterparts were not unusual.

"Yes, of course I'm game. April in Paris. What a wonderful surprise."

He winked seductively at her, and then turning to his youngest daughter, he said, "So what do you think, Lily? Does this trip get your stamp of approval?"

Lily snickered, but Alicia saw that her daughter's lips had curled into a half-smile.

"I'll be in meetings during the first couple of days. You can go shopping, visit the museums and sightsee," he said to Alicia. "The rest of the time, we'll have to ourselves. There may be one business dinner I'll have to attend, but—"

His phone vibrated, halting the conversation. He picked

it up and looked at the screen. A panicked expression flittered across his face; then it was gone in a flash, as if it never happened at all. It was fleeting, the span of a breath, but Alicia had caught it. Something about this call had distressed him. He squared his shoulders, then casually placed the phone face down on the table.

"Aren't you going to answer that?" she asked.

"It's work. I'll deal with it later." His voice sounded anxious, a sharper tone that edged up a notch in volume.

After dinner, Eliot helped her clear the table and load the dishwasher while the girls took off for their rooms: Lily to text her friends and talk to Jeff for hours, and Marston to her novel-in-progress.

Turning to Alicia, Eliot said, "Now, what would you like to do for the rest of the evening, Mrs. Gray? I'm all yours."

"What? You've no work tonight? Who are you and what have you done with my husband?" she teased. However, the phone call from earlier lingered in her mind. If it was just work, why did he hide the screen? Why did he panic?

"Never mind that," he said, drawing her back to the moment. "I've got more important things to attend to." He pulled her into his arms and kissed her passionately, leaving no question what he had in mind.

CHAPTER 3

THE NEXT DAY, Alicia backed out of the garage onto the picturesque, tree-lined street. She barely noticed the brilliant morning sunshine—neighbors walking their dogs or those on their daily run.

She had tossed and turned all night, hardly sleeping. All kinds of crazy scenarios about the mysterious phone call during dinner had flooded her brain. She'd mentioned it, casually, to Eliot as they were getting ready for bed last night.

He'd brushed it off with a, *"There you go again, blowing things out of proportion, baby. It was nothing. Just work."*

But she'd seen how the call had rattled him over dinner. Was it really about work, or was it something else?

She forced her brain to shift gears to concentrate on the road as she drove through their neighborhood on her way to the city. They'd moved to the affluent town of Weston, Massachusetts, when Eliot made partner four years ago. With luxurious homes boasting thousands of square feet of living space, Olympic-sized swimming pools, tennis courts, and lush manicured lawns, the suburb west of Boston was home to successful CEOs, lawyers, hedge-fund managers, and anyone who could afford the median home price of a million plus.

The relocation had been at Eliot's insistence. When he and Alicia were still only dating, she'd refused to let him visit her, ashamed of her tiny, run-down apartment in a rough Boston neighborhood. Right after the wedding, she'd moved into his upscale condo in Brighton, in the northwest corner of the city. She had spent many afternoons patronizing the coffee shops or taking leisurely walks in the surrounding parks. Just before Marston was born, however, they'd moved to the town of Westboro where Alicia would have been content to live and raise their family.

But it wasn't enough for Eliot. He wanted his family to have a dream home, surrounded by beauty and serenity, the antithesis of her old neighborhood. So as soon as his first partner paycheck came in, he'd bought them a six-thousand-square-foot home that included three floors for living and entertaining, with top-of-the-line everything and wired for smart technology. She was proud of the house she had meticulously decorated and turned into a warm, welcoming home, despite its size.

After battling morning traffic, Alicia pulled into the parking lot of Howell House. She volunteered three times a week at the free clinic that provided obstetric and gynecologic care to young women from underprivileged backgrounds. It was set up by Dr. Jack Witherspoon, a successful and well-respected gynecologist who also ran a private practice in Needham.

The clinic in the Jamaica Plain section of Boston was a lifeline for her, an escape from her guilt about the affluent lifestyle she lived with her family and the idea she didn't deserve it, when so many who had grown up like her were suffering. She knew the women who walked through those doors every day, many of them with conditions that had steadily deteriorated. Who had time to worry about Pelvic Inflammatory Disease or endometriosis when there were more important matters at stake, like access to food and shelter?

But her volunteer work wasn't the only reason she needed to be at Howell House this morning. She wanted to ask Jack about the possibility of a job in his private practice. She didn't care what it paid. This was about her journey of self-improvement, and what better way to start than earning a dollar?

Upon entering the office, she smiled at Monica, the receptionist. "How are things this morning?"

"Insane. The phone has been ringing non-stop, and it's only eight o'clock," she replied in a voice that sounded as if she was hosting a garden party, while keeping her eyes trained on the computer screen.

Like Alicia, Monica had dropped out of college, but during the interview almost two years ago, there had been something about the girl's cheery disposition that had prompted Alicia to convince Jack to hire the girl on the spot.

With Monica clearly swamped, Alicia turned away from the desk and swept her gaze over the packed waiting room, carefully observing the women of various ages and ethnicities. Some popped chewing gum, others flipped through magazines, while a few just stared at the pictures on the walls. A young mother bounced a fussy baby on her lap and scowled at a friend who had accompanied her. Alicia leveled an encouraging smile at a teenage girl in a ponytail and ratty sneakers. The girl's fearful gaze traveled across the room. *Probably her first time*

16

seeking gynecologic care, Alicia thought.

"By the way, all the items you asked me to purchase for Zoe are ready for her to pick up," Monica said.

Alicia returned her attention to the receptionist. "Great."

"Alicia." Monica looked up from the screen and met Alicia's gaze. "You don't have to do this, you know. It's not your fight."

"What's wrong with helping out?"

"It moved beyond helping out when you offered to pay for pediatrician visits the first year of the baby's life." Monica lowered her voice. "A year's supply of diapers and a gift card to purchase a crib? If you don't stop this, people will think we're a free clinic and a baby services and supplies depot rolled into one. Can you imagine the stampede?" Monica shuddered as though it had already become a reality.

"Jack would kill me if that happened," Alicia said. She felt a lopsided grin part her lips.

"I'm telling Zoe this is all you. Otherwise, she'll think it's from the clinic. I know you don't want me to, but—"

Saved by the bell. Monica picked up the ringing phone, and Alicia headed down the hall to her small, makeshift office, and bumped into Jack on the way.

"You're here," he stated, as they crossed in the corridor. "I want to talk to you about something."

"What is it?" she asked.

"I'll tell you when we chat," he said as he continued to walk down the corridor toward the waiting room.

"Okay. There's something I want to ask you, as well," Alicia called after him.

"Yes, fine. I'll come by once I'm finished. I have some time in between patients at nine-thirty." He disappeared, and Alicia heard his booming voice as he called out to his medical assistant.

Shutting the door of her office, she hung her double-breasted trench coat and purse on the coat rack. Officially, Alicia was just an administration volunteer, but in reality, she was essentially the office manager for Howell House. She handled patient scheduling, registration, medical records, and data entry. Jack did have a financial accountant who managed the finances for his private practice, and Mary also kept track of the operating costs for the clinic.

Alicia didn't mind the small office. With only a few wealthy donors keeping the clinic afloat, there was no room for the impractical or frivolous. The space comprised of a desk and chair, a computer, and a black filing cabinet. She had spruced it up with a couple of small plants and photos of Boston landmarks on the wall.

Alicia booted up the computer and busied herself with some data entry and then checked the schedule for the next few weeks. The clinic opened two years ago, and the patient load skyrocketed immediately, and continued to do so. She hated to think there would come a time when they would have to turn patients away because resources had been stretched too thin.

As promised, Jack appeared at her door at nine thirty—without knocking—and closed the door behind him. His stethoscope dangled from his neck. Jack was barely five foot six, in his late fifties with dark hair that grayed at the temple, pale milky skin, and cynical brown eyes. Once upon a time, Jack was her gynecologist, but once they'd forged a friendship, she had switched to another physician at Jack's private practice. He stuck his hands into his lab coat and leaned up against the file cabinet.

"What's up?" she asked.

"Thanks for referring Katalina DeLuca to our private practice. We'll take good care of her. Any friend of yours is a friend of ours."

That was odd. Kat never mentioned she was looking for a new doctor. She had never asked Alicia about her experience with Witherspoon OBGYN Associates, and she still hadn't returned Alicia's calls, either.

"Um, I can't take credit for recommending Kat. I didn't know she was looking to change doctors."

"Oh. I assumed she came to us because of your friendship. Her regular gynecologist is retiring in a few months," Jack said.

"Thanks for telling me. Although Kat and I live on the same street, we sometimes go weeks without catching up. She has a lot on her plate, making her agency a success. She probably thought she'd already told me."

Her voice lacked enthusiasm for the explanation she just invented on the fly. She wasn't sure what to think. Did Kat just forget to mention it, or was her action intentional?

"How are the grandkids?" Alicia asked, attempting to ward off Jack's curiosity. His arms were crossed over his chest, his gaze laser focused on her face.

Jack sidestepped the question. "Is everything okay, Alicia? Do you want me to refer her to someone else? She specifically requested me, asked if I was accepting new patients. I'm not, but when she mentioned your connection, I made an exception."

"Oh nonsense. It's fine."

He cast a doubtful glance in her direction but didn't pursue the matter. "Grandkids are great," he said. "Rory said his first words last week. His father missed it, like he's missed all the major milestones in the kids' lives."

She was glad he didn't press the issue. His daughter, Leanne, and her husband, Dan, had two young kids. Dan, a software sales manager, traveled extensively. Jack thought his son-in-law a good man, but Jack had confided in Alicia that his main worry was that Dan was poised to repeat Jack's own gravest mistakes. Jack had only just graduated medical school and started his residency when Leanne, his only child, was born. Long hours meant he saw little of her, and it was a regret that haunted him still. He hoped his grandchildren would not suffer the same fate as their mother: an absent father in their formative years.

"That's great, Jack. Don't spoil them too much, though. Your daughter will not be pleased."

He rubbed his hands together and belted out a movie-villain laugh. "Ha-ha-ha-ha. I shall spoil them rotten. Rotten to the core." Talking about his grandchildren always put him in a great mood.

"You really need to work on your evil laugh," she teased.

"Come on. That was epic." Then his expression turned serious. "What did you want to talk to me about?"

Alicia almost forgot her resolution this morning. Jack's announcement about Kat had thrown her off balance.

"I've been thinking about getting a job."

He raised a brow. "I certainly wasn't expecting that. Is Tillerson Brenner laying off lawyers?"

"Very funny, Jack."

"I'm serious. You live in Weston, and your husband makes piles of money. Why do you need a job?"

How could she make him understand? By his reaction, it would be no easy task. But talking to Jack presented an opportunity for a practice run before she pitched the idea to Eliot.

"Jack, I haven't earned a penny of my own since I married Eliot. Although he's proud of the life he provides for his family, I need to do this for me."

He tapped his lips with an index finger, pondering her statement. Then he said, "I think I understand where you're coming from. You want to contribute to your family in a different way from what you're used to and also gain some independence at the same time. Am I right?"

"Yes."

"I'd love to help you out, Alicia—although it would pain me, and everyone here, to lose you—but we don't have any openings in the Needham office right now."

"That's okay. But if anything pops up, please keep me in mind. It could be part-time. That way, I can still volunteer here."

"Glad to hear it." Jack began to make his way to the door but turned back, his eyebrows furrowed. "Alicia, you don't have to share anything you don't want to, but are you sure everything is okay at home?"

"Yes, Jack. Everything is fine. Our twentieth wedding anniversary is next week, and I guess it got me thinking about my past, and my future. Although I've managed to raise strong, independent daughters, sometimes I don't feel that way, personally." She couldn't believe she was confessing this to Jack. What had gotten into her?

"You should be proud of what you've accomplished," he said gently. "Job or no job. You raised two incredible kids. Eliot's career has flourished in no small part to your contributions."

As the door closed behind Jack's retreating figure, she murmured, "Sometimes I wonder if it's enough."

CHAPTER 4

ALICIA WOULD NEVER forget the scorching summer day, four years ago, when she met Katalina Torres DeLuca. When Alicia had answered the door, she'd done a double take at the stunning, Latina bombshell who stood at the entrance.

"Took you long enough to answer the door," Kat had said. "I'm melting into a puddle out here."

Alicia had liked Kat instantly, despite the envy rising up from the pit of her stomach. Kat was a breathtaking incarnation of the actress Eva Longoria in crisp, white denim shorts that emphasized her tiny waist and long, shapely legs, paired with a snow-white linen top. Her raven black hair cascaded down her back in voluminous waves. Alicia had no idea how Kat got her hair to behave in that heat.

But the most interesting accessory on Kat, Alicia observed that day, wasn't the white Birkin bag that hung from her slender wrist or the five-inch Italian wedge sandals on her feet. The two things that intrigued Alicia the most were Kat's warmth and confidence.

She had introduced herself and mentioned that she and her husband, Richard, and their son, Maxim, had just moved down the street. Kat hadn't waited to be invited in. She had simply breezed past Alicia and headed for the living room, leaving a trail of expensive perfume, a scent Alicia recognized, in her wake.

Shaking the past from her head, Alicia brought her focus back to the present. Since Kat had had still not responded to Alicia's messages, she had decided that the element of surprise would be the only way to get facetime with Kat. Alicia didn't want their friendship strained over a misunderstanding. But in order to move on, she needed to hear Kat's reason for placing her hands where they didn't belong, and so Alicia had come calling.

Late morning sunlight streamed through the large windows. A flat-screen monitor, a family photo, multiple files, and notebooks rested on a sleek executive desk. The pleasing aroma of freshly brewed coffee wafted throughout the room. Kat had spared no expense in her office space, down to the Persian rugs on the floor and expensive paintings on the wall. They were the perfect complement to the numerous plaques peppered around the office. KTM Creative Edge, a full-service digital marketing agency, whose clients included some of the most recognizable brands in the country, was also an award-winning company.

"You've been avoiding me," Alicia said in a clearly accusatory tone.

Kat flinched, then angled her body away, as though shielding it from Alicia's accusation. "I can't anymore, can I? You're here."

Kat sat behind her desk, dressed in a black, sleeveless

power dress, a braided gold necklace, and her hair in an elegant up-do. She shuffled some papers, giving the impression of the quintessential busy executive.

But Alicia wasn't impressed. She hadn't come all the way into the city to get the brush-off. "What happened last Thursday night, Kat? Eliot explained everything, but we're best friends. Tell me in your own words. Then we'll put this incident behind us permanently."

Kat picked up a thick leather notebook off her desk and quickly placed it inside the drawer, then continued shuffling papers.

"*Katalina!*" Alicia said sharply. "Why did you have your hands all over my husband?"

Kat fingered her gold necklace and paused for a moment. Then she said, "You want the sad, pathetic truth? Here goes. I thought something was going on between Richard and one of the lawyers at Tillerson Brenner who attended the party. I saw them together. Later on, as I chatted with Eliot, Richard approached. I wanted to hurt him, make him jealous. So, I…"

"You thought a provocative display would do the trick," Alicia finished.

"Yes. I'm so sorry, Alicia. I'm a terrible friend, and if you never want to speak to me again, I'll understand."

"If that were the case, I wouldn't have bothered wasting my time trying to reach you. I don't condone what you did, although I do understand. Imagine the hurt and jealousy I felt when I saw you and Eliot."

"I looked up and caught a glimpse of you disappearing. I had too much alcohol. Not that it's an excuse."

Kat clumsily brought her coffee mug to her lips, fingers

trembling. She took a sip, then said, "I didn't mean to hurt you, Alicia. What I did was inexcusable and shameful. It won't happen again."

"Make sure it doesn't. What made you think Richard was cheating?"

She shrugged. "Body language. The way he stuck to her most of the night. She made him laugh. He seemed infatuated with her."

"Did you ask him about her?"

"He told me her father is dying of Alzheimer's. She came to the party to get her mind off things. Turns out she and Richard knew each other in college. They hadn't seen each other in years until last Thursday night."

She took another sip of her coffee and placed the mug on the desk. "I feel like such an idiot. What I mistook for a romantic interlude was my husband being the nice guy that he is, trying to comfort an old acquaintance."

"We all make mistakes," Alicia said. She jiggled her foot, thankful it was out of Kat's line of vision. She had to believe Kat that it would never happen again. Believe Eliot when he said Alicia was the only woman for him, and that he would never step out on her with anyone, let alone her best friend.

"You know me and my temper," Kat said. "If something doesn't smell right to me, I react, no matter the facts. I knew it was wrong, and I felt so awful— I couldn't look you in the eye. The next day was too soon. And the next. I just didn't know what to say."

"It's a good thing I barged in on you then."

Kat said nothing for a moment, her body having curled itself into a sheepish ball. "Look, I'm in no position to ask for a favor, but please don't say a word to Richard."

Alicia waved a dismissive hand at her friend. "Eliot and I talked it over and figured you knocked back a few too many and had a terrible lapse in judgment. I mean, what were you even thinking? But you don't have to worry about either of us saying anything. Just as long as this was an isolated incident, never to be repeated."

"Thank you. If the situation were reversed, I wouldn't be so quick to forgive."

The women broke into a mirthless laugh as a printer spurred to life and spat out a few pages.

"I'm not as brazen as you to do something so ballsy. No pun intended," Alicia offered.

"That's because you're Eliot's perfect angel."

The women exchanged a knowing glance.

"He wouldn't think so if he finds out what I did." Alicia crossed her legs. "I have this recurring nightmare that Eliot finds out. He's full of rage. Then he collapses and won't stop sobbing. He walks out afterward, saying he's never coming back."

Kat pushed back from the desk, stood, and then walked around. "You want to hear a funny story?"

"Go ahead."

"When I first met you, I thought, 'This chick is too good to be true. She must have dead bodies buried in her backyard or something and tries to cover it up by pretending to be a saint. With her perfect little family, immaculate home, and charity work.' Your kids looked up to you, and just when I'd convinced myself it must all be an act, that nobody was that good a human being, you told me you were a virgin on your wedding night. I wanted to knock that stupid halo right off your head."

Alicia couldn't help but smile. Kat had always been her

staunchest defender and supporter.

"But even angels' halos slip sometimes," Kat continued. "When you told me about your bouts with depression, I thought, finally, she's human like the rest of us. I don't know… I stopped feeling as if I didn't measure up. Your struggles somehow freed me from believing I was the Wicked Witch of the West."

"No one thinks that, Kat."

"Some of my former employees may disagree with you. Anyway, my point has three parts. A, your secret is safe with me. B, you can't undo it, so let it go, and C, it doesn't change who you are. Human."

Kat always knew how to keep Alicia focused on the big picture whenever she beat herself up or had doubts. Kat came close, leaned in, and stared at Alicia without blinking. "Let the past stay in the past, *amiga*. Don't go looking for trouble. People who do, usually find it."

"You're right. How about the present then? How are you doing? Jack mentioned he's your new gynecologist."

Kat walked over to the corner of the office where the small coffee machine sat and poured herself another cup. Alicia declined when she offered her one. "I forgot to mention it," Kat said as she returned to her desk. "Things have been so crazy around here. You gave Jack and his practice a ringing endorsement. I didn't want to say anything until I was sure he had a new patient opening. Luckily, he squeezed me in."

"It's fine. Your hectic life—it takes a lot of time and energy to build an empire."

Kat cackled. "I wouldn't go that far."

"Why not? You started this agency from nothing, and now it's a big deal, not only in Boston but all over the country."

Kat had started KTM Creative Edge out of her New York apartment after working as an art director for two well-known advertising agencies. She'd steadily built up her client list of companies who needed her agency's expertise in social media, content marketing, and brand building.

Business was good, but when Richard moved the hedge fund he co-founded, York Capital Investments, from New York to Boston, it changed Kat's business, too. Eliot had helped her land Tillerson Brenner as a client, and she'd been on a roll ever since.

Kat sighed heavily as she leaned back into the Tegan Leather executive chair.

"What?" Alicia asked. "I know that sigh."

"I'm fine," Kat said. "Really."

"You're doing a lousy job of convincing me. What's wrong?"

She swiveled the chair from side to side. "Maxim hates me. He practically called me a terrible mother."

"Why?"

"Not sure. He says all I do is work. I'm never around. That's all I can get out of him."

"Come on, Kat. He's a teenager, for goodness sake. Their hormone shifts can make them say awful things. You should be lucky the boy wants you to hang around at all! Marston and Lily practically banned us from their space when they were Maxim's age."

"But did they call you a terrible mother when they were Maxim's age, or ever, for that matter?"

"Well, it's not the same thing. You run a successful business. It's not easy to get there and then stay on top, especially for a woman. You work your tail off. I'm sure Maxim is proud of you and he—"

"Don't make excuses for me, Alicia. Richard wanted more children, but I refused. I made a trade-off."

"A trade-off?"

"If I wanted to make the business a success, I couldn't do it with more kids on my hip. So, I had to choose. But look at Richard! I fully supported him when he wanted to uproot our lives from New York. He works long hours and travels all the time, but Maxim doesn't call *him* a bad parent."

Alicia said, "It's never easy for us mothers. I don't regret staying home and raising a family, but not a day goes by when I don't ask, what if? What if I had finished college? Even gone on to grad school? What if I didn't have to drop out of college to take care of my sick mother? We're always second-guessing our choices, but it doesn't mean we made the wrong call."

Kat pressed her lips together in a tight grimace. "Even so, it hurts that Maxim is right. I chose my job over him. I'm not there for him, to take him to school once in a while. I work late most nights and don't have dinner with him or help him with homework. I put my ambition first, and until lately, I never felt the need to apologize or feel guilty about it."

Alicia's heart ached at her friend's pain. Was her behavior at the party a cry for help, so much so that she mistook Richard's offer of comfort toward an acquaintance for a romantic overture and then came on to Eliot?

"You're not one to back down from a fight," Alicia said. "Richard should talk to Maxim, help him understand."

"He already tried that. It didn't work. Maxim is as surly as ever. He has a mouth on him, too."

"What does Richard say about that?"

"That Maxim is just acting out, that it's part of growing up, that it will pass."

Both women went silent. Alicia didn't know how to help her friend. Eliot would have a coronary if one of their girls disrespected her. Lily tried once. She'd told Alicia to shut up and to stay out of her face, and that she hated her.

Eliot had roared when he heard his daughter. "Don't you ever talk to your mother like that again!" He'd made Lily's life miserable for an entire month: no friends over, no TV, phone, no outings. Alicia had felt awful about it and had tried to get Eliot to ease up on the restrictions, explaining that Lily had simply picked up a nasty habit from her peers, but he hadn't cared. Lily served out her full sentence of punishment, and to this day, she never had another mean word to say to her mother.

Alicia stood and stretched out her arms. "Hug?" The women embraced. "Things will get better. You're not a bad mother, okay?"

Kat let out an exaggerated sigh. "If you say so."

"I say so because it's true. Now get back to work. Award-winning empires don't run themselves."

CHAPTER 5

E LIOT'S PHONE VIBRATED. A text message.

Alicia: Are you on your way home? Dinner's ready.

He typed back.

Eliot: Sorry, baby. Working late. What did you make?

Alicia: Salmon with garlic roasted potatoes.

Eliot: Sounds delicious.

Alicia: When will you be home?

Eliot: In a couple of hours.

Alicia: Okay.

He placed the phone back on the nightstand.

"Who was that?" The woman lying next to him rolled over, adjusting the bed sheets.

"My wife."

"What did she want?"

He tossed her a sideways glance. "Since when do you care?"

"I don't," his companion said, her tone laced with contempt.

He sat up and massaged his neck, an attempt to rub out the stiffness. It had been a long day at the office, discussing and preparing strategy for the upcoming meeting in Paris. One of the firm's global telecom clients was rapidly expanding into Europe and parts of Asia. As the lead U.S. attorney, he needed to bring his A-game.

He had no interest in getting into a fight about his wife. In fact, he made it clear to Faith that Alicia was an off-limits topic, but her folded arms and the ever-present pout signaled she had other ideas.

"Not tonight, Faith. I have a lot on my mind."

"That's your excuse every time. I'm tired of it. What are we doing, Eliot? You won't leave her, but here we are, yet again."

"I said not tonight, Faith." He growled, impatiently. "You never had a problem with this arrangement in the past. What's changed?"

He slipped out of bed, crossing the floor naked as he headed for the bathroom. He took a quick shower, toweled off, and returned to the bedroom. His navy-blue Brioni suit and dress shirt were neatly draped over the back of a chair, and he dressed quickly. Faith sat up in bed, her elbows propped up against her knees.

"You have to tell Alicia. It's time."

"The answer is the same as the last time you floated that ludicrous idea. An unequivocal no."

"Then why are you here, Eliot?" she shouted. "If Alicia is so wonderful, why do you want me so bad?" She let the sheet drop provocatively, but it wasn't going to work.

He glared at her. "My wife is none of your concern. You made it clear from the beginning that you couldn't care less how our arrangement might affect her. As usual, you only cared about what you wanted. Get this through your head. I'm not leaving Alicia, not for you, not for anyone else."

"You want to have your cake and to eat it, too, is that it?" she asked bitterly. "Your perfect little family to show off to the world, your friends, and co-workers." She looked at him through flat, narrowed eyes. "Or maybe it's because she doesn't satisfy you. That's why you keep coming back for more. Isn't that right, Eliot?"

He drew in slow, steady breaths. He refused to get angry or defensive. He wouldn't allow her negative energy to dictate his actions.

This little, one-bedroom, luxury hideaway in Chestnut Hill offered the anonymity he needed for these meetings, and the sixteen-mile drive to home and eighteen to the office made it a perfect location—not too close, but not too much of a drive, either. He had given Faith his time and energy, two of his most valuable resources, and he made no further demands of her. Yet, it wasn't enough.

He walked over to the bed and sat next to her. In a calm, moderated tone, he said, "Faith…" The girl's eyes glimmered with hope. "You know I love spending time with you." He lifted her chin with his index finger, looking her dead in the face. "But you don't get to change the rules because you're greedy and overreaching. I never promised I would leave Alicia for you nor did I spin some fairytale about us having a future together. So, if this arrangement no longer works for you, you're free to walk away."

Her eyes glistened. The chin tremors reminded him of a petulant child about to throw a major tantrum.

She screamed, "You're a cold-hearted bastard, Eliot. I hate you!"

He would never relent, no matter how many times she acted out. Faith saw his wife as her competition and couldn't stand it, couldn't fathom why Eliot stayed with Alicia, when he could have a beautiful, glamorous doll like her.

With unusually large brown eyes, a small gap between her front teeth, and a curvy figure, Alicia didn't qualify as gorgeous by society's narrow standards. Eliot didn't care. What attracted him to Alicia was her undeniable radiance, a creamy cinnamon complexion that emitted a luminous glow that made it seem unreal. But what cemented his profound love and affection for the woman was her big heart, a heart as vast as the ocean. And when Alicia smiled, daisies bloomed, he was convinced of this. She was an integral part of his existence that extended beyond his heart. She was in his blood, his veins, every cell of his body.

"Grow up, Faith," he said as he stood to leave. "Stop behaving like an entitled little brat."

CHAPTER 6

"I SPOKE TO KAT, yesterday," Alicia said to Eliot, as she placed a jug of milk into the refrigerator. He leaned against the kitchen island, sipping his gourmet coffee. They'd had this morning ritual since the early days of their marriage. Coffee together in the kitchen before he took off for work. Sometimes she convinced him to have a proper breakfast with her and the girls before he left.

He pulled a face. "I thought we put the issue behind us."

"We did. But I wanted to be clear that it can't happen again. It's not something I could stay quiet about. She's my best friend, Eliot—a face-to-face chat was the only way to get things out in the open."

He placed his mug down on the island. She ambled over and stood next to him.

"How did the meeting go?" he asked.

"She admitted she avoided me out of embarrassment. That the whole incident was a drunken lapse in judgment never to be repeated. She's dealing with a lot at home," Alicia added.

"How so?" He took another sip of his coffee, his curious gaze fixed on her.

"Maxim thinks she's a terrible mother."

"Ouch. That's gotta hurt," Eliot said. "She overcame so many obstacles to get the business where it is now. Maxim's rejection must be a slap in the face."

"Exactly. I sense the pressure of running the agency and the issues at home are getting to her."

Eliot added, "As an only child, I can't imagine how he must feel, both parents working long hours. Missing that maternal presence in his life. On the other hand, Kat's not only responsible for making the agency profitable, but she also has employees who depend on her success for their livelihood."

"No wonder she flipped out at the party last week," Alicia said, sympathetically.

She started to walk away, but Eliot grabbed her hand and pulled her toward him. He gazed down at her, his mahogany eyes moist with tenderness.

"What?" she asked.

"The kids and I are lucky to have you."

"I'm lucky, too. You work hard to give us a great life."

"What I'm saying is, I wouldn't be where I am if you didn't hold our home and family together. You always step up and never complain. There were so many times when I could have done better at helping, but you never called me out."

Eliot always complimented her on what a great wife and mother she was. However, she'd caught something different in his tone just now. She couldn't put her finger on it. Was it gratitude that he didn't find himself in the same position as Kat—his children hating him?

"We're a team. We balance each other out. Besides, you working all the time comes with great perks. I'm looking forward to Paris."

"You need a break sometimes, baby. This trip is a great idea. I wonder who thought of it?"

They grinned like two teenagers anticipating sneaking away past curfew. She stroked his cheek. There was no such thing as the perfect life, but they came pretty darn close. What did she have to complain about? Her husband adored her. Her kids were happy, healthy, and thriving. She lived in one of the wealthiest zip codes in the country. She could have anything she wanted under the sun. So why, then, was a cold finger of unease clawing at her heart?

He pulled her out of her musings when he said, "Speaking of Paris, I need to grab the file from my study." He excused himself and left, but not before planting a kiss on her cheek.

The sound of a vibrating phone startled her. She glanced at Eliot's where he had left it next to his briefcase on the island. It vibrated again, but she couldn't see the screen from her position. The strange call from the other night materialized before her eyes. It was probably nothing, just work, but she still inched closer to the phone.

People who go looking for trouble usually find it. Kat's warning echoed in her mind.

Should she check his phone? What if Eliot caught her? The dang thing just kept on vibrating. It was taunting her, daring her to have a peek. Impulsively, she reached out and pulled the phone closer to her.

Nathan Hunt, Tillerson Brenner.

Footsteps approached. Alicia quickly pushed the phone

back to its original spot near the briefcase and eased over to the opposite end of the island. She clumsily picked up her coffee mug and took a large swig. The liquid scalded her tongue, and she bit back a scream. No point in drawing attention to herself.

By the time Eliot came into full view, she was a vision of contented domesticity, a housewife enjoying her morning coffee in her gorgeous, state-of-the-art kitchen.

"Are you all packed for tomorrow?" he asked.

"Almost done. I picked out a few suit-and-tie combinations for you, too."

He picked up the phone and slipped it into the pocket of his suit jacket. After he grabbed his briefcase, he said, "Thanks, baby." He kissed her on the lips and then headed out.

CHAPTER 7

ALICIA STOOD UP from the kitchen table, where she'd been hunched over her laptop since Eliot left, and stretched, feeling reassured. She felt ridiculous for peeking at his phone this morning. Ashamed of herself, if she were being honest. Clearly, Eliot was telling the truth when he said it was work calling during dinner last week—the call that had caused him to panic. How could she have doubted her husband? His corporate clients were often demanding, and his office, probably Nathan, had most likely called to address some problem that had popped up out of the blue and Eliot hadn't wanted to deal with at the time. Or perhaps Nathan was part of the legal team heading to Paris, and he needed to check something.

She picked up the bottle of water next to her computer, twisted the cap, and chugged it down. The refreshing liquid quenched her thirst and also recharged her mind. She'd been staring at a screen all morning, researching colleges around the Boston area that offered public administration degrees, the first step in pursuing her goals.

Alicia had said nothing to Eliot about it yet. She wanted to have a firm plan before broaching the subject. Should she return to Suffolk University or transfer her credits to a different school? It depended on which school provided the fastest route to a bachelor's degree.

The doorbell rang. She closed her laptop and went to see who it was.

Rina Stark, her neighbor from three houses down, stood at the entrance, her hair in a semi-messy bun. Before Alicia could greet her, Rina's narrow face beamed.

"The kids are at school, David is working, and I'm all alone with these ludicrously delicious donuts. You want some?" She waved them under Alicia's nose as if the box were a fine perfume. Alicia never could resist Krispy Kreme donuts. She took the box and stood back from the door, inviting Rina in.

"So, what's new?" Rina asked as she pulled out a chair at the kitchen table.

"Same old, same old." Alicia moved her laptop out of the way and placed the box of donuts on the table. Rina was a lovely woman, but a notorious gossip, so Alicia thought it wise not to confide in Rina, just yet, about heading back to college. Otherwise, Alicia's business would be all over the neighborhood before she had a chance to discuss it with her family.

"Are you trying to get me fat?" Alicia greedily eyed the donuts as she made coffee for her and her neighbor. Alicia had a weakness for the crispy-on-the-outside, fluffy-on-the-inside, melt-in-your-mouth treat. She didn't care that it was basically fried dough with glazed icing on top. It was insanely delicious. Sometimes, after Eliot left for work and the kids were off to school, she would indulge herself with a second cup of coffee.

Rina had busted Alicia one day when Rina dropped by unexpectedly and had been in on Alicia's little secret ever since. But she was aware of Rina's own secret vice that she kept from David, her husband, so they were even.

"That's the thanks I get for being so generous, huh?" Rina said. "I should take them back with me."

"No!" Alicia objected and pulled the box toward her, away from Rina, in case she carried out her threat and took them back.

"I thought so," Rina said with a devious grin.

"What's new?" Alicia asked.

"I'm bored. Needed a change of scenery and some adult company."

Boredom followed Rina at every turn. Alicia guessed she missed her old job. Rina had worked as a product management director for a software company in Waltham until she fell in love with the CEO, David Stark. David was still technically married and in the middle of divorcing his first wife at the time. It had caused a huge scandal within SummitTec and with Rina's conservative Indian family who had briefly disowned her.

Once their first son, Jacob, was born, Rina had taken a break from work. It lasted two years, and two more sons followed. Now both motherhood and marriage had lost their luster for Rina.

"Why don't you just tell David you want to go back to work, even if it's part-time?" Alicia asked, finishing off her first donut and reaching for another.

Rina evaded the question by asking, "Can we sit outside?"

Taking the quickly depleting box of donuts with them, the women walked to the patio and flopped down on the white sectional seating adorned with yellow and blue cushions. The

Mediterranean-style outdoor patio was the perfect place to laze away a suburban morning. A large clump of purple and pink allium, sweet-scented globe-like flowers, created a stunning yet calming effect in the surrounding garden.

Rina reached into the front pocket of her jeans and pulled out a single cigarette and a lighter. She lit the cigarette, took a long drag, and then exhaled.

"How long are you going to get away with that before David finds out?" Alicia asked, watching Rina relax into the cushion as the nicotine hit.

"What David doesn't know won't hurt him. I quit for him and the kids. Besides, I only do it once in a while. No big deal."

Rina continued to puff on her cigarette, swatting the smoke with her free hand. She stared at a flowerpot for a while, as if thinking deep. Then she said, "If I go back to work, it can't be at SummitTec. It's been almost ten years since David and I got together, but I'm sure some members of the old guard are still there who'd love to make things awkward."

"Oh, Rina. It's all in the past. Besides, you were already a successful woman in tech before you met David. You will be again, wherever you go."

"Yeah, but I've been out of the game for so long. There are new platforms now, new ways to develop software. A lot has changed. It will be like starting all over again. I don't want to go through all that, with three kids in the mix."

"Why not take a few refresher courses? There are tons of online classes now," Alicia said. "You just need to brush up, that's all—give yourself a little confidence boost."

Rina sighed and took another drag on her cigarette, staring out into the garden this time.

Alicia watched her friend. Despite Rina's honesty about her work-related anxiety, Alicia sensed there was something else on her friend's mind. She had clearly brought the donuts to butter up Alicia and the cigarettes to calm herself. From experience Alicia knew that it was only a matter of time before Rina's real reason for visiting would make itself known.

Rina blew out a puff of smoke. "Are you coming to book club tomorrow?"

"I can't. Eliot is taking me to Paris in the morning. We're celebrating our twentieth wedding anniversary."

"Oh, Paris in April! That'll be wonderful," Rina gushed, tapping Alicia on the knee. "I'm so jealous. David is always working. It's hard to plan anything, and with three little kids, almost impossible. Ugh."

"Eliot's going for business, and it happened to coincide with our anniversary, so we're mixing business with pleasure."

"I hope you're packing something naughty that will blow his mind. And promise me you will do tons of shopping. Bring something back for poor Rina?"

Alicia laughed. "I'm sure I'll find ways to occupy myself while Eliot's working."

"Are the girls staying with the DeLucases?" she asked.

Ah, here we go. The innocent question wasn't so innocent. The real reason for Rina's visit. *Kat.* Rina never liked Kat from the moment she moved into the neighborhood. Rina thought Kat was too flashy, brash, and overtly sexual. *Trying too hard,* Rina called it. Kat didn't think much of Rina, either; the two women despised each other, and Rina never missed an opportunity to bash Kat.

"No. Lily will stay over at Colby's house, and Marston over

at Veliane's. I think they would rather hang out with friends while we're away."

"I don't blame them for avoiding the DeLucases."

Alicia inwardly rolled her eyes but leaned forward in anticipation of what Rina's latest stab at Kat would be. "Why's that, Rina?"

With an insincere apologetic glance, Rina stumped out her cigarette in an ashtray on the table. "Maxim has been getting into trouble at school. Makes you wonder what's going on in that house."

Usually the stuff that Rina came out with was petty tittle-tattle, but after Alicia's conversation with Kat the other day, this new revelation was jolting. Alicia worried at the speed with which the news had reached Rina already.

"What kind of trouble?" Alicia probed.

"Like you don't know."

Alicia didn't want to betray Kat's confidence that Maxim had been giving her a hard time lately. Why hadn't Kat said anything about it during their conversation? And how did Rina find out? Her kids were eight, five, and three years old, respectively. Maxim was a freshman at Weston high school, and neither Lily nor Marston, who attended the same school, had said anything to Alicia.

Rina needed to feel comfortable divulging information if Alicia was going to get to the bottom of this, so her response was diplomatic. "You know teenagers, they're always acting out."

Rina scoffed. "Maxim punched a classmate—I'd hardly call that acting out. They also found him smoking in the boys' bathroom."

"Who told you all that?"

"Oh, you know, Alicia..." Rina leaned back into the sofa. "People talk. Kids talk. Before long, everybody's in the loop."

Apparently, everybody but me. "Kat never let on," Alicia said, then immediately regretted the slip. She wanted to extract information from Rina, not the other way around.

Rina responded with her trademark sass. "Why would she tell you her kid is an out-of-control little snot? You may be her best friend, but you're the perfect mother with the perfect kids. Maybe she's ashamed, feels like she can't measure up as a mom."

Alicia averted her gaze. A painful lump formed at the back of her throat. Guilt. How could she sit here gossiping about her best friend with a woman who loathed her?

Alicia said, "Maxim's a good kid who's obviously struggling."

"You see the sunny side of everything, Alicia, but it's clear he's acting out because of her."

"Don't say that, Rina. Kids act out for different reasons. We can't know for sure. Oftentimes, it has nothing to do with the parents."

"And that long-suffering husband of hers, Richard. He deserves a medal for putting up with her."

Anger spiraled from the pit of Alicia's stomach. Rina's digs at Kat were usually innocent enough, but this was going too far. She wouldn't allow Rina to unfairly criticize Kat.

"Everyone struggles at one point or another. Don't you think you're being just a tiny bit unfair to Kat?"

Rina huffed and folded her arms, her opinion set. Nothing would change her mind.

Alicia still reeled, however. Something wasn't right. First, Kat hadn't mentioned Jack was her new gynecologist until Alicia mentioned it. Then that incident at the cocktail party.

And now Maxim was causing trouble at school, and Kat failed to mention that, too. Was her best friend going off the rails and was too proud to ask for help? Kat knew Alicia's deepest, darkest secrets, so why didn't Kat feel comfortable confiding in her? She had to find out what was really going on.

Alicia jumped to her feet. "Thanks for stopping by. I still have some packing to do. Tell Mary Beth that I'm sorry I can't make book club. But I'll be at the next one. Marston is writing her first novel. Perhaps it will be our pick one day."

"That daughter of yours is going places," Rina said, stealing the final donut before making her way back into the kitchen ahead of Alicia. "I can't wait to read her book."

"Yes, but that's a long way off. With high school graduation and college coming up in the fall, she has a lot on her plate."

"How is Eliot handling his firstborn heading off to college soon?"

"He's excited for her, but as a parent, he's nervous."

Rina didn't respond as she made her way down the hallway with Alicia on her heels. Rina opened the front door and paused in the entryway. "How are you and Eliot, anyway?" she asked.

"We're good." Alicia scratched her cheek, slightly taken-aback by the question. "Why do you ask?"

"No reason." Rina's gaze wandered off down the street before refocusing on Alicia. "You and Eliot are a great couple. I would hate to see anything change that."

What did that mean? The icy finger of unease Alicia felt this morning returned.

"Oh, don't worry," Rina said, as if reading the fear on Alicia's face. "I'm just saying I admire you and Eliot as a couple. You two made it to twenty years. That milestone is rare these

46

days. Cherish it. Protect it, no matter what."

"Protect it from what?"

"I have to go." Rina stepped outside and walked briskly down the driveway. "Enjoy Paris!" she called with a final wave.

CHAPTER 8

A LICIA WAS HOLED up in her bedroom, busying herself with packing for the trip tomorrow morning. Alone in the room, events of late buzzed around her brain like troublesome insects.

Kat's struggles with Maxim and why she hadn't shared how serious things were. Rina's strange comment and Eliot's suspicious phone call.

Alicia grabbed a few dresses from the massive walk-in closet and dropped them on the bed for closer inspection. At home, her wardrobe was simple, with mostly solid colors and separates. In the summer, she preferred pretty, floral dresses and anything with polka dots. But for this trip, she needed a chic, stylish wardrobe and appropriate jewelry. If there was anything the Parisians knew about, it was style. Looking at the selection, she made a mental note to pack the gorgeous, diamond Cartier bracelet she received as a fifteenth wedding anniversary gift. Eliot had said that she deserved an exquisite jewelry collection, and he never passed up an opportunity to bring home something that sparkled.

As she returned to the closet to pull out another load of outfits, her brain worked backward. No matter how hard she tried to convince herself that there was nothing there, she couldn't let go of the phone call that had caused Eliot to panic. Before Rina's visit, Alicia had brushed it aside as nothing, but her neighbor's passing comments had put her right back in the thick of doubt and misgivings.

You and Eliot are a great couple. I would hate to see anything change that.

Alicia ran her hands down the fine wool of Eliot's dark-gray suit. The scent of his aftershave lingered on the fabric. Eliot often received work-related calls at home, but she had never—in the twenty-one years he worked for Tillerson Brenner—seen him panic like he had that night. There was something about his reaction that had convinced Alicia that the call was personal, not business. And how did Nathan Hunt, who buzzed Eliot this morning, fit into the puzzle? If he did at all. Would Eliot freak out if it was Nathan who'd called during dinner? She *needed* to find out.

She pulled out the suit and a crisp white shirt. After she finished packing two large suitcases, she walked over to the open bedroom window and stuck her head out. The sun warmed her face, and a light breeze ruffled a few strands of her shoulder-length hair.

She closed her eyes for a moment before drawing her cell phone from her pocket, holding it in one hand. Her index finger hovered over the screen. *What are you doing?* She filled her cheeks with air and then let out a long puff.

She locked and unlocked the screen, mumbling to herself for another minute or two about what to do. But she was determined. She had to know. She would make the call and put her paranoia to rest.

She dialed the main line for Tillerson Brenner. After only a couple of rings, the receptionist picked up.

Alicia cleared her throat and mustered up her most confident voice. "Nathan Hunt, please."

"I'm afraid Mr. Hunt no longer works at this office."

"Oh, which office does he work out of?"

The receptionist's voice was stern, but not quite impolite. "Sorry, ma'am, I'm unable to give out that information." Then she thanked Alicia for calling and hung up.

Alicia turned the information over in her head. Did the receptionist mean that Nathan Hunt was merely based out of another location or that he no longer worked for Tillerson Brenner? Besides Boston, the firm had U.S. offices in New York, Los Angeles, Silicon Valley, San Francisco, Atlanta, and Washington, DC. Would she have to call all six to locate Nathan?

A brilliant idea unexpectedly occurred to her. She sat down on the bed and placed the call, putting the phone on speaker to free up her hands. She grabbed a pillow and squeezed it to release the nervous energy building inside her.

"Is your LinkedIn profile still active?" she asked.

"Well, hello to you, too, Alicia. And, yes, I've still got LinkedIn. Why?"

"Yes, sorry, Rina. I need a favor."

"What kind of favor? We only saw each other a couple of hours ago."

"Something came up. Can you look up someone on LinkedIn, anonymously?"

"Yes, sure. I would have to tinker with the profile privacy

settings, but I can do it. Who are you looking up, and why can't you do it yourself?"

"I don't have a Linkedin account," she answered.

"Oh," Rina said, coming to her senses. "You know there is a thing called Google."

"Can you just do me this favor, please?" Alicia pleaded. She double punched the pillow.

"Okay, you've got me, I'm intrigued," Rina said. "Who are you spying on?"

"Are you going to help me or not?"

Rina's three-year-old screamed in the background.

"Oh, here we go. He's been screaming since I picked him up from preschool. I've got to go, Alicia, but text me the name and I'll see what I can do," she said before hanging up.

The next twenty minutes were excruciating as Alicia busied herself with the last of the packing. When her phone pinged on her bedroom dresser, she stuffed the passports she had been holding into her handbag and grabbed the phone. A text message displayed.

Rina: Check your email.

Breathless with anticipation, she opened up her email account. The message from Rina appeared at the top. She clicked on it. The body of the email simply said.

Hope this is what you're looking for.
Cheers.

There was an image attached. It was a screenshot of the LinkedIn page; Nathan Hunt looked to be in his mid-thirties and his profile stated he was a litigation attorney with Tillerson Brenner out of New York. He had attended New York

University and Cornell for law school.

Alicia couldn't work out why she was disappointed. What else did she expect to find? The Linkedin profile only confirmed that Nathan Hunt worked for Tillerson Brenner. So why had Eliot looked so afraid the other night? Unless Nathan wasn't the one who'd called. She hadn't seen his phone's screen, so she had no idea whether or not it *was* Nathan. Recalling that Eliot had claimed that the dinner interruption was work related, this morning she'd assumed that the call had been from Nathan.

Oh, this was hopeless. The two calls might have absolutely nothing to do with each other, which put her right back where she started, with out-of-character suspicion and paranoia. What if she was making something out of nothing?

But then, Eliot wouldn't have placed the phone face down on the table if it were Nathan or another colleague calling. She would bet money on it.

CHAPTER 9

W HEN ALICIA STEPPED into the lobby of the Four Seasons Hotel George V, her worries and concerns vanished. The opulence and beauty of the place took her back to her wedding day. Eliot had given her a fairytale wedding at an antebellum mansion near Atlanta, and Alicia had been blown away by the beauty of it. But now, she stood in the lobby of this luxury hotel, once a 1928 art deco building, in Paris, that made their wedding venue seem ordinary by comparison.

Magnificent works of art hugged the walls. The polished marble floor shone so beautifully she almost felt bad for standing on it. The laughter of guests milling about, waiting to be checked in—mingled with the fragrant aroma of the fresh floral arrangements of stunning peach, pink, and fuchsia in towering glass vases—produced a euphoric feeling.

Everywhere she turned, a rush of excitement swooshed through her veins.

The hotel itself stood at the heart of Paris' Golden Triangle with its high-end boutiques, fashion houses, and the most iconic sites in the city. She could see herself whiling away the few afternoons she had to herself in this fabulous city.

As if the lobby wasn't luxurious enough, when they arrived in their room, Alicia gasped. The lavish duplex suite boasted a Louis XVI theme: romantic, elegant yellows and creams, rich fabrics, fine art, and a colossal four-poster bed. Two huge floor-to-ceiling windows let the beautiful spring light in.

Alicia threw open the doors that led to their private balcony. Iconic views of the Paris skyline greeted her. The Eiffel Tower stood splendid and proud, surrounded by the heartbeat of the city, spread out like a large canopy of architectural wonder. She closed her eyes and reveled in the cool air caressing her skin. The sound of humming traffic below gave her the sense that there were still surprises in store for her.

She felt warm, gentle arms wrap around her.

Glancing up at her husband, she said, "This place is perfect, Eliot. It reminds me of our wedding."

He wiggled his eyebrows. "That's why I picked it. It's the perfect place to celebrate twenty years of marriage."

She giggled when he nibbled on her earlobes.

"We don't have to go out if you don't want to," he whispered suggestively. "We can have lunch right here in the room, and dinner, too."

She turned around, so they were face-to-face. "No way. I'm looking forward to dinner at Le Jules Verne. We've never been there."

He pouted dramatically. "You're such a spoil sport."

"Arnie called in a lot of favors with the Paris office to get us reservations on short notice. The waiting list goes on for months. Can you imagine, dinner at the Eiffel Tower?"

"Okay, okay, you've convinced me. Le Jules Verne, it is, for tonight." He kissed her on the neck. "As long as I can have you for dessert."

Without thinking, she pulled away. "Can I ask you something?"

"Anything."

"I need an honest answer."

"One honest answer coming right up."

"I'm serious, baby." A light breeze blew strands of hair across her cheek. She tucked them behind her ears.

He searched her face for signs of distress. "What's going on?"

"Is everything okay at work?" she asked.

He took a step back. "Of course, babe. Why would you ask me that?"

She shrugged. "Oh, I thought something terrible happened, and you were trying to protect me from it."

"What gave you that idea?"

"The other night at dinner. I know you said it was nothing, just work, but you placed the phone face-down after you ignored the call. That was unusual. You take work calls when you're home all the time. But this was different. It upset you."

There. She finally got it out of her system. This trip was her truth serum, and she had no choice but to bring the question out in the open if she wanted to enjoy her Parisian holiday. If she wanted honesty from her husband, she couldn't keep things bottled up and sneak around behind his back.

He pulled her into his arms and stroked her hair in a smooth, soothing motion. "You have nothing to worry about, I promise. Arnie works hard to keep me happy. Rival law firms have been trying to lure me away for years and haven't stopped."

She broke their embrace again. "Then what was the other night all about?"

"I had a rough day, tense negotiations. Coming home to you and the girls calmed me. It helped get me out of that negative head space. The last thing I needed was to spend more hours on the phone with my boss when I should be spending precious time with my family."

It was a reasonable explanation. Eliot worked hard, often too hard, for his firm. It made total sense that after a long day, he just wanted to forget the pressures of his job.

"That's a relief. You had me worried. Sometimes I forget the intense pressure that goes with your job. You handle it so well."

LE JULES VERNE sat on the second floor of the Eiffel Tower. The muted, sensual ambience of laughter, murmured conversations, and clanking glasses and silverware enhanced the panoramic views of the Paris skyline. Four hundred and ten feet above the now glittering nighttime version of the city, the place buzzed with a radiant energy and dreamlike quality.

For her first night out in Paris, Alicia had carefully chosen her outfit: an ivory, button-detailed, ruffled midi dress by Matériel, with seams at the waist and a softly pleated skirt. She liked the designer's precise tailoring and clever draping, which made it easy to flatter her figure. She accessorized with gold strappy sandals and a gold satin mini tote covered with embellishments. Her special Cartier bracelet added glamor and sparkle to her ensemble. Eliot, who didn't even have to try to look debonair—and who would look dapper in a trash bag— had ditched the tie and settled on a white, open-collared dress shirt and linen sport coat.

Once they were seated, Eliot ordered a bottle of 1996 Dom Perignon, the same champagne they drank when they toasted each other on their wedding night. Alicia was touched that he remembered.

They agreed on the seven-course tasting menu for dinner. She had her eye on the scallops with lime zest and caviar, while Eliot leaned toward the Foie gras.

The waiter appeared and poured their champagne. After he disappeared, Alicia shifted in her chair. Her eyes roamed around the restaurant and at the view outside the windows. Her wandering gaze caught Eliot's attention.

"What is it?" he asked.

She didn't want to ruin the mood, but something else was on her mind. A relaxed Eliot would be agreeable, so why not?

"I've been thinking about going back to school to finish my bachelor's. Maybe even grad school afterward."

"You have?" He leaned in and caressed her arm. "Baby, that's great."

"You're not just saying that to make me feel good, are you? Because this is important to me. I'm not sure whether to go back to Suffolk or transfer elsewhere, but this could be really good for me now that the girls are almost grown."

"Seriously, baby. I'm so excited for you."

She'd hoped that Eliot would react positively, but she paused before continuing. "I've also been thinking about getting a job, too. Maybe part-time."

"Oh, wow. A job, as well as going back to college. You're taking on a lot." He slowly withdrew his hand from her arm. "Why do you need a job?"

Alicia glanced at the waiter serving the dinner on the

table across from them as she tried to gather her thoughts. She needed to choose her words carefully, make Eliot understand.

"I love our family, and I feel lucky that I was able to stay home and raise our children. But I need to find out what else I'm capable of, besides being a housewife. There's nothing wrong with that. Believe me, I appreciate how hard you work to provide the lifestyle we enjoy." She looked out at the glittering night sky, as though it would provide encouragement. She returned her gaze to Eliot. "I need to rediscover who I am outside of being a wife and mother."

He listened attentively without interrupting her. Then he said, "I understand your wanting to return to school. Quitting when your mother fell sick and becoming her sole caretaker meant you couldn't finish your degree. But I worry you'll be stretched too thin by taking on a job, as well. Think about it. You already volunteer most days at Howell House, and with a full course load, plus your duties at home, your life will become chaotic and stressful."

She opened and closed her mouth several times. She appreciated his concern that he didn't want her stressed out. On the other hand, if she went back to school and got a job, things would change on the home front. She wouldn't be around as much, and Eliot might have to take on more at home. Would her husband be that selfish?

She lowered her gaze and then whispered, "Sounds like you're trying to talk me out of it."

He leaned in and lifted her chin with his index finger. "Alicia, all I want is for you to be happy. What I don't want is you taking on too much and being overwhelmed and exhausted. You've been taking care of everybody. First your mother, then our children and me. I'd be a self-obsessed jerk if I didn't support your goals, which I'm behind a hundred percent, but it needs to make sense."

"What does that mean?"

"Say you went back full-time, then it makes sense to get a job in your field of study afterward. Do you still want to study public administration?"

"Yes, with a non-profit management minor."

"So, you're leaning toward returning to Suffolk, then?"

"I still haven't decided. It depends. If another school offers a faster route, I'll take it."

"I'm so proud of you." He lifted her hand and kissed it. "And I do appreciate your sacrifice for our family."

"What sacrifice?"

"You waited. In the past ten years, you could have been out there, taking over the world. But you didn't. You stayed home, for me and the kids. But now that they can fend for themselves, it's your turn. Unless that was your plan all along?"

She cracked a smile. "Yes, that was my plan all along. To wait until the kids were older so I could return to school unfettered. Genius, huh?" She tapped her temple twice.

"You got that right. Eliot didn't marry no fool." He leveled a wicked, seductive grin at her, the one that made her heart dissolve into liquid fire. He leaned in, and she met him halfway. Forgetting they were in a public place, they were swept up in a deep, sensuous kiss she didn't want to end. Paris in spring, with sweeping views of the city and the twenty thousand lights of the Eiffel Tower, was the perfect backdrop.

She was thrilled he had come around. His initial anxieties about getting a job had made her nervous, but she understood his logic. He only wanted the best for her and their family. It would be a lot of work, but she would return to school full-time so she could finish her degree sooner, rather than later. Plus, with more and more classes being taught online, it would be easier to balance her family life, too.

Eliot held up his glass of champagne. "To you, baby, our family, and the future."

She clinked her glass with his, wholeheartedly embracing the promise of a future filled with optimism and hope.

WHEN THEY RETURNED to the suite, Eliot synched the wireless floor speaker to his iPad playlist. The opening notes of "Perfect Symphony", Ed Sheeran's duet with Andrea Bocelli, enveloped the room. Alicia inhaled the fragrant aroma of raspberries and citrus emanating from the bountiful bouquets of exotic roses.

"Dance with me," he said, extending a hand.

She molded her body to his—a body that still thrilled her after twenty years. When Andrea Bocelli's bold, dazzling tenor reverberated throughout the room, she wrapped her arms around Eliot's neck, rested her head against his chest and moved with him in a seamless, sensual rhythm.

"How did I get so lucky?" she asked.

"I'm the lucky one," he said. "I landed my perfect angel."

That halo is about to fall off your deceitful little head, isn't it?

She bit her lips and stayed quiet. *If only he knew.* She buried her face deeper into his shirt, breathing in his cologne to calm her racing heart.

Eliot's voice jolted her back to the present. "I have a confession to make."

Her heart thrashed around in her chest, and thoughts raced around her head. What was he about to say? Was this about the phone call? Had he lied to her all along? She lifted her head from his chest and looked him in the eyes. Even by candlelight, she caught the anxiety-riddled intensity in his deep, mahogany gaze.

"What is it?"

"You're not the only one who wants to fulfill a dream."

"Oh?"

He hesitated, unsure of himself. Eliot possessed unwavering self-confidence, so when he revealed even the smallest crack in the armor, that worried her.

"I know we never discussed it, but after we lost Jonathan, I wondered if we should try again. I know the pain we both went through, but he did give me hope that we could grow our family. Then tonight, when you brought up returning to school, I thought, that's the end of that dream. I know how selfish that sounds, but I guess I never got over losing my boy."

Her body shivered. Her knees went weak and she pulled away, crumpling onto the nearby sofa. Eliot joined her, but she couldn't look him in the face and instead gazed off to the side, focusing her attention on a wall painting of a Bed & Breakfast surrounded by lush trees near a lake. She couldn't go back to that time. It was the most horrific experience of her life, losing their son at sixteen weeks.

But Eliot didn't know the whole story. The secret she and Kat had been keeping from him. And no matter how much guilt consumed her, he must never know the truth. It was the only way to preserve their family.

Eliot put his hand on hers. "I'm sorry, baby. I shouldn't

have said anything—"

"No, no. I'm sorry. I know it was hard on you too, losing him. After the miscarriage, I didn't want to think about another baby. Maybe I was afraid the same thing would happen again."

He cupped her face and planted a long, unhurried kiss on her lips. Then he said, "It was so sudden. One minute everything was perfectly fine and the next, just like that, he was gone."

"These things happen sometimes," she said, as if the vague justification should satisfy him.

"But it hurt so much when you pushed me away afterward," he said.

She held her breath. "What?"

"You wouldn't let me go with you to the follow-up appointments after the miscarriage. You were adamant about going alone."

How was she going to get out of that one? *This is what happens when you tell lies.*

"I'm..." she began.

He continued. "I felt as though you were shutting me out. It was a tragedy for us both, but you kept me at arm's length."

Her lips trembled. Tears circled. She whispered, "I don't want to talk about this anymore. It's too painful."

He hugged her tightly and apologized profusely. "Please forgive me. That wasn't fair of me. You'd gone through a major trauma—you weren't yourself at the time."

You have no idea.

Alicia pulled herself together. "No, Eliot, *we* went through a major trauma. I don't ever want you to think that it didn't happen to you, too, that your feelings didn't matter. You were Jonathan's father, and his loss still haunts you."

He stayed quiet and rained kisses all over her face and neck. Before long, she let go of the grief and guilt, surrendering to the sensual onslaught. "Happy anniversary, baby," he said. "You're my heart, my love, my forever."

Alicia was half asleep when an irritating, buzzing sound pulled her from the edge of blissful rest. She opened her eyes slowly. A soft glow sprang from Eliot's side of the bed. But there was no Eliot. She reasoned he must be in the bathroom. Half-drunk with sleep, she dragged herself across the bed and reached for the phone on the antique nightstand. She wanted the whirring to stop, decline the call. She picked up the device, rubbed sleep from her eyes, then stared at the screen.

Nathan Hunt

Alicia hit the red 'decline' button and dropped the phone back on the nightstand. She was now wide awake. Once she crawled back to her side of the bed, she tried to fall back asleep. What on earth was so urgent that Nathan would call Eliot at this hour—after midnight? What time would it even be in New York? The time zones had confused Alicia's body clock, but surely nothing could be that urgent, especially since it was highly likely that Nathan would know about the Paris meeting.

A naked Eliot returned from the bathroom and slipped under the covers.

"I thought you were asleep," he said, spooning her.

"I was. Your phone woke me up. Nathan Hunt called. Remind me to tell him off."

CHAPTER 10

S ORRY TO BARGE in on you like this, Jack" Alicia said. "Donna told me your next patient isn't for another hour or so."

Jack gestured for her to take a seat in his office. "No problem at all, Alicia. How was Paris?"

Eliot's confession in Paris about wanting another child and his reflections on what had happened to their son had shaken Alicia more than she cared to admit. The situation called for drastic action if she wanted to keep her family intact. So, the moment she returned from Paris yesterday, she had called the receptionist at Jack's Needham office and hightailed it over for his earliest availability this morning.

"Paris was wonderful. Thanks for asking, but Jack, I need to talk to you."

"Oh, sounds serious. What's on your mind?"

"Evidence."

"I don't follow."

"Evidence of what happened three years ago. Eliot's asking questions, but he must never find out the truth."

"I thought you said he accepted your explanation. What changed? Why is this an issue all of a sudden?" Jack picked up a croissant from a paper plate next to the photo of Leanne and the grandkids on his desk, and bit into it.

Alicia sighed wearily. She was still jet-lagged. So much happened in Paris and her head still spun, but she'd decided to tackle one problem at a time. The most important problem first: the one that could blow up in her face and ruin everything if she didn't do something fast.

"While we were in Paris, Eliot mentioned trying for another baby. It seems that losing Jonathan hit him harder than I suspected, but now he wants to add another member to our family." She explained Eliot's probing questions and how the guilt had almost sent her into a complete meltdown.

"Yes, but I don't see where I fit in," he said, wiping off croissant crumbs from his mouth and sipping his Starbucks latte.

"Is there any way you could, um, accidentally lose the paperwork?"

"Pardon me?"

"It's a lot to ask, I know. But files go missing all the time. Are there any notes in my file that differ from what we talked about? What Eliot knows?"

Jack took another sip of his latte, then broke off another piece of croissant and popped it into his mouth. As he chewed, the tension grew heavy.

What if Jack doesn't want to cooperate with this crazy scheme?

Finally, he spoke. "Alicia, you're protected by doctor patient confidentiality and HIPPA. There's no reason to be concerned."

"You don't know Eliot," she said. "He brought up the fact that I never wanted him to accompany me on follow-up visits. I didn't know it had bothered him all this time. To be frank, I didn't think he'd noticed. So, what else could he be wondering about?"

"You're worried he'll keep asking questions and demand proof?"

"Exactly. Once he gets started, he won't stop."

"Alicia, the only way I would give up your file to anyone but you would be by court order," Jack reassured her. "And Eliot has no grounds for that."

Was she unraveling, losing her common sense? Jack was right. Eliot had no reason to come poking around. She was the one who needed to remain calm and stop making foolish moves. If she didn't pull herself together, Eliot would definitely get suspicious, and that was the last thing she needed.

CHAPTER 11

J ACK'S REASSURANCE, YESTERDAY, that her secret was safe provided Alicia only a temporary reprieve from panic and anxiety. In their place, new fears sprung up like stubborn weeds. She stood at the kitchen counter and scowled at the typed note after reading it for the third time.

Someone's husband is lying.
Can you guess whose?

Was this a joke?

She'd gone through the stack of mail she'd picked up from the mailbox before dinnertime. It was the usual: bills, junk mail, and a reminder that she needed to take her car in for servicing. Then the plain envelope with no return address caught her attention. She'd almost missed it, because it was hidden at the bottom of the stack.

A riddle from an anonymous sender that insinuated Eliot was lying. Was she supposed to take this seriously? She shook her head vigorously, as though prying loose the ridiculous idea.

Clearly, it was a hoax. Wasn't it? Someone just trying to wind her up. And, yet, she couldn't explain the fact that her name and address were on the envelope. The sender obviously knew her, where she lived, and that Eliot was her husband. She turned over the information in her head, wondering what someone would have to gain by sending the note. One thing was certain. This was no accident.

Her hands trembled. Fear swooped down like a murder of crows, eager to ruin her peace. They had returned from Paris two days ago, giddy, more in love and committed than ever. Now this.

No. She wouldn't allow some anonymous person to get inside her head. She had no interest in playing this game, whatever it was. She ripped up the note and envelope into tiny pieces and dumped them into the trash.

CHAPTER 12

Y OU PULLED A fast one, Alicia," Kat said, as they sat at the dinner table later that evening. "We found out from Lily that you had snuck off to Paris with your man for a romantic getaway without telling anybody, and now look at you. You're glowing." She winked at Alicia. Turning to Eliot, Kat said, "Good job."

Alicia blushed and partially covered her face with one hand. "It wasn't like that. Eliot was working most of the time."

"I bet he was," Kat said, cheekily.

"Katalina, there are children at the table," Richard said. "Tone it down."

"Oh, please. They hear and see much worse on the Internet."

"Still. This is a family gathering."

Kat waved away his statement and sipped her drink.

Alicia had invited the DeLucases over to help smooth things over with Maxim. She'd prepared beef wellington and roasted fingerling potatoes with fresh herbs and garlic, which she paired with a five-year-old California pinot noir for the adults.

At least for this evening, the DeLucases would be together as a family. Alicia had warned Kat that if she even thought about working late tonight, she would drive to Kat's office and drag her to dinner by her hair.

Still concerned about Rina's gossip, Alicia had asked Lily and Marston earlier if they'd heard anything about Maxim getting into trouble at school. Her daughters had confirmed what Rina said, but they thought that their mother already knew, that Kat had said something.

Maxim was sitting next to Lily at the opposite end of the dining-room table. His honey-brown eyes radiated defiance, aimed at his parents, mostly his mother. Then he twisted his handsome face into a scowl.

Alicia had been observing Richard and Kat since they arrived. Other than Richard's earlier admonishment to tone down the conversation to G-rated, the two never spoke and barely acknowledged each other.

"Hey, Lily," Maxim said, elbowing Lily. "Are you still dating that weirdo Jeff?"

An indignant Lily said, "He is not a weirdo. Jeff is unique and quirky. That's what I like about him."

"Quirky is just another name for weirdo." A smirk materialized on Maxim's face. "Who says 'over and out' to end every conversation? Is he in the military?"

Alicia knew that Maxim and Lily often teased each other. It wasn't in malice, though. Maxim was only ten years old when his family moved into the neighborhood. Marston babysat him frequently. He had grown up around the girls and was comfortable with them.

Lily rolled her eyes. "What's your beef with Jeff, anyway?"

"No beef. I just think you could do better. Find yourself a real boyfriend."

"And who would that be?"

"Ahem." Kat made a show of clearing her throat. All eyes shifted in her direction. She said, "Guess who made the cover of *Tigress Magazine?*"

"What?" Alicia squealed. "Kat, that's incredible. Congratulations."

A round of congratulations from Eliot and the girls circled the table. Kat beamed. Richard's expression remained neutral. Maxim double downed on shooting daggers at his mother.

"Tell us more. How did this happen?" Alicia asked.

"One of my clients is friendly with the editor-in-chief. They were happy with the work our agency did for them, and she recommended me for a cover story. The issue comes out next week in print and online."

Alicia was so proud of her friend. What a tremendous honor, and finally a little sunshine to lift her spirits. *Tigress* was a business magazine that helped women scale their businesses and featured articles, tools, and advice on leadership and how to unleash their inner tigress.

"I have an idea," Alicia said, bobbing up and down with excitement. "I'm throwing you a party at the country club. You deserve to be celebrated, so we'll make it a fun night. We can invite your staff and clients, so just send me a list with their contact info and I'll do the rest."

"Can we invite our friends, too, so they can learn from a female entrepreneur who's crushing it?" Marston asked.

"That's a great idea, kiddo," Eliot said.

Excited chatter took over the table as they discussed

plans for the party. It would be next week, to coincide with the magazine release, and there was so much to plan, so much to do…

A thunderous clap split the air, followed by another and another, slowly building to a crescendo that brought the chatter to a slow halt.

Maxim was standing and applauding his mother. But by the look on his face, it wasn't a compliment.

"Congratulations, Mom. You did it again. Made a fun family gathering all about you. You can't stand not being the center of attention for five whole seconds. It must be so exhausting."

Eliot cringed. The girls' eyes popped wide. Richard stared down at his plate. A fake smile froze on Kat's lips like someone on Botox overload.

Alicia's heart rate kicked up several notches. She had suggested this dinner. Now, it was a bust. Things were way past bad.

"Aren't you excited at your mother's wonderful news, Maxim?" Eliot said, turning to the teenager, now seated again. "She works hard, and she's receiving some well-deserved recognition. We're all proud of her."

"Maybe she should put some of that effort into being a better mother." His lips curled in disgust.

Alicia observed Eliot glaring at Richard as if to say, "Do something."

But Richard pretended that he hadn't seen the stink-eye directed at him and ignored Eliot's non-verbal cue.

Kat let out a joyless chuckle. "Maxim believes in honesty. He holds nothing back."

"You should try it sometime, Mom," he said. "But I won't hold my breath."

"Maxim, we're all friends here. We care about you," Eliot said. "Where is all this anger coming from? Is there something wrong?"

Maxim grunted and pulled the hood of his sweatshirt over his head.

"Don't do that at the dinner table," Kat said. "It's rude. Take off the hood."

With defiance radiating off him like an energy field, Maxim did the opposite and pulled on the strings of the hoodie, further covering more of his face.

Silence pervaded across the table. The dinner was over. Eliot suggested that Richard take Maxim home. He didn't object. Marston and Lily maintained their incredulous looks and eventually retreated to their rooms. Alicia told Eliot she would hang with Kat for a while and then escorted her out onto the patio.

The evening air was still warm as they sat together. Alicia watched her best friend struggling not to fall apart.

Kat was quiet. She rubbed her eyes, then slumped into the enveloping comfort of the sofa. Kat rarely brought down her walls, but it was clear that Maxim's words had cut her.

"Why didn't you tell me it was this bad?" Alicia asked gently. "I thought you were exaggerating when you told me he hates you." She thought it best not to reveal what Rina had said about Maxim acting out at school, as well. No point in kicking Kat while she was down.

"I don't know what to do," Kat choked out. "He gets more rebellious every day. I'm avoiding my own kid now."

Alicia moved to sit closer to her friend and placed her arms around her. "We'll figure it out. We won't let you go through this alone. Maxim loves you. We just need to get to the root of his anger, find out what's really troubling him. It can't just be about you working all the time."

Kat wept into Alicia's shoulder. In loud, straining breaths, the entire story poured out.

"I missed several baseball games at the beginning of the season. I had meetings with a major high-tech client, and it came down to KTM Creative and another agency. They were leaning our way, but they needed a nudge."

Despite having never been in the same situation, Alicia could understand the difficulty of making the decision of doing whatever it took to land a lucrative client, even though it would cause chaos at home. Her friend was truly caught between a rock and a hard place.

"We won the account," Kat continued. "That's when my relationship with Maxim torpedoed. New clients, with the kind of money they threw at us, came with excessive demands and aggressive timelines to deliver the campaigns. Things spiraled from there. I had more missed games, events, dinners, breakfasts even."

"Where was Richard? What was he doing? Surely, he noticed Maxim had a problem with your absence?"

Kat lifted her head from Alicia's shoulders, wiped her tear-stained cheeks, and tucked the loose tendrils of hair behind her ears.

"We're not in a good place. I'm sure you noticed tonight."

A dog howled in the distance. The night air had cooled as they sat outside. Alicia lit the firepit to keep them warm. This might be a long night. "We need more wine," she declared. She headed inside and returned with two glasses and a bottle of merlot, then poured them each a glass.

Flopping down next to Kat again and handing her a

generously filled glass, Alicia said, "Yes, Richard did seem disinterested tonight. It surprised me when he showed no excitement about your news and did nothing to reel in Maxim when he mouthed off to you. It's as if he's checked out."

"Always so polite, Alicia. You can say it. He's lost interest in me, in our marriage."

"Oh Kat, Richard adored you—"

"*Adored.* As in past tense."

Both women fell into contemplative silence as they sipped their wine. Kat inhaled hers and was soon two glasses ahead of Alicia who couldn't keep up.

"What are you going to do?" Alicia asked.

"What do you mean?"

"Well, you have to tell Richard to knock it off with the nonchalance. Confront him, make him tell you what's going on so you guys can fix things. This affects Maxim, too."

Kat emptied her third glass of wine and placed it on the table. She said, "What's the point. I don't think he cares, anymore."

"Marriage is a bumpy road. You can't give up because you encounter potholes." Alicia's words bounced around her head like ping-pong balls. They mostly shouted at her. *Hypocrite. Phony.* Here she was dispensing marriage advice when she was keeping a monumental secret from her husband, and then she topped it off with domestic espionage. Then there was the strange note. She had not shared it with Eliot or anyone else. Another secret to add to the list.

"You can talk all you want. You're married to a gorgeous hunk of a man who still has you on a pedestal after twenty years of marriage, and two kids," Kat said. "He just whisked you off for a romantic getaway to Paris. Tell me, how are you in a position to feel my pain?"

The words jabbed at Alicia. She had no response to Kat's anguished yet accurate statement. Helplessness swirled around her like thick black smoke.

Kat had always been there for Alicia, but now her friend needed her, and she had come up short. Alicia had to think of something to help Kat before it was too late.

CHAPTER 13

ELIOT WALKED INTO the WorkSmart building on Atlantic Avenue. He scuttled up the stairs to the offices of KTM Creative Edge. He wanted to surprise Katalina. Given the disastrous dinner last night, she needed some cheering up. During their morning coffee, Alicia had suggested he drop by to check on Katalina. His office in the financial district was only half a mile from her business, so it made sense.

In the reception area, he inquired whether she was in a meeting, and when the receptionist said she wasn't, he knocked on her office door and poked his head in. "How are you doing, Katalina?"

"Oh, Eliot! What a surprise. Come in, come in. Sit down."

He pulled out the chair on the other side of her desk and sat. "You don't have to pretend with me. I'm sorry about last night's debacle. Did Richard remember what today is?"

She shrugged. "Does it matter, anymore?"

"Sure, it does. What's more important than family? No matter how many years it's been since your brother's death, he should understand what a terrible loss that was for you."

"Maybe it's karma. Life with me isn't always easy."

Eliot didn't want to criticize another man and the way he ran his family, but he had grown protective of Katalina, and he was here as a friend, a shoulder to lean on. Not that Richard DeLuca was Eliot's enemy. Their relationship was cordial, but they weren't drinking buddies.

Katalina had lost her brother, Arturo, five years ago, and to this day, it was clear that the guilt still ate away at her. She was on a visit home to Miami and had insisted that he run to a liquor store to pick up a particular brandy for a special family recipe. He'd refused, telling her that he had somewhere else to be and he didn't want to be late. She'd pressured him until he'd caved.

Arturo had stumbled upon a robbery in progress. The perpetrator had shot him at point-blank range. Eliot knew that every year on the anniversary of his death, Katalina lived the nightmare all over again, blaming herself for the tragedy. How the particular brandy shouldn't have mattered or that she should have gone herself. If she had allowed her brother to stick to his own plans for the evening, he would still be alive. Or had she asked him earlier in the day, he wouldn't have come upon a crime in progress. Eliot was used to her going on and on with the what-ifs.

"Hey, we all do and say things we regret," Eliot said in a soothing voice.

"Don't you have anything better to do than babysit this hot mess?" she asked with a wry smile.

"Well, if you're a hot mess, you're the most beautiful one I've ever seen."

There was a short, awkward pause. Eliot bent down and

picked up the gift basket he'd brought with him and placed it on the desk in front of her. "I brought you goodies to cheer you up. A few audiobooks, some business and leadership-type bestsellers, stress balls, a dartboard in case you want to kill somebody—just imagine the face on the dartboard. And a few bottles of wine. Don't drink them all in one go. Finally, Godiva Chocolates. Alicia told me that chocolate always helps when you're stressed."

"Will you think I'm a lush if I started in on the wine now?" she said with a nervous chuckle. "It's only eleven in the morning, but it's always Happy Hour somewhere, right?"

"No judgment here," he said. "Just take it easy."

Another awkward pause.

"I never got the chance to apologize for the other night," she declared, filling the silence.

He waved her off. "No apology necessary. You had a tough night."

"I mean it, Eliot," she insisted. "When I think of what I did, well, it's a miracle that you and Alicia still speak to me. I told her if the situation were reversed, I wouldn't be so forgiving."

"She's quick to see the good in everyone. Your actions hurt her, though. She thought you betrayed her. I mean, *we*."

"Is that why you took her to Paris, because you felt guilty?"

The comment landed like a slap on the cheek. It stung. Anger churned in his chest. "I don't need a reason to take my wife anywhere. Alicia and I discussed the situation the morning after it happened. I defended you."

She shot him a sour look.

He took it down a notch. "Paris had nothing to do with you at all. Alicia deserves to be swept off her feet, now and again."

"Well damn, Eliot. You sure set me straight. I wasn't trying to put down Alicia by implying you had ulterior motives for taking her on the trip."

"Yes, you were. But I forgive you." He stood up. "I have to go. I just came by to say that I care. Congratulations again on the *Tigress Magazine* feature. I'm looking forward to the party. Alicia is going all out."

"She's too good to me. I don't deserve her friendship."

Eliot said nothing on his way out.

CHAPTER 14

ALICIA ARRIVED AT the country club a half-hour before the party's official kickoff at six. She trusted the staff who had impeccable taste and service, but she wanted to give the place a once-over and iron out any last-minute issues before the guests started to arrive. With all but five having RSVPed yes, a total of forty guests would be attending.

With stunning views of the eighteenth green and the Boston skyline, the Wyndham room was perfect for a late-April celebration as spring marched on.

A table loaded with extra copies of *Tigress Magazine* sat near the entrance. Kat, in a Stella McCartney pant suit and flawless makeup, dazzled on the cover. She was the epitome of the successful, in-control boss lady the headline alluded to.

"Make sure you get photos of Arnie Tillerson and anyone else from Tillerson Brenner together with Kat, once she arrives," Alicia said to the photographer. "It should be on the shot list we discussed."

She imagined the flashes from his camera creating the

Hollywood red-carpet feel as uniformed servers floated throughout the room, enticing guests with a variety of scrumptious appetizers. "It's really important," she added.

After the photographer assured her that he had everything under control, Alicia glanced at the wall clock. It was already after six, and people were starting to arrive. As she moved toward the open bar, Lily and her boyfriend, Jeff Barnes, intercepted her.

"Hi, Mrs. Gray. Thanks for letting us crash your party," Jeff said. "I told Lily I think it's cool that she's surrounded by powerful women, like you and Mrs. DeLuca. She has some great role models to look up to, although she's already a strong woman in my opinion." He flashed a megawatt smile, revealing teeth white enough to qualify him for a toothpaste commercial.

"Isn't he the best?" Lily gushed. She wrapped her arm around his waist, as if laying claim to her enlightened man before someone snatched him away. "He's not at all intimidated by girl power."

"It is my pleasure," Alicia said. "We have crudités, nuts, and meatless appetizers, so help yourself." Jeff was vegan, and she'd made sure to add items to the menu so he and any other non-meat eaters wouldn't starve.

"Thank you. Um, is Mr. Gray around?" Jeff's eyes darted around the room.

"He'll be here soon." Alicia chuckled under her breath. Jeff was afraid of Eliot, who took every opportunity to promise he would turn Jeff into mincemeat if he messed with Lily. Eliot thought Jeff was a nice kid, but Eliot didn't want him taking liberties with his daughter.

"Maxim and Richard are here," Lily said. "But no Kat."

"She likes to make an entrance," Alicia said. "I bet she'll be here any minute now. In the meantime, I'll say hello to Maxim and Richard."

Kat made her entrance at six forty-five, on the dot, wearing a body-flattering, pink halter dress, paired with strappy sandals with crystal embellishment. Her hair and makeup were flawless. The room erupted in applause as she sashayed in and immediately began preening for the camera. She laughed and gestured appropriately, as she worked the room like a pro.

A half-hour later, she moved toward Alicia with a beaming smile on her face. *She really does look stunning*, Alicia thought, but as Kat got closer, dismay clenched around Alicia's chest like an iron fist.

She's wearing my bracelet! What the...?

The fiery brilliance of the eighteen-karat gold and diamond Cartier piece almost blinded Alicia. It was identical to the bracelet Eliot had gifted her on their fifteenth wedding anniversary, five years ago, the one she'd worn to dinner at the Eifel Tower. An exact replica now adorned her friend's wrist.

Alicia had worn the bracelet to a charity gala at the Museum of Fine Arts in Boston, and Kat had gushed over its beauty. It was extraordinary, but what made it priceless to Alicia was the special inscription.

Alicia and Eliot had been at a hotel in the Berkshires celebrating their anniversary and had spent the entire day in bed. Her jaw dropped when Eliot, with a grin as wide as the Great Plains, opened the dark red box and presented her with the diamond-studded piece, as a tribute to their passion and romance. Before he placed it on her wrist, he'd read her the inscription.

To Alisia. My heart. My love. My forever.

As she'd gazed at the spelling that demonstrated the proper pronunciation of her name, Alicia recalled her mother, Margaux, telling the story behind how it came to be. One day, while pregnant with Alicia, Margaux stood in line at a bakery when the man ahead of her greeted the server who wore a nametag, with the name, *Alicia*. The man was British and called the server "Alisia". Her mother had been so taken with the elegant pronunciation, she'd decided Alicia would be the perfect name for her daughter, but with the British pronunciation.

However, the plan backfired. As a kid, no matter how many times she corrected teachers, classmates, and strangers alike, they all stuck with the American pronunciation. After a while, she just gave up trying to correct them.

Eliot had fallen in with the crowd, calling her "Al-ee-sha", but that day she'd realized that he hadn't forgotten her mother's story. As the bracelet glittered on her wrist, Alicia had been overcome with Eliot's thoughtfulness. That bracelet was so special to her, not because it was Cartier, but because of what it symbolized—a man who cherished her.

Kat had said that it was the most romantic story she had ever heard. She'd even used the phrase "swoon worthy." So why was she wearing the exact same one?

"Oh, Alicia, thank you, *mi amiga*," Kat said, embracing her friend. "Tonight is just wonderful! I appreciate you so much."

It was wonderful that Kat was in high spirits, grateful and happy. Mission accomplished. The party was a success. But Alicia's stomach flopped. A trickle of sweat ran down her back. Should she say something? Would it be petty to ask about the bracelet now, when her friend was on such a high?

Kat said, "I wasn't sure about this evening. I thought celebrating my accomplishment might be in poor taste, what with everything going on with Maxim, but you showed me how important it is to mark these moments, Alicia. You stepped up for me, big time."

"Happy to do it," Alicia responded. "You've had a rough time lately. We lift each other up, right?"

"You do that better than anyone else." Kat lowered her voice. "I tease you about your halo and being a goody-two-shoes, but I wish I were more like you."

Alicia smoothed her dress and patted her hair. Kat's unexpected admission hung awkwardly in the air. She would laugh out loud at the irony if she didn't feel like a drunken hippo had just crashed into her. Kat, wanting to be like her. *Ha, ha, ha.* Was that why she showed up wearing the identical bracelet to the one Alicia owned?

"So you bought one, huh?" She pointed to Kat's left wrist.

"Oh yes. It was a mistake to wear it, though."

"Why is that?"

"Richard bought it for me last month. He remembered how I kept going on and on about yours and the story behind the inscription."

You heard that story four years ago. "Well, he has an excellent memory. Is there an inscription?"

"No," Kat whispered, sadly. "Right, must go mingle—it is a party in my honor, after all!"

Later in the evening, Alicia found herself standing beside Richard DeLuca in a corner of the room that offered an unobstructed view of the party. What she saw concerned her. Over the past hour, Kat had gone back and forth to the bar—four times and counting. She was also snatching flutes of champagne from passing servers.

"Is Kat okay?" Alicia raised her concern to Richard.

"Katalina is skilled at looking out for number one. If I were you, I wouldn't waste my time worrying about her."

In the dimly lit space, Alicia studied Richard. His voice was strained. When he wasn't jangling the keys in his pocket, he continually rubbed his temples. He leaned into the wall as if he would fall if he didn't use it for support. Then he yawned. He actually yawned.

"Are you and Kat okay, Richard?"

He gave her a one shoulder shrug, then lowered his head. "Is any marriage ever really okay?" Then he looked up at her. "She doesn't deserve one shred of your kindness, you know that, don't you?"

He offered up no further explanation but simply turned away and headed toward the exit.

CHAPTER 15

Your husband has a secret.
Can you count the many lies?

ELIOT'S NOT CHEATING. Eliot's not cheating." She chanted the phrase several times more, pacing up and down the bedroom floor. Another note had appeared in the mailbox thirty minutes ago. Same as last time. Another cryptic message typed on plain white paper. No signature. No return address.

Alicia sat in the rocking chair across from the massive four-poster king-sized bed with the note in hand. She rocked back and forth. The motion helped sooth her chaotic thoughts. The chair was a baby shower gift from her mother-in-law when Alicia was pregnant with Marston. She had spent many a night rocking both her babies to sleep or soothing their fussiness. Today, she needed some soothing and assurances of her own.

They were happy she told herself. She and Eliot. No marriage was perfect, but they were one of the lucky few. Alicia only had to look at Kat and Richard's relationship to be reminded of how good she had it.

Eliot had explained why he'd placed his phone face-down that night. The man had been exhausted and just wanted a break from work, a breather from the electronic leash. And the call in the middle of the night in Paris was probably a simple time-zone confusion. Someone was obviously out to get her, wanting to stir up trouble by sending these ridiculous notes. She had no clue who would do such a thing, and she didn't care who was behind the hoax. If anything, she felt sorry for them, that their lives were so empty that they felt the need to harass other people—her in this case.

But she couldn't let them get away with it. She wouldn't be bullied, and she knew just where to find the answers.

ALICIA STOOD AT the consultation desk of Cartier's Diamond Salon on Boston's Newbury Street—a mile-long street lined with nineteenth century Brownstones and hundreds of shops and restaurants, which made it a popular destination with tourists and locals. The space wreaked of opulence and luxury—floor-to-ceiling gold columns, plush carpeting, and display cases loaded with engagement rings, bridal jewelry, and special pieces for gifting.

With the messages implying that Eliot was cheating and Kat's brazen display at Arnie's party, along with the dubious story that Richard had purchased an identical Cartier bracelet for her, Alicia could no longer pretend that the three occurrences were mere coincidence.

She'd concocted a story in advance of her arrival to the store. Her husband had bought her the Love Bracelet as a fifteenth wedding anniversary gift and had a special inscription engraved into it. The piece had gone missing for a while, and she feared it might be lost forever. When it didn't turn up, she finally told her husband, and then shortly after, she overhead him tell their daughter that mom was so upset about the missing jewelry that he was considering surprising her with a replacement.

"But I found the original, you see—silly me. It was hidden in my jewelry case all along—thank goodness. I wanted to check if he'd ordered another, so I could cancel it, and make up for my silliness." Alicia directed a radiant smile at Patrick, the sharply dressed associate with minty breath and an impressive man bun.

"You must be so happy it turned up," Patrick said. "Let me look up some information for you." He tapped a few keys on the computer and concentrated on the screen.

"Looks like you're safe." He drew his attention back to Alicia. "Mr. Gray has not purchased a replacement. The original he bought five years ago is the only record we have."

She placed a palm over her chest. "Oh, that's good to hear. I can't wait to tell him that I found it. The original has sentimental value to me. The inscription, the first time he read it out loud to me. Anyway, sorry… I'm rambling. Thank you, Patrick. You've been so helpful."

She slid her purse over her shoulder and turned to walk out of the store, when Patrick said, "Try not to lose the matching earrings. Not that I would mind the commission if they needed replacing."

Alicia froze. "Earrings? What earrings?"

"Don't tell me you already misplaced them," he teased. "They're the matching earrings to your bracelet. In yellow gold and diamonds. Mr. Gray bought them a month ago."

CHAPTER 16

"M OM, DID YOU see the bracelet Kat wore to the party yesterday?" Marston asked, as the family sat at the dinner table that night. "It's exactly like the one Dad bought for your anniversary."

"Not exactly, honey. Mine has a special inscription on the inside."

Alicia's foot bounced under the table. She wiped her sweaty palms on her jeans. Marston's observation was like picking at a fresh wound. Alicia had no appetite. The bombshell Cartier store revelation was four hours ago, but she was still reeling from it.

It served her right for playing Sherlock Holmes. She just wanted to find out if Eliot had purchased Kat's bracelet. Turned out her friend was telling the truth, that *her* husband had bought it for her. So, who the heck did Eliot buy earrings for?

"I saw that, too." Lily chimed in with a questioning frown. "She flaunted it, like she wanted everybody to notice."

Alicia continued to pick at her food.

"Yeah," Marston said. "That's a lot of bling. People noticed."

Alicia ventured a glance at Eliot, searching for a reaction, but his face remained neutral as he continued to eat his dinner.

"Dad, don't you think it's weird?" Lily said.

"What, sweetheart?"

"Kat's bracelet," Lily said. "Get with the program, Dad. Kat has the same bracelet as Mom. The one you got her for your fifteenth anniversary, five years ago. It's tacky as all get out. Mom and Kat are best friends, for crying out loud."

"Maybe she liked it and wanted to treat herself," he remarked.

"Come on, Dad. If Colby bought the same dress that I did for prom and showed up to prom wearing it, I would flip out on her. It's the girl code. Same as not dating your friend's ex kind of thing. You don't run out and buy the same jewelry as your best friend, especially when you know it was a special gift from her husband."

Marston served up an enthusiastic, "That's right," and nodded her complete agreement with her sister. "No offense to Kat, but that *was* tacky. Especially since Mom threw her that party."

"I guess I'm outnumbered," Eliot said. "I don't think Katalina meant any harm, though."

Just like she didn't mean any harm when she grabbed your crotch. Alicia stabbed at her food with more vigor.

"The bracelet is only the beginning," Marston said, in a raspy voice that mimicked the stereotypical horror movie trailer voice-over.

The girls and their father burst out laughing.

Alicia did not.

TWO HOURS AFTER dinner, Alicia let out a loud, frustrated groan, slammed her laptop shut and headed for Eliot's study. She knocked once and then entered.

"That piece of junk I call a computer is driving me nuts. I'm in the middle of downloading information, and it just kicked me out. When it's not doing that, it holds my files hostage when I try to open them. I need to borrow your laptop for an hour or so."

He looked up from reading a document and smiled up at her. "Come here," he said, patting his thigh. "Why don't you just buy a new computer? You've been complaining about problems with this one forever. It's old. Replace it."

She sighed. "I've been avoiding the hassle of figuring out which make and model I should get. Gigabytes, speed, and storage capacity and all that. Plus transferring all my files to the new model."

"They have people who can help you with that."

"Okay, you got me. I don't have an excuse. But I have to finish what I was doing. I need to borrow yours."

"On one condition?"

"What's that?"

He pointed to his cheek.

How could he behave like an attentive, flirtatious husband while he was buying expensive jewelry for another woman? Should she confront him right here, right now? *And say what? That you thought he bought a bracelet for Kat and went behind his back to find proof, and oh, by the way, while you were on your little espionage outing, the store clerk accidentally spilled the beans?*

"Fine." She reluctantly kissed him on the cheek. "Happy now?" she asked.

92

"Yes. Now, you can borrow my computer. And get a new one. Tomorrow. No excuses."

She scooped up the laptop from the desk, and as she walked away, Eliot swatted her behind playfully. "Don't work too hard."

She padded back down the hallway to the space she called her office but was so much more than a workspace. It was the place she could be alone to reflect, think, dream, or just mellow out. To take some time to herself away from the busy goings-on of looking after a family and her duties as a corporate wife.

Her office was larger than her old apartment, and she made it a point to fill it with beautiful things. Fresh flowers twice a week, scented candles, a gorgeous antique sofa, a bookshelf with mostly hardback first editions, photos of her and Eliot at glamorous parties, along with travel and vacation shots. But it was also where she kept old photo albums with pictures of life with her mother, after her dad walked out. Looking at them broke her heart, but they were her most cherished possessions.

Alicia tried to log in to the computer and failed. She'd forgotten the password Eliot had given her a while back. She thought about it for a minute and recalled it was his mother's maiden name, Scott, in combination with the date and year he was accepted into Harvard Law.

She tried it, and it worked. She returned to the University of Massachusetts website, where she had been before her computer glitched. She read the requirements for transfer students and began creating an account but became stumped by some of the form's requirements. She couldn't find the answers on the website, so it was probably best to email the admissions office first. She didn't want to mess up her chances for a new kind of future before it had even begun.

She clicked on the mail icon. Annoyingly, Eliot had forgotten to log out of his email. She'd have to switch accounts. However, as she tried to find the settings icon, she noticed something strange about the inbox. It was almost empty. Eliot valued efficiency and cleaning out his inbox was the kind of thing he would do, but what was weird was the number of emails in his draft folder to the left of the screen—seventeen in all.

Why hadn't he sent those messages? It was unlike Eliot to keep such a tidy inbox but not do the same to his drafts folder.

Alicia swatted away the troublesome thought. It was nothing. Her anxious brain was playing tricks on her. If he had something to hide, he would have come up with some plausible excuse why she couldn't borrow his computer. He hadn't done that. Instead, he had willingly turned over his laptop without a second thought.

She squirmed in her seat, unable to get comfortable. If he had nothing to hide, there would be no harm in looking in the folder. There wouldn't be anything upsetting in it, right?

Alicia dragged the mouse to the drafts folder and hesitated. Her brain issued a silent scream, egging her on.

She clicked. To her surprise, none of the messages had a subject line. Before she lost her nerve, she scrolled to the top of the page, double clicked on the most recent message, and read it.

A vicious chill hit her at the core.

CHAPTER 17

ALICIA COVERED HER mouth to suppress the wounded scream threatening to burst out of her. She wanted to run away, erase what she had just seen. But her body wouldn't cooperate. Her muscles froze. Oxygen fled her brain. Her breath caught. She couldn't breathe properly. Air reached her lungs in short, anguished bursts.

It was right there, in black and white. The anonymous notes were correct. Eliot and another woman. A woman who had just exposed a major crack in Alicia's marriage. No. Scratch that. A 9.0-type earthquake on the Richter Scale.

To: Eliot Gray
From: Empress Faith
Subject: Our future

I'm tired of sharing you with her. I love you. I would do anything for you. Doesn't that count for something?

From: Eliot Gray
To: Empress Faith
Re: Our future

This is getting tiresome, Faith. We agreed. No emotional attachments.

From: Empress Faith
To: Eliot Gray
Re: Our future

Oh. I get it. She's too good to do the things you do with me. Your precious Alicia. It's not fair. Maybe we should call things off.

From: Eliot Gray
To: Empress Faith
Re: Our future

You're a grown woman, not a child. Act like it. Stop calling me on my personal cell phone.

From: Empress Faith
To: Eliot Gray
Re: Our future

Maybe I should tell Alicia all the crazy things we do in bed. What you like, how you like it...

From: Eliot Gray
To: Empress Faith
Re: Our future

Do that, and I'll make you regret it.

Time ceased to exist. She didn't know how long she had been staring at the screen, absorbing every word of the exchange, or when tears began to flow down her cheeks and soaked her chest. The intimate back and forth was one long draft message that was never sent.

Despite the evidence staring her in the face, a small part of her, deep in the crevices of her mind, hoped that this was a mistake. It just was a misunderstanding. Her interpretation was wrong. This was clearly someone playing a cruel game. This couldn't be the truth. Her loving, brilliant husband wasn't cheating on her.

Kat's warning came roaring back again: *People who go looking for trouble usually find it.*

Why did she open his email? What was she expecting to find? Not this. Anything but this.

She wiped her tears on the sleeves of her blouse, took a loud, aching breath, and guzzled down the bottle of water she had brought with her. There must be something wrong with her, because any normal woman would have exited the email folder, powered down the laptop, and called it a night. But not Alicia. She wanted to learn more. Prove there was some mistake.

She clicked on the 'sent' folder and found only three emails. She opened the most recent one, and gasped, yet again. It was the itinerary for the trip to Paris, a week ago. Eliot's administrative assistant, Erica, had emailed the itinerary to his personal email account. But then Eliot had forwarded it to this Faith woman. Alicia clicked the down arrow to see her email address: Empress Faith.

Was she serious? Empress?

Other pieces of the puzzle clicked into place: Nathan Hunt's call in Paris. Eliot's email telling Faith to stop calling his personal cell phone. *Nathan Hunt must be Faith.* That was why Eliot had panicked at the phone call during dinner, and that was why he'd said nothing when she'd complained to him in Paris about Nathan calling so late.

He'd known it was his mistress.

CHAPTER 18

ALICIA AWOKE EARLY the next morning before Eliot did and left the bed.

She'd hardly slept all night, only crawling into bed after he was asleep. She couldn't stand the thought of him spooning her the way he usually did, not after what she had discovered. She had wept into her pillow—silent, gut-wrenching, body-wracking, going-to-kill-him sobs.

What about the sweet things he'd said to her only a week ago? Were they all lies? She'd been married to the man for twenty years. He hadn't been pretending in Paris. Alicia was sure of that. Or at least she thought she was. Every word seemed genuine, every touch, every kiss.

Then how do you explain his betrayal?

With each question, fresh waves of misery had assailed her last night. Sometimes it hurt so badly, she thought her heart would explode onto the bedsheets.

After showering away some of the night's pain and squeezing a few drips of eye drops into her eyeballs, she looked and felt better. She had to act as though everything was normal. No hint of trouble in paradise. She couldn't reveal what she had discovered. Not yet.

"You were up early. I reached for you, and you weren't there," Eliot said, as he walked into the kitchen an hour or so later.

"I wanted to get an early start. Your coffee is here," she said, pointing to the mug on the kitchen table.

"Thank you, baby." He pulled out the chair across from her and sat. "I'm working from home this morning, so I can hang out with you for a while before I head into the office later."

"That's great. The girls will be happy to see you at the breakfast table before they leave for school."

She took a sip of her coffee, then decided she would keep herself busy. She would get a big hearty breakfast going. They would have breakfast as a family, like normal. Everything was normal.

Except it wasn't.

Breakfast didn't go as planned. She'd prepared a western omelet, French toast and a fresh fruit platter. The girls woke up late, scurried into the kitchen, barely said hello before announcing they would grab something to eat at the school cafeteria.

"I guess it's just us," Eliot said. "I'm digging in."

Her stomach churned at the idea of food. She imagined herself puking all over his lying, lowdown, dirty-rat of a face.

"I'm not hungry," she said. "I have to get going soon. Need to check out a new computer. You said no excuses, right?"

She meant it as a joke, but her heart wasn't in it and her delivery came out weak and unenthusiastic.

A concerned frown framed his inquiring eyes. "Is everything okay, baby?"

Don't you "baby" me, you lying snake!

"Why wouldn't it be?" She laughed. "Is everything okay with you?"

"Everything is fine."

"Are you sure?" she pressed. She was giving him a chance to come clean.

"Yes. What's going on, Alicia?"

"Be honest, Eliot. Are you happy? If you're not, tell me. We can fix it."

She didn't mean to come off as pathetic, but the pain was eating away at her like some corrosive acid that destroyed everything in its path. She didn't know how long she could keep up this ruse of normality. Discovering the affair had blindsided her. So had the earring purchase, which he'd clearly bought for Faith. The matching earrings to her anniversary bracelet. The total rat!

There had been no signs that anything was wrong in their marriage. Didn't it usually start with the couple fighting over the silliest things, drifting apart, and barely communicating except about the kids? Then the cheating spouse would withdraw affection. There had been none of that. They were still as crazy about each other as they had been since day one of their relationship. Or so she thought.

"Where is this coming from? Are you feeling all right?" Eliot's brow furrowed. He reached out his hand to hers, but she pulled away.

"Please, Eliot," she pleaded. "Don't lie to me. If you're seeing someone else, it will take me a long time to get over the betrayal, but people make mistakes. You're human. I promise you I won't give up on us. Whatever has caused you to stray, we can work it out."

He looked her dead in the face. "Alicia, I would never cheat on you. I love our family. I love you with every fiber of my being. There is no one else. You're it, my heart, my forever. You know my father and I have our issues, but the one piece of advice he gave me that was worth anything was 'don't mess with the home base'. You and the girls are my anchor in this crazy world. I can't, wouldn't, mess with that."

She hadn't known it, but there was something even more painful than discovering your husband's infidelity: his denial of cheating. She wanted to scream at him, tell him she knew he was lying and that she had proof. Her voice, however, had deserted her.

She didn't expect an outright confession. Dodging the issue, sure. Playing dumb or trying to make her look like she was nuts, fine. But to lie with such confidence, sincerity, and poise... Well, she'd never expected that from Eliot.

"Okay," she said, defeat clouding her voice.

This was neither the time nor place to fight this battle. She would regroup. Give him one more chance to tell the truth. Right now, she needed a strategy. This was unfamiliar territory for her, and she had to learn how to navigate the terrain. Now, she understood how her mother must have felt when she'd found out Alicia's father had been unfaithful. The discovery had changed her mom. She had never been the same after that. Alicia believed her mother mourned her father's leaving up to the day she died.

Eliot stood up and came around to her side of the table. He sidled up next to her. "Baby, what's this really about? Where did you get the idea that I'm cheating on you?"

She forced a smile but didn't answer.

"I promise, I will never leave you. How else can I reassure you? What's really bothering you?"

"Who is Nathan Hunt?" she blurted out.

He froze. Then his facial muscles relaxed. "He's a lawyer with the firm. We work together."

"Why did he call you at midnight? If you work together, he knew you were in Paris last week."

He loosened his tie and then turned away from her.

"There was some information for the Paris project that I needed. I asked Nathan to call me the minute he had it, no matter the hour. I realize the call disturbed your sleep, but it's nothing for you to worry about. Just work."

She had backed herself into a corner. She couldn't confess now that she had looked up Nathan Hunt and knew that he was a litigation lawyer out of the New York office. The likelihood that he and Eliot worked together was slim. Possible, but unlikely.

Eliot specialized in project finance, helping large, multi-national corporations negotiate terms and agreements with lenders and investors. Nathan sued or defended companies from lawsuits, depending on the client's needs. Alicia wasn't a lawyer, but she knew that there was no obvious connection between the two specialties of the company that would justify the two men working together.

However, in the digital world, any name could be assigned to any phone number in a contact list, so Eliot could have assigned Nathan's name to Faith's number to deflect suspicion. It was the perfect cover. The lengths he'd gone through to deceive her stabbed at Alicia's heart.

"I'm sorry for jumping to conclusions," she said, eager to

end the conversation. "Your job is demanding. Sometimes that means getting calls at odd hours."

He kissed her on the cheek. "It's okay. I understand why you were suspicious. There's no need to be. I'm not going anywhere. You're stuck with me, whether you like it or not."

I'm not going anywhere.

The email exchange flashed in Alicia's mind. Faith was upset that Eliot was still married to her. He'd made it clear that he had no intention of leaving Alicia. So why the hell was he cheating?

CHAPTER 19

YOU'RE PRACTICALLY SHAKING, Alicia. What's happened?" Kat said, as she and Alicia sat down on the patio sofas.

She'd invited Kat over out of desperation. It was best to speak to Kat face-to-face before the girls came home from school and caught them. They might accidentally mention it to Eliot, and he would think it odd that Kat was here in the middle of the day, given her hectic schedule. Though Alicia had been upset about the bracelet situation, all that paled in comparison to what she'd since discovered. And right now, she needed a friend, a listening ear. Kat was discreet. She also knew Eliot well and would be objective, tell Alicia what she needed to hear, not what she wanted to hear.

"Eliot is cheating on me."

Kat's face dropped. "I'm sorry, I didn't hear you. What did you just say?"

"You heard me."

Kat whispered something under her breath in rapid

Spanish, a bunch of expletives, Alicia was sure.

Kat abruptly stood up. "Stay there. We need alcohol." She raced into the kitchen. It was just after one in the afternoon, and Alicia had barely eaten all day, but in her current state, she didn't object to downing alcohol. Kat would drink most of it, anyway.

Returning with a bottle and two glasses, Kat plonked down on the sofa and poured generously. "You're gonna need this." She thrust the glass into Alicia's hand. "*I'm* gonna need this!"

She took a gulp and then placed the glass down on the table. "Okay, start from the beginning," she said. "Tell me everything. We won't get emotional until I'm ready to kill Eliot and that *perra*, whoever she is."

The entire story came tumbling out of Alicia, punctuated by bouts of hiccups, breathlessness, rambling and hot, bitter tears. Kat held on to her hand and listened attentively.

The exchange via email came roaring back, the words slicing through her anew, as if she had just made the discovery for the first time. After she had no more tears left, she sat up straight, and wiped her face with the back of her hand.

Kat refilled Alicia's glass of wine and insisted she drink it all.

"He lied right to my face, Kat. If you'd heard him, you would have thought I belonged in a psych ward for even bringing up the idea."

"Eliot came to see me a few days ago, to cheer me up. He remembered it was the anniversary of Arturo's death. I apologized again for the incident at Arnie's. He was cool about it, but I asked him if he felt guilty and had taken you to Paris to make it up to you."

The hairs on Alicia's arm stood at attention. Eliot never mentioned that he and Kat had discussed the incident at

Arnie's. He was the one who'd insisted that they put the "ugly incident" behind them when Alicia had confronted him the morning after.

"Anyway," Kat continued, "he got upset, yelled at me for suggesting he felt guilt over it. Now, I'm wondering if I hit a nerve. What if Eliot in fact did take you to Paris because, A, he felt guilty that he was cheating, and B, he wanted to throw you off the scent that he was being a bad boy?"

The possibility hit her with the force of a freight train. She had previously questioned herself about Eliot's behavior in Paris and if it meant what she thought at the time. Whether or not he was being genuine or was just pretending. She'd been so sure that he was genuine, but considering Kat's observation, she began to doubt herself.

"Do you think he's going to leave me?"

"Oh, Alicia, he—"

"According to those emails, that *woman* has been pressuring him to do just that, but he'd told her to knock it off. This morning he swore up and down that he would never abandon me, or our family."

"He wouldn't, Alicia. He couldn't." Conviction rang in Kat's voice. "Eliot would be a shell of a man without you and the girls. That's why he told the home-wrecker to cut it out."

Emotions bubbled up through Alicia's chest again. "I can't go through what my mother did, Kat, I just can't."

"You're not your mother, and the circumstances are different. Your father left you and your mother penniless, and you guys did what you needed to do to scrape by. It's not the same situation here."

"How is it any different?" Alicia asked. "He knows how

I grew up, that my father leaving left a hole in my heart that never healed. How could he even consider doing that to Lily and Marston?"

"Let's not get ahead of ourselves," Kat said. "Nobody is going anywhere. Eliot needs a reality check, a painful one, but you two are meant for each other."

"I used to think so. What I don't understand is why. I mean, is there something wrong with me? Do you think he wanted the beautiful, glamorous career woman all along and got stuck with me instead? Is he acting out now?"

Kat expelled a loud sigh. "If you weren't already hurting, I would slap you for making that idiotic comment."

"Come on, Kat. I'm just a boring housewife, nothing exciting. Maybe this Faith chick is all the things I'm not. I bet she's drop-dead gorgeous. Eliot likes beautiful women. You can't deny that."

"Forget what I said. If you don't stop, I am going to slap you," Kat threatened. "Men like Eliot don't do anything they don't want to do. He wouldn't have married you if he didn't want to. He wouldn't have hung around for twenty years. Besides, some men cheat because they can. Stop making this your fault."

Alicia couldn't bring herself to smile, but in that moment, she was so grateful for her best friend's no-nonsense ways. "Thanks for having my back," Alicia said. "I can't believe my life has become a walking cliché. While we were in Paris, we talked about our future as empty nesters. What do I have to look forward to with two grown daughters in college and a husband who could walk out at any moment?"

"Everything. You have *everything* to look forward to. If Eliot won't end the affair, divorce him, take all his money, and live life on your terms. You can do anything you want, become anyone you want. No limits."

"You make it sound easy."

"It is. You gave him twenty years of your life and two beautiful daughters. I'm rooting for you guys, but you don't deserve this treatment. Eliot has obviously lost his mind. If he can't appreciate what he has, then he deserves to lose it all."

Alicia had given little thought to what would happen if Eliot continued his affair. From his performance this morning, it looked like the likely outcome, unless she confronted him with the proof she had. But could she do that? Was she ready to drop that ax on her marriage?

"Show me the emails," Kat said.

"I can't read them again," Alicia protested. "It gutted me the first time."

"No problem. Just open the inbox, and I'll take it from there. Tell me where to look."

"Okay." She led the way inside to the kitchen table where her brand new laptop sat. However, when she launched her Internet browser and typed in Eliot's email password, she got an error message. She frowned in confusion. "That's weird."

"What?" Kat asked, leaning over her shoulder.

"The password doesn't work."

"Maybe you typed it in wrong."

Alicia tried again, her fingers tapping the keys slowly, ensuring she didn't make a mistake this time. But she got the same message again, either the email or password was incorrect. "I don't understand why it's not working."

"He changed the password, didn't he?"

"Oh, my goodness." She leaned back in the chair. "I'm

playing cat and mouse with my own husband. And I can't mention that the password has changed because he'll want to know why I tried to access his email."

"But if you say nothing, he'll assume he's safe," Kat said.

"Exactly." She blew out a puff of air from her cheeks. "But someone else knows."

"What are you talking about?"

"Someone's been sending me anonymous notes, implying that Eliot is hiding a secret, that he's been lying to me."

Kat shook her head and muttered under her breath. "When did this happen?"

"The first one showed up last week. Then I got another one yesterday."

"But how? You just found out he was cheating. Do you have them still?"

"I didn't believe the notes at first. I just threw them out."

"What are you going to do?"

"Wait him out. He can't lie forever."

"And then what?"

She didn't know.

CHAPTER 20

N OTE NUMBER THREE arrived a few minutes after eleven the next morning.

You're running out of time.
Don't be taken by surprise.

Why would she be caught by surprise? She already knew Eliot was unfaithful. Yet the sender had taken the time to warn her, as if there was more to the story. *You're running out of time. Don't be taken by surprise.* Was she missing something?

After the note appeared, Alicia left the house, hoping that a change in scenery would give her some perspective about what to do next. She found an open booth at the Starbucks on Main Street in Waltham, five miles from home, and sat down with her laptop. As the email browser loaded, she diverted her gaze from the screen to take in her surroundings. A stalling tactic. Blenders whirred. Patrons placed their orders. The coffee grinder was on full blast. The smell of coffee collided with the other drinks the café served and produced a sweet, candy aroma that wafted throughout the space.

Once her attention returned to the screen, she loosened up her fingers and typed a message to Faith.

From: Alicia Gray
To: Empress Faith
Subject: Eliot Gray

Faith,

I imagine you know who I am. It must be a shock to hear from the woman whose husband you're sleeping with, but I thought we should be adults about this. Eliot has a family. A family that existed before you came along. You have no right to ask him to desert our daughters and a twenty-year marriage for a temporary fling. Have some respect for yourself. Leave us alone. It won't end well for you.

Alicia Gray

She hit send. If she'd hesitated, she would have talked herself out of it. She had no idea what would happen next, but she gave herself a mental high-five for having the courage to send the email and not let it languish in a draft folder.

Butterflies roiled in her stomach. She asked the young girl at the table next to her if she'd mind watching her things while she went to grab a cup of coffee. Alicia wasn't sure she could drink the coffee despite the dryness in her mouth, but she needed to do something; she couldn't just sit there. The line was about five people deep, so not too long to wait. As she moved forward, she forced thoughts of what she'd done out of her mind. If Faith had the guts to respond to her email, it would take a day or two, surely. Instead, she resolved, once she returned to her laptop, she would send that email to the admissions office she'd been meaning to and continue gathering the documents and information she would need to launch her return to the classroom.

Except, Alicia was wrong. In the ten minutes that elapsed between hitting send on the email, waiting in line for her coffee, and returning to her spot, a response had come in. And it was vicious.

From: Empress Faith
Re: Eliot Gray

What a sad cliché you are. The clingy wife, desperate to hold on to a husband who doesn't want her anymore. Have some dignity. Eliot only took you to Paris because he pitied you. Did you think it meant anything? We were in contact the whole time. He couldn't wait for the farce to be over.

Empress Faith

Her breathing stalled. When she caught her breath again, she covered her mouth, as if to hold the shock and fear inside. The savage, cruel truth was laid bare before her eyes. This woman's crushing words were nothing less than the deadly avalanche of lava, ash, and gas spewing from a dormant volcano. Its only goal: her complete destruction.

Alicia barely remembered leaving the café. The girl who'd watched her laptop flashed a look of concern as she bundled her stuff, knocking over her newly purchased coffee and dashing out the store. She didn't know how she ended up on the Mass Turnpike, heading East to Boston. She wasn't aware of how fast she was driving or of other cars on the highway. She didn't remember stopping at the toll booth to pay the toll or which exit was the right one. All she knew was that she needed to speak to Kat. She didn't want to be alone right now. Her friend always knew how to pull her back from the ledge.

She whipped out her phone once she arrived at Kat's Atlantic Avenue building and sent a text.

Alicia: I'm just outside your building. Need to talk. It's urgent.

She hit send and waited for a response. One came a few minutes later.

Kat: Come on up. Meet me in the conference room, wrapping up a meeting.

By the time she arrived at the door of the sleek conference room, she could barely breathe. Kat's employees filed out, casting puzzled looks at her bedraggled state. She entered to see Kat sitting in her chair gazing out at the view of the city. Alicia closed the door behind her.

Kat turned around. "What's going on? You're freaking me out."

Alicia plopped down in the chair closest to Kat. "You were right," she croaked.

"About what?"

"Eliot. He took me to Paris to ease his guilt because he was seeing another woman."

Kat squinted in confusion. "What are you talking about? I was just running my mouth when I said that—"

"Turns out you were right," she said, her breath shaky.

"What happened?"

"I'll show you." She took out her computer and pulled up the email she'd gotten from Faith.

Kat rubbed her eyes after reading the email. "I can't wrap my head around the kind of person who would send you this message. It's cruel. Obviously written by a shameless whore. Do you have any idea at all who this woman is?"

"I don't," Alicia whispered.

"A co-worker of Eliot's? Didn't you tell me about a woman who brazenly flirted with him right in front of you at a barbecue last year?" Kat snapped her fingers, trying to recall the name. "Barbara Sellers. That's her."

"You think? Alicia asked. "She goes by Faith in the emails."

Kat gave her the "Are you kidding me?" look. "You think Side Chick Babs is going to use her real name when luring away other people's husbands?"

Alicia had all but forgotten about Barbara, a snobbish, high-on-herself attorney who sometimes worked cases with Eliot. The first time Alicia met Barbara, the woman had not hesitated to unleash a thinly veiled insult at Alicia.

She recalled the disdain on Barbara's flawless made-up face. "*Oh, from the way Eliot talks about you, I was expecting someone different...*"

Apparently, Alicia didn't measure up to Barbara's expectation of what Eliot's wife should be. Had Eliot given her an opening, implied that things weren't great at home?

"I don't know what to think," she said.

"Well, I do," Kat said. "We're going to write back to Little Ms. Home Wrecker."

"What? No way."

"Yes way. She wants to be nasty, let's show her she doesn't scare us."

"Kat, I don't think that's a good idea. Things may escalate."

"Good. Let them. Let her spill her guts and tell all. She's met her match. This is your husband of twenty years, Alicia.

You can't let some random side dish think she can just swoop in and take everything from you. No. Show the *perra* who the real empress is."

Before Alicia could take back the laptop, Kat began to type, wasting no time in composing the perfect response. Alicia still had doubts about this approach, but Kat was right about one thing: Alicia couldn't allow this woman to steal her husband and break up her family. Alicia owed it to her daughters to put up a fight.

A couple of minutes later, Kat handed her the laptop. "What do you think?"

From: Alicia Gray
Re: Eliot Gray

Women like you are common and cheap, a dime a dozen. The way you responded tells me you have no class. No shame. Eliot will NEVER be serious about you. Why do you think he kept you his dirty little secret? Because that's all you'll ever be.

Alicia swallowed hard. The response was harsh and didn't sound like her at all. But she wasn't herself. Everything had changed.

"Are you sure, Kat? This woman might be psychotic, capable of much worse than mouthing off in an email."

"Alicia, the woman is sleeping with your husband, and she insulted you," Kat said indignantly. "How much worse can it get? She's in the wrong, and you want to back down? If I were you, I would hunt her down, scratch out her eyeballs, and then jam them down her trampy throat."

She could always count on Kat to get to the point in her uniquely creative way; she couldn't allow Faith to think she had won. But this would be the last message. A drawn-out back-and-forth would be childish.

"Okay, you've convinced me," Alicia said. She hit send and stood up from the table.

"Don't give her any power over you, Alicia," Kat said. "You're Eliot's perfect angel, remember? If he was serious about Faith, he would have packed his bags a long time ago."

But what was stopping him from doing that any day now? Her husband had looked her dead in the face and lied when confronted. At this juncture, Alicia wasn't sure what she was fighting for.

CHAPTER 21

I MEANT WHAT I said, Eliot. This can't go on any longer. You have to tell Alicia everything. It's better to rip the band-aid off. Your daughters are almost grown. What's the point of waiting?"

Eliot had snuck away from the office and driven the twenty minutes to the apartment in Chestnut Hill. Faith stood in front of the bedroom mirror, teased out her short curls, and then re-applied lipstick. Eliot flawlessly executed a Windsor knot on his Italian silk tie.

He had to end it before his life imploded. He'd completely forgotten he'd left his email account open when he'd let Alicia borrow his computer. He wasn't sure if she'd read his messages, but he couldn't take the chance. How could he have been so careless? He'd let his arrogance and complacency get the better of him after getting away with seeing Faith for so long. What a stupid, rookie mistake.

Other than her questions about Nathan Hunt, Alicia had exhibited no signs of a wife who suspected her husband was cheating. Those questions had worried him, but now, he had to be extra careful and break off the relationship with Faith before any further damage occurred.

He would not lose the love of his life and his daughters. He would not give his prick of a father the satisfaction of seeing him fail. Eliot Gray, Sr, would love nothing more than to see his son lose his family.

"You screwed up yet again. You had it all and you couldn't keep it together. You're such a disappointment." Then his father would shake his head in that way Eliot had dreaded as a kid and walk away as though he detested being in the same room as his firstborn.

Eliot put on his jacket and said, "I made myself clear, Faith. What do I need to do to prove to you that I meant what I said? I'm not leaving Alicia. I'm not abandoning my daughters. I can't put it any simpler than that. Bringing it up every time we meet will not yield a different outcome. My family stays intact."

She turned around. "Right. Because you need your perfect little family intact for the cameras. Ladies and gentlemen, senatorial candidate Eliot Gray, his mousy homemaker wife, and their lovely daughters. Yay." She clapped in mock applause.

"Watch yourself, Faith," he growled. "My patience is wearing thin."

She edged closer to him so they were eyeball to eyeball. "Ooh, I'm so scared. I'm tired of being your dirty little secret, Eliot. Alicia deserves the truth, that her hero husband is a big, fat, lying zero who has been cheating on her for years. How about that?" She poked him in the chest with an index finger.

Eliot grabbed her face. His fingers dug into her jaw. He applied enough pressure to keep it steady. Her eyes bulged with

119

fright. Eliot was not a violent man, but this time was different. Everything was at stake.

"This is my final warning. Keep Alicia out of your delusions. If you make any attempt to contact her, repeat any of this garbage you've been spewing, I will kill you." He released his grip and wiped his hands on his wool pants, as if touching her made his skin crawl.

Faith stood silent, shaken, unable to move or speak. Tears trailed down her face.

Eliot picked up the last of his things and turned to leave. But as he walked away, he heard two words that stopped him dead in his tracks.

"I'm pregnant."

CHAPTER 22

ALICIA CLOSED HER eyes and stretched. She'd finally finished her transfer student application to UMass. She'd taken advantage of rolling admissions, and it felt good to power down the laptop, not to mention pleased to have taken the first step on her new adventure. She picked up her phone from the desk to set the alarm before she went off to bed when her email inbox, the last app she used, popped up before she could punch in her passcode.

Alicia's stomach dropped.

There was a new email from Faith.

She dreaded reading the response. Should she open it now? Probably not the best idea before bed, but could she sleep, knowing what was lurking in her inbox?

She tapped the screen.

From: Empress Faith
To: Alicia Gray
Re: Eliot Gray

Listen, you ugly cow. It's over. We're starting a new

family. Your days as Mrs. Eliot Gray are numbered. Just accept it, Alicia. You're old news, his past.

Empress Faith

New family? With trembling fingers, she tapped the attachment in the email and for the second time that week, an avalanche cascaded over her. The attachment was a photograph. A sonogram, to be exact.

Eliot was having a baby with his mistress.

Alicia hunched over in the chair, as if her skeleton could no longer hold her. The photo shot straight through the heart. Numbness overtook her. She couldn't muster the energy to cry.

The world moved in slow motion. A thick, horrific, nightmarish fog had a stranglehold on her thoughts, emotions, and physical state. She trembled as if it were freezing cold instead of a warm spring night.

Was this her punishment? Was God still angry with her for what she'd done? She had prayed with Tina, her pastor's wife, and she'd assured Alicia that she was forgiven because Christ had died for her sins as it says in John 19:30: *it is finished.* And she'd thought it was. But look what was happening now. It didn't seem finished.

The tears suddenly broke like a dam, and then the wounded howling began, followed by heavy crying that made coherent speech impossible. She was so deep in her misery she didn't hear the door open.

"Mom, what's wrong?"

She jerked upright, placed the phone face down on the desk and wiped her face with the back of her hand as Lily came farther into the room.

"Mom, are you okay? You look terrible. What's going on? Should I get Dad?"

"No," she said sharply. She took Lily's hand for emphasis. "It's okay, baby. I'm fine."

"Then why were you wailing?"

Alicia hated lying and she hated liars—like Eliot—but she had to protect her child. "I was thinking about your grandmother. About when I lost her, how it felt to be all alone in the world at twenty years old."

"It's okay, Mom. You're not alone anymore. You have us."

Lily placed her arms around her mother and hugged her tight. What would she do if she didn't have her girls?

"And when you get old, I won't send you to a nursing home," Lily promised. "You can come live with me and my family."

Alicia chuckled. "Thank you, Lily. It's nice to know I have options."

"I wish I had met her—your mom. Grandma Ella is great and all, but it would have been nice to know my maternal grandmother, too."

"She would have loved you. You're like her in so many ways."

Lily took a seat on the antique sofa. "Tell me how I'm like her. You never talk about her much. Is it because it makes you sad?"

"Well, a little. Your grandmother was feisty. She wouldn't want us crying. She cursed out the landlord one time because he refused to fix a broken window. I thought he would evict us because she mouthed off to him. She wouldn't back down, though. She withheld the rent and got in his face when he made demands. Eventually, he caved. Only then did she pay the rent."

"Wow, she does sound fierce."

"She was. She told the guys who hung around the

neighborhood, 'undesirables' she called them, that if they even so much as looked at me sideways, she would cut off their you-know-what."

"What about Grandpa Reginald? What was he like? You never talk about him, ever. That's not healthy, Mom. You're stuffing your feelings."

Tell me about it.

"You're chatty tonight, Missy," Alicia said, changing the subject. "Did you need something?"

"Yes. I came to tattletale on Marston."

"What's going on?"

"Marston is not okay, Mom."

"What are you talking about? What's wrong with her?"

"It's the real story behind why she won't go to prom. She's hurting. It was more than Brandon asking someone else instead of her. She's going to kill me for telling you, but I can't watch her suffer anymore. She would rather die than tell you."

Alicia switched to mama-bear mode. Forget her husband's deceit—the lying rat. Her daughters were what mattered now.

CHAPTER 23

"I S EVERYTHING OKAY, Eliot?"

"What?"

His administrative assistant, Erica Jones, asked again, "Is everything okay? Do you need some tea or coffee? Can I get you anything? You seem distracted."

"I do?"

"Yes. You asked me to schedule a meeting with Tom Pfeiffer at JC Stanfield. But you already spoke to him last week about his issues with the Sterling pharma project."

Eliot rubbed his temple as if trying to remember.

"You told him if he wouldn't play ball, you would advise your client that another investment bank would be a better fit and have them divest their assets from JCS."

"Oh, yes. Yes. The ball is in Tom's court now. I'm sure he'll tell me what I want to hear soon. Not to worry."

He sat behind his cluttered desk. File folders, documents, pens, and notebooks were strewn all over. This was not normal for him. He liked things neat and organized. What was happening to him? Thank goodness he had Erica to keep him on track.

"Have you spoken to Alicia lately?" Eliot asked her casually. "Perhaps she tried tracking me down at the office and you forgot to mention it?"

She wrinkled a curious brow. "No. Alicia rarely calls your office line, if ever, and even if she did, I wouldn't forget to tell you. Is something wrong?"

Faith's bombshell revelation from yesterday afternoon had shaken him. Long after he returned to the office, it continued to rattle around in his head. He'd lost his focus on work. He was making ridiculous inquiries, and Erica, by the look on her face, thought he'd left his brain on the breakfast table this morning. But he needed to be sure Alicia didn't suspect a thing.

"Nothing's wrong. Everything is great," he reassured Erica.

The possibility that Faith was lying to force him to end his marriage was real. However, if she was telling the truth, that would be the least of his problems. He would not ask her to terminate the pregnancy. He couldn't do that. So, how was this going to work? Two separate families and never the two shall meet? That was a fool's errand.

The fallout would be far-reaching. It would devastate his daughters—Lily, who was a Daddy's girl and who wanted to be a lawyer like him, and his sweet, quiet Marston, who was so much like her mother. How would he find the courage to tell them that they had a new sibling? And what about the rest of his family? His sisters, Summer and Dana, who adored Alicia. Ella Scott Gray, the kind, dignified, loving woman he was proud to call Mamma. He would lose her respect.

But what terrified him most of all was the thought of

losing Alicia and the family they'd built together. They were about to have a son who would carry on the family name before he was so cruelly snatched away when Alicia suffered the miscarriage. The news that he got another woman pregnant would break her.

He'd met Alicia Thomas, the girl with a smile that could light up the night sky, twenty-two years ago at a Boston restaurant. Eliot was in his mid-twenties, fresh out of Harvard Law, and a newly minted associate at Tillerson Brenner. His childhood best friend, Sam Robinson, had come for a visit, and together with a couple of young lawyers from the firm, they'd headed to a casual dining spot in the city after a long day.

When she'd arrived at their table to take their drinks order, Eliot had noticed her smile right away, and then her shyness, intoxicating as it was.

"When does your shift end?" he had asked.

She'd gaped at him, as if no one had posed that question to her before and she didn't know what to make of it.

"See, now you scared her," Sam said. "Way to go, Eliot."

"Sorry if I came on too strong," he said with a smile. "I thought I would ask you first before the other guys in here get the same idea. What's your name?"

She hesitated. Then, in a light pleasant voice, she said, "I'm Alicia." She pointed to the nametag he'd pretended he hadn't seen.

"Well, Alicia, it's nice to meet you."

He kept his eyes fastened on her. The poor girl was so flustered her hand shook when she wrote their orders on the notepad. After she took off, his friend razzed him.

"She's too good for you, Eliot," Sam said. "Too sweet and innocent. Did you see how quickly she wanted to get away from you?"

They had all thought it was funny and had a big laugh at his expense, but she'd intrigued him. Though Alicia was shy, he'd observed a sadness in her eyes. He wanted to learn who or what had put it there. He'd resolved to show up at the restaurant the same time, every evening, hoping to run into her until he gathered up enough courage to ask for her phone number.

She had stirred something in him he couldn't explain. The more he learned about her, the more he knew she was *the* one. The realization had stealthily crept up on him and then whacked him over the head. Until that moment, he had no desire to be tied down. He was young and had his entire life ahead of him. At the time, he'd thought he would be in his early thirties, at least, before he considered marriage.

Yet, two years later, on his twenty-seventh birthday, he and Alicia were married in a lavish ceremony at an antebellum mansion in his hometown of Atlanta.

"Eliot, are you with me?" Erica asked.

"Sorry? Yes, sure." He stepped out of his perfect past, back to his messy present.

"Why are you worried about Alicia tracking you down at work? She's not that kind of wife."

His phone buzzed. When he looked at the screen, his stomach roiled. Then with shaky fingers, he declined the call. "I'm not worried. She had a minor emergency the other day and couldn't reach me, that's all."

"I would tell you right away if she called. She's so thoughtful. I still can't believe she baked me that birthday cake and brought it into the office."

"That's my Alicia. Sweet and thoughtful."

His phone buzzed again.

He ignored it a second time.

"Someone wants you." Erica raised an eyebrow. "I'll leave you to it," she said, heading back to her desk.

Nathan: Tell her or I will!

Eliot needed time alone to sort his thoughts. He put his phone on his desk, leaving the message unanswered, and moved to the window, both hands in his pockets, and looked out at Faneuil Hall Marketplace—a Boston landmark set around a cobblestone promenade. The bustling crowds enjoyed music, entertainment, and the convenience of multiple shops, restaurants, and pubs.

He would not panic. It was more important than ever that he maintained control over his emotions. This was a test. Faith wanted to see how far she could push him. If she insisted on this little game of hers, he would simply checkmate her. He would make sure she lost everything.

CHAPTER 24

M ARSTON, BABY, TELL me what's going on."

"Lily told you, didn't she?"

Alicia smiled. "Yes, she did. Yesterday. I'm glad she said something, though. She's worried about you. So am I."

"I told her it was no big deal. She has such a big mouth."

Alicia had knocked gently on Marston's door and joined her eldest daughter in her bedroom. It would be easier for her to confide in her mother if she were in her own space. The room perfectly suited her personality: mellow, simple and elegant. The décor and beddings were various shades of buttercup yellow, purple, and lavender. A few photos lined the walls—mostly of the family and a few with Marston with her teammates from the track team. A large bookshelf containing classics and modern books in various genres dominated the room.

"Come sit next to me," Alicia said. She patted a spot on the small sofa near the window.

Marston silently complied.

"Lily said there was more to the story of why you don't

want to go to prom?"

"Mom, I really don't want to talk about it. I don't know why Lily said anything. Brandon asked someone else to the prom. I was upset because I thought he liked me, thought we had a connection. I was wrong. He picked somebody else. End of story."

Alicia knew that wasn't the end.

The scent of the lilac blossom candle perched on the desk filled her with calm. She embraced the feeling. No matter how long it took, she would be patient and non-judgmental until the entire story came out. A small part of her felt guilty that she hadn't picked up the clues, subtle or otherwise, that something was bothering Marston. Alicia was usually in tune with her daughters, but lately, she'd been so caught up in her own drama she'd missed that her baby needed her.

"Did Brandon explain why he asked this other girl instead of you? He owes you an explanation if you had some form of relationship."

"Oh, there was nothing like that, and it didn't matter, anyway. So, why would I bother to ask? It wouldn't have changed anything."

"If you thought there was something between you, why didn't he have the guts to tell you if he didn't feel the same?"

"Mom, he's an eighteen-year-old boy. You assume a maturity on his part that he doesn't have. You give him too much credit."

"Maybe I do. But Marston, you're an intelligent, thoughtful, mature girl who doesn't do anything on a whim. Brandon must have done or said something that led you to believe he liked you. So, I can only assume he's behaved like a big-time jerk, somehow?"

Marston stood up and folded her arms. Her eyes glistened.

Alicia looked at her daughter, knowing that all she needed was a little push, a nudge to tell her mother everything.

"He *was* a jerk," Marston said. "But I don't see what good talking about it will do. I'm done with him. We don't speak, and I avoid him like the plague. That works for me."

"Tell me what happened, baby," Alicia said gently. "No judgment. I promise."

Ever since Marston was a kid, she had a tendency to bottle things up. Even when she got angry, she didn't react like other kids by yelling, screaming, or crying. As she got older, she got better, but she still tended to hide her true feelings, not showing any weakness.

Luckily—until now—Alicia's girls' upbringing had been secure, happy with little to no drama. But it wouldn't be long until they were out in the big wide world where Alicia could no longer protect them.

Marston sat back down next to Alicia, and she took her daughter's hand and listened as she began to speak.

"I hate him, Mom. I hate him so much. He's a big, fat liar. I can't believe I ever thought he was special. I thought he was different, but he's not. He's just a lying jerk. I never should have let him in."

Alicia pulled her daughter into her arms as the tears began to flow. "Shh, now. It's okay. He doesn't deserve you. But there's still a silver lining here. Now, you're free to be with someone who truly cares for you, and when you find him, his words and actions will match up. That's a sign of the real thing."

Marston continued to sob into her mother's chest. Alicia sensed there was still more to the story as she thought of her daughter's words: *I shouldn't have let him in.*

Alicia didn't want to jump to conclusions, but her already anxious mind skipped to the worst-case scenarios. She and Eliot were open with the girls about sex and had promoted abstinence, no sex until marriage. So far, so good. Or was she a naïve mother who didn't want to face reality?

"Marston, did Brandon pressure you into doing something that you weren't ready for?"

Deep, gut-wrenching bawling followed the question. Alicia gnawed at her lip until she tasted blood.

Marston turned to pick up her favorite stuffed elephant and hugged it for dear life. Eliot had won it as a prize during a day trip to Canobie Lake Park five years ago. She'd wanted the toy so much, and the fact that her dad had won it for her made it special. Despite the fact that she considered herself too old for cuddly toys, Cocoa never left her room.

"Did he force himself on you, Marston?"

"No, Mom. We both agreed. He said he loved me. But it was awful, Mom. Awful and painful. He was so gross, like he just wanted to get it over with. Then the next day, he acted like nothing happened and treated me like I had cooties."

Alicia's jaw clenched again. How dare this undeserving loser of a boy use and discard her daughter like she was nothing?

She hugged Marston tight, then kissed her face and forehead. "I'm taking you to see Dr. Rawlings to make sure everything is okay."

Marston didn't object. Was that a good thing?

"I don't mean to be indelicate, honey, but did he use protection?"

"I insisted." She uttered the words with firmness.

Alicia exhaled deeply, relief washing over her.

133

"Mom?"

"Yes."

"Please don't say anything to Dad. It's humiliating enough as it is. He'd go postal if he found out."

Alicia had so many questions. When did this happen and where? Did the girl Brandon asked to the prom make Marston feel uncomfortable? Girls that age could be cruel. But Alicia didn't want to overwhelm her daughter. Her self-esteem had already taken a serious beating.

"I won't tell Dad yet." She cautioned her daughter. Although she hated Eliot's guts right now, he had a right to know what was going on with his child. "But listen, Marston, honey, I don't want this awful experience to define future relationships for you. Some guys don't know when they have a gem. Ha, pretty much all guys don't."

"I feel so stupid that I fell for his lies. Now, I can't take back what we did. I wish I could."

"Don't beat yourself up, baby. Brandon is an immature jerk, and unfortunately, the world is full of them. Just leave him and what's happened in your rearview mirror. There is a perfect guy out there for you who will see how amazing you are. He will be so thrilled to be with you he won't believe his luck. And most importantly, he'll respect you."

She shrugged. "I guess."

"I know this is the last thing you want to think about, but have you given any more thought about going to prom with Veliane and Syra? I don't think you should miss out. Prom is an important rite of passage. Don't let this foolish boy ruin your fun."

"Lily said Jeff's cousin Will isn't going to his prom either. He's a senior at Boston Latin. Lily's got this idea of Will and

134

me double dating with her and Jeff. Will and I texted a few times, and he said we should go if I agreed, but I told him I didn't think so. My heart just wasn't in it after what happened with Brandon."

Alicia's heart soared. There was hope. But it had to be Marston's choice.

"Lily is very protective of you. If Will was a jerk, she would have shot down the idea and not even suggested it to you. He sounds like a nice boy, but it's up to you."

"I'll think about it."

"Good. Now I need to remember to make a hair appointment at Crystal's for the both of you."

Marston leveled a *Don't push it, Mom* gaze at Alicia. But she smiled.

"No pressure. Just in case you decide to go. You don't want to miss out, and you can cancel if you change your mind."

Alicia crossed her fingers behind her back, willing Marston to accept Will's offer. Since there were no salons in or around Weston that catered to African-American hair, Alicia and the girls often took the thirty-minute drive into Boston. At this late stage, she might have to be extra sweet to Crystal to fit them in.

"Okay, Mom. No promises. I only said I would think about it."

"That's all I'm asking."

CHAPTER 25

R INA STARK PUFFED out a plume of cigarette smoke. It burned Alicia's eyes, even though her seat was on the opposite end of the patio sectional. But she forgave Rina because she had brought another box of Krispy Kreme donuts.

"Come on. Spill the tea," Rina said impatiently. "What's going on?"

Alicia stuffed half a donut into her mouth and chewed. After she swallowed, she said, "You have to keep this confidential. You can't go blabbing to anybody."

Asking Rina to come over was a risky proposition, given her penchant for gossip. But Alicia needed someone who wasn't privy to her marital problems. Someone worldly. Rina fit the bill.

"I'm offended. Who am I going to tell?" Rina said, holding one hand to her chest in mock offense whilst stubbing out her cigarette in the ashtray with the other.

Eliot's mistress is pregnant.

The thought replayed over and over in Alicia's mind. And now this painful, messy dilemma was a cruel reminder of how foolish she'd been. She'd let her guard down, thinking Eliot was different from her father. She should have had a backup plan, a solid Plan B in case things didn't work out. She might never have needed it, but instead, she had gambled everything on forever with Eliot.

She was a naïve, unsophisticated, twenty-two-year-old when she married him. A plain Jane from the wrong side of the tracks who couldn't believe this gorgeous, Ivy League educated lawyer from a prominent family wanted to marry her.

She'd promised him she would be the best wife. She dreamt of a secure upbringing for her children, in a home with a mom and dad, showered with unconditional love. She thought she had that perfect family, but recent events had forced her to take a closer look, and the truth had revealed itself. She'd made the same mistake as her mother, by marrying a cheater.

"I need the name of a good divorce lawyer. A real shark at the top of his or her game."

"Why?" Rina asked. "Wait, you and Eliot—"

"No, don't be silly," Alicia quickly reassured her friend. "I ran into a friend from my old neighborhood. We lost touch and then she showed up at Howell House of all places."

Rina blinked in confusion. "What does that have to do with a divorce lawyer?"

"She's in an awful marriage and looking for a way out. He's a cheater, emotionally abusive, and lost all their money. She's on food stamps for goodness sake."

"That's terrible. But if things are so dire, how can she afford a top-notch divorce lawyer?"

"That's where I come in. I'm helping her out. I want to do this for her and her three children. Give them all a fresh start."

Rina lit another cigarette, took a drag, and then exhaled. The smoke floated through the air in a semi-circle. "Hmm. That's interesting. He's a cheater, huh?"

"And a liar, a terrible combination."

Rina took another slow drag, her eyes boring into Alicia.

Feeling hot under Rina's gaze, Alicia broke eye contact, darting her vision around the patio, before she refocused her attention on her neighbor, who was still staring at her. "So, do you have any suggestions?"

"I might. David's lawyer when he divorced his ex. Shark doesn't begin to describe this guy. She walked away with half of everything, including an impressive stock portfolio."

"He sounds perfect. Can you get me his contact details quickly? I told my friend to come by the clinic tomorrow because I might have a name for her."

Rina remained quiet, took another drag on her cigarette, and exhaled. The pleasant breeze carried away the smoke. "Alicia, please consider me a friend. I can be discreet when it counts. Okay?"

Alicia knew she had a terrible poker face, so she avoided looking Rina in the eye again, and instead pretended to roll up the sleeves of her blouse. She was not in the confiding mood. She had things to do first, like ensuring Eliot didn't suspect she knew about Faith, the baby, all of it.

"I do consider you a friend, Rina." Alicia smiled. "I wouldn't have asked you over if I didn't."

"Good," Rina said, satisfied with her friend's answer. "His name is Wesley George. I'll ask David for his information and text you the details later on tonight."

CHAPTER 26

E LIOT HADN'T BEEN able to get Alicia's attention once at the dinner table that night. She'd been talkative with the girls but had not said a single word to him since she served the shrimp-and-angel-hair pasta with greens. He'd noticed she hadn't touched her food, either as she was too busy talking to the girls. But whenever one of his daughters tried to draw him into the conversation, she'd switch the subject to something else that had nothing to do with him.

Eliot was confident that she hadn't found out about his pregnant mistress, but Alicia's behavior was unusual. He'd made sure to wipe clean any email communication between him and Faith from his computer and had deleted Nathan Hunt from his cell phone contact list. He'd even purchased a burner phone and asked Faith to use it exclusively now since he shut down email communication with her. At the time, he'd thought an email draft folder was safe. With the setup he had going, there would be no messages going back and forth over the internet. Faith had the login details to his email account and would leave her messages in the folder. He would respond the same way. Well, that *had* been the plan.

He stuck his fork into a shrimp—probably with a little more muscle than necessary—and forced himself to eat. Alicia was an excellent cook, but tonight the food offered no pleasure to his taste buds, no burst of texture, flavor, or aroma. His mind churned continuously, searching for a permanent solution to the Faith conundrum. A collision of his two worlds would be catastrophic. Plans for his life, both in the present and the future, would go up in flames.

The sun was setting on his career at Tillerson Brenner, as well. Twenty-one years he'd given the firm, but he'd decided that it was time to move on. One of the two Massachusetts Senate seats would be up for grabs in a little over a year, and he intended to be well positioned to have a successful run. That meant convincing Alicia to make the transition from corporate to political wife. He knew she'd make the switch with the efficiency and elegance she always did with big life changes, as they split their time between Washington, DC, and home, here in Weston.

However, it also meant that he couldn't afford any scandals. If history was any indication, nothing sank a political campaign faster than a candidate who cheated and got his mistress pregnant. *Don't forget you threatened to kill her if she told Alicia about the affair. Voters might frown upon a would-be-murderer candidate.*

As dinner came to a close, Eliot leaned forward and whispered to his wife, "Are you okay, baby?" He didn't want to alarm the girls.

For a microsecond in time, he saw something resembling resentment flicker in Alicia's usually gentle brown eyes. Then it was gone.

"I'm fine."

"No, you're not," he said with conviction. He looked at his daughters. "Could you excuse your mother and me for a moment?"

Marston and Lily looked at each other before scrambling from the table and exiting the kitchen. Eliot scooted into the seat next to his wife and reached out to touch her forearm. She recoiled. Something was terribly wrong.

"Alicia, you're not fine. What is it? Tell me. I can help you."

"Why are you so concerned that something is wrong? Did you do something wrong?"

He flinched. "You're not acting like yourself. You don't even want me to touch you."

"I've had a lot on my mind lately, thinking about my mother. Marston graduating and leaving home in three months. Doubts about my future, whether I can pull off this returning-to-school thing. It's a lot to handle. Emotionally draining, I'd say."

"Baby, that's what I'm here for, to help you through anything," he soothed. "I can't take away the pain of losing your mother, and as for Marston leaving home, I'm afraid, too, but she's growing up so fast. We have to let go. And don't doubt yourself about returning to school. You'll do great."

"I guess you're right."

He wasn't sure his little pep talk had any effect. He had always been an expert at reading her, but this new Alicia was putting up walls and he had no clue why. If she had discovered the affair, she would have raised hell with him by now. His wife was a sweet lady, but when pushed too far, her rage turned into a hurricane, and she did things no one thought her capable of. Though he would never admit it, he was afraid of her when she got that way.

It took every ounce of her strength to hold it together, not spill her guts and confront him as the pain ate her alive. Every day without release, without telling him that she knew everything, was another day the stinging betrayal wound its way around her heart, her soul, her spirit, choking the life out of her.

His affair with Faith had tainted everything—her confidence that she was enough for him, the belief their marriage would last until they each took their last breath. She hated him for making her face the harsh reality that nothing lasted forever. She hated him for stealing her peace of mind, for making her feel fragile and insecure.

"Stop worrying so much, baby. Everything will be fine."

Baby. He had tainted that moniker, too. The first time he'd called her baby, she'd turned into a mushy, gooey mess.

It was a couple of months into their relationship. He'd come by the restaurant to pick her up at the end of her shift, but it was so busy that night, she'd ended up working overtime. He'd waited patiently in the parking lot. She was so embarrassed and had apologized profusely once she got into the car and shut the door.

He'd said, "Baby, it's okay. I understand. Stop worrying." And to show her that he meant it, he'd kissed her deep and long.

"You're right," Alicia agreed, stepping back into the present and facing a very different Eliot. "Everything will be fine."

Eliot stroked her arm again. Her skin crawled as his fingers caressed her skin. She wanted to bolt out of the kitchen and hide. Did he touch Faith that way? Did he also call her baby, make her feel like the most cherished woman on earth?

Jealousy tore through Alicia. Until now, she had not allowed herself to think about what his relationship with the other woman was like. Faith had said, in their email exchange, that he had missed her the entire time he and Alicia were in Paris, and that they had kept in touch the whole time.

She didn't know if Faith was a cunning liar, desperate to get Alicia out of the picture, or whether Eliot had made promises, assuring Faith that they had a future together. Perhaps that was why the emails were so nasty and condescending, because she knew something that Alicia didn't.

He leaned over and kissed her on the neck. The move surprised her, and she wanted to withdraw, make an excuse, run. It was too painful to have him touch her, when all she could think about was his betrayal. Yet, her breath quickened. Heat flooded her body. Despite everything he'd done, her whole being ached with the desire to touch him. *Don't give in.*

She splayed her hands over his chest and gently pushed him away.

His body went slack. His arms fell to his sides, limp and lifeless. The desperation in his voice was thick when he asked, "What's wrong, Alicia?"

"Not now. There's something else, something I didn't mention before."

"What is it?"

She hated herself for what she was about to do, but she realized just how weak Eliot's betrayal had made her. His intentions were clear, but she couldn't allow her body to dictate her actions. She needed to redirect his focus. Bring him back down to earth.

"It's about Marston. I promised her I wouldn't say anything

to you, but she's your daughter. You deserve to know what's going on."

"What about Marston? Is she okay? You're scaring me, Alicia." Eliot's face was the epitome of a concerned dad.

"She's fine, physically. Emotionally, that's another story."

Alicia provided the highlights of her conversation with Marston, offering reassurances throughout that their daughter would be okay, especially since she was no longer bottling up her anxiety.

"So, you're telling me that this worthless piece of dung violated our daughter and then discarded her like trash?"

"Eliot, it was consensual; he didn't force her. She took responsibility for her part in it."

"I don't care," he spat, then stood up. He paced the floor, his expression turbulent. When he slammed his fist on the kitchen island, she jerked back in her seat.

Eliot wasn't prone to angry outbursts. He believed people who couldn't control their anger or used it to manipulate others were weak. However, everyone has a limit. When it came to his family, his children—that was where he drew the line.

"I'm going to find that little bastard and make him crap his pants."

"Eliot, calm down. Think about Marston," she pleaded.

"That's exactly who I'm thinking about." He returned to his seat at the table, dropped his face in his hands, and let out a muffled, frustrated sigh.

She reached out to her husband but caught herself and returned her hands to her lap. Crippling guilt threatened to swallow her whole. She had successfully diverted his attention, but at Marston's expense. Alicia shifted about in her seat, unable to remain still. She raked her hair back repeatedly. How would she explain to Marston why her mother betrayed her confidence if the subject came up again? Would Marston forgive her?

Alicia pondered what it would mean to end her marriage. Cheating was one thing. When she'd first discovered the infidelity, she had decided that they would work it out. She had been willing to endure the pain, anger, and the rollercoaster of emotions. She had been willing to fight for her family.

But what was there to fight for when her husband continued to lie? How could she stay married to a man who refused to own up to his betrayal? What reassurances did she have that even if she forgave him, he wouldn't do it again? The fact remained that this disloyal man was no longer the man she married.

"Our daughter will be fine. She's strong and resilient. I wish I had her levelheadedness at that age," she said to him.

"But what about you?" he asked.

"What do you mean?"

"You keep saying you're fine, but you're not. Something's not right with you, Alicia. And I don't think it has anything to do with your mother or Marston or the stress of returning to school."

"I don't know what you're talking about."

"Don't you? First you accuse me of cheating on you. Then you turn cold and distant. I want you to connect the dots for me. The truth. What's going on?"

Connect the dots? The truth?

Those words did not just come out of his mouth. He wouldn't know truth if it hit him across the face with a crowbar. The man was a high-flying lawyer, for goodness sake. He was

145

supposed to be the smart one. And yet, she recognized this tactic, meant to make her look like the one who was holding back, the one with something to hide. Oh, the irony! Charm, manipulation, and getting others to spill the truth were part of his training as a lawyer and his natural disposition, as well. She needed to tread carefully.

He'd ambushed her earlier with his display of affection, and she almost fell for it. It would be easy to explode, give in, show her cards, and lose the game. But as long as she kept him in the dark about what she had discovered, she had the advantage.

Mimicking his behavior, she looked him square in the face, without flinching. "When have I ever kept the truth about anything from you? When have I ever lied to you, to your face? When have I ever deliberately hurt you, over and over again?"

It was only momentary, but terror flashed in his eyes. A vein popped out in his neck. Then just as quickly, a smile, meant to reassure and beguile, spread across his face.

"I can't say that you have. Your honesty is one of the things I love most about you."

"I hope I'll always be able to say the same about you."

CHAPTER 27

HER APPOINTMENT WITH Wesley George was set for three. The main office was situated on Atlantic Avenue in Boston, but she'd requested that they meet at the Wellesley location instead. Kat's agency was on Atlantic Avenue, Eliot's firm less than a mile away in the financial district. She couldn't risk running into either of them.

Wesley greeted her in the posh reception area with an outstretched hand. "Call me Wes," he insisted.

He seemed to be in his late forties, around Eliot's age, African American, with baby-smooth skin, a neat moustache, and bow legs. His suit, though expensive, was slightly loose-fitting, as if he had recently lost weight.

He ushered her into the office. A bookshelf, file cabinet, and coffee maker were strategically placed around the room. A thick file sat in the center of the desk.

After she declined an offer of coffee, they both took seats. Wes opened the file, scanned some documents, and then closed the folder.

"So, Alicia, what can I do for you? What brings you here?"

She placed her hands in her lap and nervously smacked her lips. "Exploring my options. My husband has cheated, and I no longer trust him, and I don't think I ever will again."

"I see." Wes leaned back in his leather chair and twirled a pen. "You have proof of the affair?"

"Plenty."

She rummaged through her bag for the printed copies of the email exchange between her and Faith. She handed it to Wes. He read through the first pages, then placed them in the folder.

"So, you want an estimate of what you could walk away with if it came down to it, if you decide to end the marriage?"

When he put it like that, it made her sound like a gold digger. The word sent shivers up and down her spine. She wasn't greedy. She could make do with little. Money wasn't what all this was about, but she couldn't be selfish either. She had to look out for Lily and Marston. Make sure that college tuition, health insurance, a trust, and investments were set up so they could continue to enjoy the lifestyle they had become accustomed to, and so on.

As for herself, she just didn't want to end up like her mother, struggling after her father abandoned them. She only needed enough funds for a fresh start somewhere. A small apartment with enough room to accommodate the girls when they came to visit, with enough left over to finish up her degree. She had no idea what she would do about a job to earn a steady income, but she would cross that bridge when she came to it. Once she got her degree, who knew what path lay ahead for her?

Perhaps Kat would have pity on her and hire her. As what though? Gosh, she was pathetic. Eliot had all the power, and here she was in a divorce lawyer's office with no cards to play.

"I'm not asking for the world or to stick it to Eliot if that's what you're thinking. I just want my girls to be okay and have a little something for myself to start over. He's the one who cheated. I devoted twenty years of my life to him. That should count for something, right?"

"Your girls are sixteen and almost eighteen?" he asked.

"Marston turns eighteen in July, two months from now. Lily will be seventeen in January of next year."

"Do you think he will contest the divorce if you file?"

She hadn't considered that. Would Eliot refuse to let her go? He was stubborn, and his family meant the world to him. But he'd forfeited that family the moment he cheated. When the time came, she would simply reason with him, explain why she couldn't stay married to him anymore. He would have to relent in the face of her irrefutable proof—the vicious emails from Faith, the sonogram.

Yet, despite his betrayal, her endless moments of paralyzing fear and doubt, and Faith's disturbing claims, she knew deep down in her soul that Eliot still loved her. He always would.

She inhaled deeply. "Honestly, Wes, I don't have a great answer. Does that complicate things?"

"Not at all," he affirmed. "In fact, it would be in his best interest to settle quickly and painlessly."

"Why do you say that?"

"Did you have a prenup?"

"No. We married young. Eliot had just graduated law school, a first-year associate at Tillerson Brenner."

Wes nodded then asked, "How much does he make? Do you know the state of your finances, assets, property, investments, stock portfolio, that sort of thing?"

149

Wes should just write *stupid idiot* in big red letters on her forehead right now and spare them both the embarrassment of her ignorance. Eliot handled the family finances. She never got specific because she figured he was better at that sort of thing than she was. However, he always informed her that they were financially secured and that she never had to worry.

He gave her access to his American Express Centurion card, and she had another backup credit card, a household expense account, and a checking account in her name. But who was she kidding? That was all money Eliot earned.

"Eliot is a partner and makes eight figures, but I'm not sure about the exact number. There's the house we live in, the vacation home on Martha's Vineyard, and the one in Acapulco. Oh, and he's also a partner in his father's sports agency. I'm not privy to the details of the stock portfolio or other investments."

"Don't worry. I did some digging. It's nothing concrete, but enough to give me an idea of what we're dealing with." He leaned in. "Alicia, I don't think you have anything to worry about. I've been doing this a long time, and I can count on one hand the number of clients who were in the position you're in."

"What position is that?"

"Your children are almost adults. They can decide which parent they want to live with. Custody issues and the destruction of a family notwithstanding, it often comes down to money. Your husband can afford to be generous is all I'm saying."

She pondered his statement. Was he right? Twenty years, two children, laughter, joy, pain, love, passion, loss. It would come down to a bunch of documents that said, *Thank you for your loyalty these past twenty years, but your services as a wife are no longer required. Please accept this severance package as a token of our appreciation. Goodbye.*

"You keep saying I will be fine. What does that mean?"

"If the divorce is uncontested and even if it is, it means, Alicia, you could walk away with a multi-million-dollar settlement."

Alicia sagged deeper into the chair. She had difficulty forming a response to Wes' pronouncement. Instead, she peered down at her left hand. The platinum wedding band and dazzling diamond engagement ring suddenly felt heavy and out of place. How had she missed the signs? She replayed every possible scenario in her head, round and round, looking for the tiniest sliver that might have indicated there was a growing chasm in her marriage, but she came up empty. Until the mysterious call he'd claimed was work-related three weeks ago, she'd had no reason to suspect Eliot of cheating.

There were no changes in his behavior to suggest he was growing bored or restless. His attention to her and the family never waned. He didn't pick random fights with her or exhibit any secretive behavior. The sizzle factor in their physical relationship still made her weak in the knees. Yet, she couldn't shake the feeling that she had missed something crucial that had seemed insignificant at the time.

She recalled the day he proposed. At twenty-two years old, she had been naïve in believing that the fairy tale would last forever. It just had to.

He had rented out an elegant, private event space at an exclusive Boston restaurant. Large bouquets of pink and blood-red roses, seemingly endless candles in vases decorated in Swarovski crystals, and large balloon clusters adorned the space.

"Eliot, what is all this? It's not my birthday," she had said to him.

"I know it's not your birthday, baby. But I'm hoping by the end of the evening, it will be the birth of a new beginning for us."

"What do you mean?"

"Alicia, you're the kindest, most selfless person I've ever met, with the biggest heart. You possess a light and an innocence that's so intoxicating that I wonder if I'm good enough for you."

When he got down on one knee and reached into his pocket, her heart had stopped.

"Alicia Gail Thomas, I don't deserve you. I'm not a perfect man, but I never knew that I was capable of loving someone as deeply and completely as I do you. I can't let you go. I want you to be my wife. Say you'll marry me."

She had stood dumfounded, gaping at him as if he'd just said something thoroughly obscene and scandalous. He'd held out a small, black jewelry box and popped open the lid to reveal a diamond engagement ring that put the blazing candlelight in the room to shame. She was convinced it was a fake. It had to be. She'd only seen rings like that in movies or on the fingers of wealthy celebrities. Girls like her didn't get to wear them.

"So, what do you say?" He'd smiled up at her, nervous, yet hopeful.

"Um, yes?" Her answer was but a squeak.

He'd raised a brow.

"I mean, yes. Yes, I'll marry you."

Fast forward twenty years later, an entire lifetime, and everything had changed. The fairytale was fractured, the princess broken-hearted and confused. Her prince charming had turned out to be a lying, manipulative philanderer. And nothing in the kingdom would ever be the same again.

152

CHAPTER 28

THE ENTIRE FAMILY sat at the breakfast table as they had many times before. Though the sight pleased Alicia, a melancholic mood snaked its way around her heart. Could this be one of the last times they all sat at this table, in this kitchen, and had breakfast together? Alicia glanced at her daughters. So young and vibrant. Secured. The happy family they had been born into would remain so. Only it was a lie.

"Have you decided about prom yet, Marson?" she asked, sipping her coffee.

"Not sure, Mom. It's too much work. I have to find a dress, shoes, jewelry, and put on makeup. Spend at least three hours at Crystal's for the hair appointment. Besides, all the limos are booked, and there might not be any tickets left. And I don't want to stress out Will."

"Marston, Marston, Marston," Lily chimed in, shaking her head. "Lame excuses, all of them. You can wear one of the dresses I bought. I settled on the red one, so you have two to choose from. You can borrow jewelry from Mom if you don't want to wear yours. You and Will can share the limo with Jeff and me and Colby and her date… And Jeff and I got an extra pair of tickets in case you changed your mind." She beamed at her sister, as if she'd planned it all along.

"You shouldn't miss out on your prom, kiddo," Eliot said. "If you don't go, you'll regret it. You've been working so hard. No one deserves to have a fun night out more than you, right, Lily?"

"Dad's right," Lily concurred.

"Tell you what." Eliot grinned. "I'll throw in the house on the Vineyard into the mix. You can all head out after prom and spend the rest of the weekend with your friends. I'll drive down to chaperone. And don't worry, you won't even know I'm there."

"You would do that for us, Dad?" Marston asked, her eyes wide.

"Yes. You and Lily should enjoy yourselves with friends. Anything for my beautiful girls." Eliot turned to his wife and gave her a knowing smile.

Alicia pursed her lips and smoothed her clothes to keep her hands busy. Her chest ached. Her daughters were so happy. She resented Eliot for putting her in this position. She lived in a constant state of indecision, which could only go on for so long. Eventually, she would have to confront him, decide if her marriage was worth saving. His mistress knew Alicia by name, knew they had taken off for Paris. For goodness sake, the woman had had the itinerary. That said a lot. As much as it pained her to admit it, Eliot cared for this woman. Alicia retched at the thought.

"You okay, Mom?" Lily asked, with a worried expression.

"I'm fine, honey. Eat your eggs."

"Okay. You looked like you were about to barf just now."

Yes. I want to vomit all over your father's lying, deceitful face.

"My stomach is a little unsettled, that's all. Nothing to be concerned about."

Eliot focused on her intently. "Have you been feeling that way lately or did this just happen this morning?"

"This morning. As I said, I'm fine."

Alicia was sure that after their conversation last night he wouldn't be convinced, but he dropped the matter.

"So, prom's a go, then?" she asked Marston. Anything to take the spotlight off her and keep Eliot from asking questions.

Marston relented. "All right. I guess I'm going to prom."

AFTER THE GIRLS left for school and Eliot for the office, Alicia took a cup of coffee and her phone to the patio. She wanted to feel the sun on her face, absorb the serenity of the morning, admire the beauty of the blooming flowers. A half hour where everything was right with the world was all she needed to calm her nerves.

She sipped the coffee, placed the mug on the table and punched up her email. The message at the top of her inbox stopped her cold. It was from Faith.

The serene half hour Alicia had planned was in danger of dissolving. Did she really need to read a message from a hateful woman of questionable morals, who took every opportunity to insult her? Faith called Alicia an "ugly cow" in the last email exchange. From Faith's messages, Alicia imagined that Eliot had landed himself an immature, entitled twenty-something. A classy, mature woman would not respond with such a superficial sentiment. Not that Alicia was generalizing.

But she needed facts and information to strengthen her

case for or against divorce, help her make a final decision. Faith's acidic tongue was just the ticket. One last email. Alicia would read one last email and rid herself of the whole side-chick-tormenting-the-wife mess.

From: Empress Faith
To: Alicia Gray
Subject: He's serious as a heart attack

Alicia,

You claim Eliot isn't serious about me. See the attached photos. What more proof do you need?

Empress Faith

The last time she opened an attachment from Faith, it was a sonogram. Alicia's fingers tingled. She tapped the first photo. A real estate listing appeared on the screen. A beautiful colonial with a lush green lawn, a winding driveway, surrounded by tall, leafy trees. The house was listed in Brookline, a suburb twenty minutes away.

Was she supposed to infer that Eliot and Faith were moving into this house? Did the girl really think a photo of some random listing was going to convince Alicia it was over? She almost laughed until she tapped the second attachment to launch the document.

A purchase and sales agreement for 32 Hyde Park Avenue in Brookline opened up.

Her stomach dropped when she came to the signature line and saw the scrawl she would recognize in her sleep: Eliot Gray.

CHAPTER 29

ALICIA GAVE THE heavy door knocker a workout, banging so loudly that the sound ricocheted up and down the street.

Rina answered the door, her eyes flaring with annoyance. "My goodness, Alicia, what's going on? You scared me half to death—I thought it was a home invasion or something. You could have just texted."

"She thinks she can swoop in and steal my life," Alicia said, not waiting to be invited in and hurrying past Rina into the spacious hallway. "Who told her she could have him? Who? Who told her she could rip my children's father from them? What kind of hateful, mentally deranged woman thinks this is okay?" Alicia's breaths were wheezing, with each inhale, her whole body shuddered with agony and fury.

Rina's eyes bulged out of their sockets, completely lost apparently. She remained silent and gestured toward the sunroom as Alicia's tirade continued.

"It is not okay. I need to know who she is, Rina. Today.

Right now. Then I'm going to make him wish he had picked a different restaurant that summer evening, twenty-two years ago."

A sobbing Alicia collapsed onto the sofa in Rina's gorgeous sunroom, the May sun slicing through large bay windows, its lemon glow mocking Alicia's misery.

"Alicia, what's happened?" Rina spoke for the first time.

"You said you were a friend, Rina. That you could be discreet when it mattered. Did you mean it?"

Rina peered over at Alicia. "You already know the answer to that question. Otherwise, you wouldn't be here."

"You have an advanced degree in computer science, right? Programming, coding, stuff like that?"

Rina nodded.

"So, you can hack an email account and find an IP address?"

"Yes."

"I need your help."

"I guessed as much."

"Eliot's been cheating on me, and his mistress has been sending me these awful emails. She says he's leaving me. Sent me a sonogram and a purchase and sales agreement for a home in Brookline, with Eliot's signature on it."

Rina sat still, her face impassive, as if nothing Alicia said was shocking.

"Why are you so calm?"

"Because you're a terrible liar."

"What?"

"I knew when you asked me to recommend a divorce lawyer that you were asking for yourself, not some 'friend' from your old neighborhood. I didn't want to push. Figured it was none of my business. But now you're asking me to do something illegal, so it *is* now my business."

Despair gnawed at Alicia. She was desperate, and Rina knew it. What would she do if Rina refused to help her? "Are you saying you won't help me?"

"I'm not saying that at all."

"But you want something in return for helping me?"

Rina shook her head. "No, but before I start anything, I need to be sure you want me to do this."

"Yes, why wouldn't I? That's why I'm here. I need to put a name and a face to the woman who's been tormenting me and threatening to dismantle my family."

"The wife always thinks she wants the details, but sometimes, Alicia, you're better off not knowing."

Was this a warning? There was no logical reason Alicia could see for Rina saying it might be a good idea to back off. "What do you mean?"

"Things aren't always as they appear."

The statement further deepened Alicia's confusion. Rina wanted to help but something was stopping her.

"Please, Rina," she begged. "I'm fighting for my family, my marriage. When I saw his signature on the sales agreement for the house, something inside me snapped. I won't hand over my husband to this woman. It doesn't matter if Eliot and I eventually collapse. I owe it to my daughters. They can't fight her for their dad, so I have to do it for them."

"I feel for you, Alicia, but before you take this step, is there any chance you and Eliot can work this out? I'm guessing you haven't told him any of this?"

"No. That's why I want information about her. He can dismiss the emails, the sonogram, and the house as someone messing with me. But naming her and presenting details about her… He can't lie his way out of that."

Rina sighed and stood up, leading the way to the home office where her computers were set up. All kinds of tech gadgets, cables, USB ports, and something that looked like a small circuit board spanned two desks. Alicia had no idea what any of this equipment was, or how they worked, but just as long as they did, that was all she cared about.

After Alicia provided Faith's email address, Rina typed faster than Alicia thought humanly possible. Data populated the computer screen, coding, a series of numbers and letters. A stone-faced Rina continued her task with an intense focus, as if she wasn't Rina, but some crazy computer genius in action. This task seemed to get her juices flowing. Alicia now understood why she yearned to return to the workforce.

"If she uses a Virtual Private Network, VPN, when she signs online to communicate with you, it would hide her IP address," Rina explained, never taking her eyes off the screen. "There are also firewalls to get through."

As Rina typed and clicked and scrolled, for what felt like eternity, Alicia paced the room. She had no idea how long this would take or whether Rina would be successful. Alicia didn't want to think about that. How else would she find out who Faith was?

Rina turned in her office chair to face Alicia, a pained expression marring her face.

"What? What did you find?"

"Your husband's mistress lives in this town. On this street."

CHAPTER 30

I DON'T UNDERSTAND," ALICIA said, through quivering lips. "Are you sure it's not a mistake, some technical glitch in the results or something?"

"No, Alicia. It's not a mistake."

"Well, who on our street would Eliot be having an affair with? Faith sounded young and immature. I could tell by the things she said to me. She must be in her twenties. Goodness, what a cliché! The man goes through a mid-life crisis and takes up with a woman in her twenties to make him feel young and vibrant."

"Not always. There are exceptions to every cliché."

"What are you saying? What does this information mean?"

Rina looked away.

"You're scaring me. What else did you find out?"

"I extracted details, down to the actual address."

"Who is it?" she asked. Her eyes darted from Rina to the screen and back again.

"Katalina Torres DeLuca."

Alicia shook her head. "No. No way. It's a mistake. Check

161

again. There is no way that Faith is Kat. Kat wouldn't say those things to me. She wouldn't try to steal my husband. Maybe someone visited her house and used her computer to make it look like she's the one sending the emails?"

"Then the person would have to go to her house every time she wanted to message you."

She had arrived looking for answers, but she had found only more questions. What Rina uncovered made no sense. There had to be a logical explanation.

"Last week I visited Kat at her office in Boston and showed her the email. She wrote a response and showed it to me before I hit send. How could she have done that if she was Faith?"

"You told her about this?"

"Well, yes. We're best friends."

"Oh, Alicia," Rina said. Her voice oozed with pity. "I tried to warn you."

"What do you mean?"

"The notes."

Alicia's mouth hung open. "You were behind the anonymous notes?"

"Yes. I hoped that you'd see, find out for yourself, but you didn't."

"Explain." Alicia almost growled.

Rina gazed at Alicia with compassion. "Alicia, I like you. You're a wonderful woman. I couldn't just sit by and let this happen. You know that Katalina and I have had our differences, but I didn't just dislike her because she flaunted her looks and her body."

"Go on."

"David saw her and Eliot on Atlantic Avenue, outside her

office building, kissing, with their hands all over each other. That was two years ago."

Alicia let out a harsh breath and said nothing. She just stared at Rina. Nausea snaked its way up from her stomach. "Two years? You said two—"

She stalled. Couldn't get the words out. Too many things were happening inside of her at once. The weight of betrayal pressed down on her as though an African Elephant just stumped on her chest. Alicia breathed in and out, but no matter how deeply she inhaled, she couldn't get enough oxygen. Her life had turned into a soap opera. Kat was her best friend. No, Alicia considered Kat a sister. Alicia loved her friend. They lifted each other up, supported each other. But this?

"Oh, Alicia, I'm so sorry," Rina said. "David didn't know what to make of it, so he asked me to keep quiet. He didn't want me sticking my nose where it didn't belong and causing trouble."

"Two years," Alicia croaked. She couldn't wrap her head around it. "They've been carrying on behind my back for two years? Kat pretended to be my friend, my champion, all the while she was sleeping with my husband, plotting to destroy my family, my life?"

"What are you going to do?" Rina asked.

It was a logical question to which she had no answer. Richard DeLuca, in his own subtle way, had tried to warn Alicia by telling her that Kat didn't deserve her kindness. But she hadn't gotten it, just like she'd missed Rina's alerts by not taking the notes seriously. Loyalty to Kat had blinded Alicia.

The cruel things she'd said in those emails played on every one of Alicia's insecurities. In retrospect, it made sense. Who knew her better than her so-called best friend? What better way to dismantle her life than to leverage insider information?

Alicia drew herself up slowly to her full height, strengthened by a new resolve. "I'm going to make sure that Kat never comes near my family again."

CHAPTER 31

ELIOT PLACED HIS briefcase on the cherry-wood coffee table. He had just wrapped up a meeting with a potential client who didn't want to sit in a stuffy conference room and so had asked Eliot to his hotel instead. The large, floor-to-ceiling windows and overall atmosphere of the hotel lobby were much more conducive to real conversations than soulless meeting rooms the client had said. Eliot was inclined to agree.

He stood up and made a left in the direction of the hotel's restaurant, intending to grab a quick lunch before he headed back to the office. But as he turned toward the bistro, he almost collided with another guest. "Sorry," he mumbled, and continued walking.

"Eliot. Eliot Gray."

He turned around. There was something familiar about the stranger. The man inched closer.

"Wes George!" Eliot boomed. "My goodness, man, how many years has it been?"

"Too many," Wes said. The men shook hands enthusiastically.

Eliot and Wes had been in the same class at Harvard Law, and together with Damon Hill, they had jokingly dubbed themselves the "Legal Bros". They were the only African-American men in their class and had stuck together throughout their time at Harvard. Eliot hadn't seen Wes since they both attended a gala recognizing the city's top lawyers, five years ago.

"Still with Wilson & Carlyle?" Eliot asked.

"No. I moved on to greener pastures. Davidson & Lynch."

"Oh. Family law."

"Yes. I mostly handle divorce cases for high-net-worth clients. I hear you've done well for yourself at Tillerson Brenner."

"I have no complaints," Eliot bragged.

Wes lowered his voice. "I'm sorry to hear about you and Alicia. I thought you two would go the distance. As an old friend, that makes me sad. This is off the record obviously."

Eliot frowned. "What are you talking about?"

Wes rubbed his chin, confused. Then he held up his hands and slowly backed away. "It's clear I've said too much. It was good seeing you again, Eliot." He headed for the bank of elevators without a backward glance.

Eliot's stomach fluttered, and suddenly his suit was too thick and tight and wouldn't let him breath. Then the truth gut-punched him, rendering him breathless. *You complete idiot. How could you have missed the signs?* All of Alicia's recent behavior suddenly made sense. *She knew.*

He flopped down in the same seating area he'd occupied with his client moments earlier. He needed a minute to get his breathing back to normal and for his brain to process everything. For any other client, Wes could get in serious trouble for breaking client privilege, but Wes was speaking as an old friend, not an attorney. He was giving Eliot the heads-up.

Divorce? Alicia wanted a divorce? It didn't make sense. When she'd asked about Nathan Hunt and thought he'd been cheating on her because of that phone call in Paris, he'd shut down those concerns with unequivocal denials and reassurances that he wasn't going anywhere. If she had proof, she would have already confronted him. What was he missing?

A sickening realization dawned on Eliot. There was only one explanation. Faith had carried out her threat. *"You have to tell Alicia about us. I'm tired of being your dirty little secret."*

Eliot whipped out the burner phone from his briefcase and typed a text message. Rage flowed through his fingers into every word.

Meet me at the apartment in thirty minutes. If you don't, I will dismantle your life, piece by piece. Starting today.

CHAPTER 32

TELL THE TRUTH," Eliot snarled. "The pregnancy is a fake. You made it up."

"No, I didn't. I *am* pregnant."

She had arrived at the apartment before he did. His rage had morphed into red-hot boiling fury on the drive over. Now that he was face-to-face with her, in the center of the living room, he let it all out.

"I want proof. I bought a pregnancy test. You're going to take it while I stand outside the bathroom door. Then we'll have our answer."

Panic flittered across her face. Her body tensed even more. *Gotcha.*

"I don't have to do anything, Eliot. If you don't believe me, that's your problem, but I'm not taking that test, so you can stop waving it in my face."

"Okay then." He pulled out his phone.

"What are you doing?"

"Calling Arnie Tillerson. I warned you I would dismantle

your life starting today if you continued to be a problem. Remember it was me who got you Tillerson Brenner as a client for your agency. Well, I can take it away, just as easily. The first of many dominoes to fall."

"You wouldn't," she challenged.

"You went after my family. I'm about to give you a nasty dose of your own medicine. What did you say to Alicia?" he demanded.

"Nothing."

"You're lying again."

"So, sue me," she quipped.

"Is this a joke to you?"

"Well, yes. You getting all high and mighty, as if you hold all the cards."

"Meaning what?" Eliot pushed.

"If our affair is no longer a secret, Alicia will divorce you and take half your money. Your reputation will be tainted, and no one at Tillerson Brenner will respect you. You'll be damaged goods. You know Arnie takes the firm's reputation very seriously."

"I'm not in the least bit concerned."

"What about your Senate ambition? Can you imagine the scandal? An affair with a married woman, your wife's best friend no less. You can forget about the female vote for starters."

He pretended to consider everything she said, but he had already made up his mind. "I'm willing to take the risk. My personal reputation may take a hit, albeit temporarily, but my skills and talent are irrefutable. Law firms all over the country have been after me for years. I'll simply move to another city. As for Alicia divorcing me, I'll make sure that never happens."

Panic replaced her smug attitude. Her eyes went wide. She

backed away from him. "You'd throw away the senate run, your life's dream, just like that?"

"If it came down to a choice between Alicia and becoming a U.S. Senator, that's easy. Alicia wins."

He inched closer, standing directly in front of her. "You overplayed your hand. I warned you. I gave you plenty of chances to stop the madness, but you wouldn't."

"All of this, why?" she pleaded. "Because you won't leave your precious Alicia, hmm?"

"Do you want to revisit the pregnancy story, Katalina?"

"Okay. I'm not pregnant. But Alicia believes I am. Well, Faith." She smiled. It was diabolical and chilling, a predator anticipating the kill.

"Meaning what?"

"Well, your little wifey and I had a tête-à-tête going." She paced the room. "I sent her a sonogram of our baby, told her you were leaving her, and threw in a couple of creative adjectives in our communication. She did not like 'ugly cow'. I told her you only took her to Paris because you felt sorry for her.

"And the poor thing, she was so crushed, she came running to her best friend, Kat, broken hearted and pathetic. Admitted she was just a boring housewife, and you probably fell for someone more beautiful and exciting. I pitied her. I only wish I could have confirmed how much more beautiful and exciting your mistress is." She tossed her hair back, as if she was in a shampoo commercial.

Eliot clenched and unclenched his fists. Blood rushed through his head. Coherent thoughts escaped his mind. He couldn't lose control of the situation, however. He would not hand over a victory to Katalina. What she did was unusually cruel, a callous disregard for Alicia's feelings and well-being. How could Katalina hurt her like that?

Hypocrite!

"You're a miserable wretch, and I wish I had seen it before. Richard wants out of the marriage, and your only child cannot stand the sight of you, so your alternative was to beat up on my wife."

He picked up a throw pillow off the sofa and jammed his fist into it to calm his fury. "What? You thought I would leave her after Richard dumped you? Was that the plan, why you constantly threatened to tell her about us if I didn't leave her?"

"You're no better than me, Eliot," she said. "You've been cheating on her for years. Don't stand here and pretend to be a Boy Scout. We're both two terrible human beings who hurt your poor, precious, Alicia."

"I finally understand why you despise her so much." Eliot guffawed. "You're jealous. That's it. You want to be like her. You want to be the kind of mother she is. The kind of wife she is. You wish you had her heart—kind, generous, caring. You couldn't pull that off even if you had a personality transplant!"

"Pfft. Please, Eliot. If I woke up one day and I was whiny, insecure, desperate-for-approval Alicia, I would kill myself."

"Shut your filthy mouth! You don't get to say her name anymore."

"Because she's so perfect, right? Well, let me tell you about your perfect little angel, Alicia."

"I'm not interested in anything you have to say. We're done!" Eliot turned toward the door and began to storm out.

"Oh, Eliot. You'll want to hear this. Trust me," Kat cooed from behind.

Eliot performed a three-sixty on his heels and marched up to her again, his height towering over her slight figure.

"I don't think so. You should have listened to me. But listen to me now. I'm not leaving Alicia. Richard will end up dumping you. A man can only take so much. Maxim has all but written you off. Sounds to me like you'll end up alone." He practically spat the last words. "Exactly what you deserve."

He hovered above her for a moment longer and took a deep inhale before marching toward the door.

"I could have given you the son you always wanted, Eliot, since Alicia didn't want to," she called out to his retreating form.

He turned around, his expression sour. "It's over, Katalina. Please, if you have one shred of dignity left, just stop. Stop with the drama and the lies." He turned the doorknob.

She shouted, "The miscarriage Alicia had three years ago wasn't a miscarriage. It was an abortion."

CHAPTER 33

ELIOT HAD NO idea how he made it home without a major accident. As he sat in the driveway, his head on the steering wheel, his entire body trembled—aftershocks from the earthquake that had rocked him to the core.

At first, he'd thought it was just another one of Katalina's vile tricks. She'd proven herself to be so cruel already it wouldn't have surprised him. But as the details unfolded, he'd known she was telling the truth. Somehow, it all made sense.

When Alicia found out she was pregnant, it had been a cause for celebration for them both. However, because she was thirty-nine, they'd agreed that she should undergo an amniocentesis, a medical test that checked for potential genetic problems in pregnant women over thirty-five that could affect the baby. During that test, at sixteen and a half weeks, doctors had confirmed that they were having a boy. Excitement had overwhelmed him. Finally, a son to carry on the family name. He'd immediately called his parents and sisters who'd been overjoyed at the news.

Then the worst happened.

A week prior, Alicia had said she'd been feeling stressed and that she needed some time away at a hotel and spa to relax and refresh. She didn't want her agitation to affect the baby. She hadn't told him where she was headed, but she'd promised to check in daily. He hadn't wanted to push the issue, knowing it would cause more stress.

It was only when she'd returned, a few days later, that he'd found out about the miscarriage. She'd said she had experienced extreme cramping and back pain and had somehow made it to Jack's office, where he'd confirmed the diagnosis. Eliot's world had collapsed when he'd heard the news, but he never questioned it. Why would he?

He wasn't a doctor. But thinking back, it had never made sense to him. Nothing on the scans had indicated a problem. Alicia was healthy, and so was the baby. She'd sailed through her pregnancies with Marston and Lily with ease. Yes, she was a little older, but they'd had every reason to be optimistic about her carrying the pregnancy to term.

Only now did he see it for the deception it was. Alicia had planned to get rid of his son, and she knew she would need time to recover. That was where the sudden desire for some time alone had come into play.

According to Katalina, Jack Witherspoon had performed the procedure and had helped her cover it up by providing evidence that matched up to her story, that it was a late miscarriage, which typically occurs between thirteen and twenty weeks. After the abortion, Alicia had checked into a hotel to recover under an assumed name. When she'd finally returned home, she was still weak. It had taken her almost a month to recuperate.

"Sometimes it just happens," Alicia had told him. "Other times it's an abnormality or genetic defect."

Remembering that dark time, blood rushed through his ears. He lost track of his thoughts. Next thing he knew, his breathing had become truncated and erratic. He was blubbering and couldn't stop. It was as if all the grief he had stuffed deep down at the initial loss, because he'd wanted to be strong for Alicia, now erupted in one fell swoop—raw, penetrating and merciless.

He thought he knew his wife. Never thought her capable of carrying out such a betrayal, cover it up, and lie to him for years. If Katalina hadn't spilled the story to diminish Alicia in his eyes, how long would she have kept the truth from him? But what Elliot really wanted to know was why?

CHAPTER 34

ALICIA WAS SITTING in the rocking chair in the corner of their bedroom, near the window.

"Why, Alicia?" Eliot asked.

She leveled an icy gaze at him. She had been crying, her eyes red, her face swollen. "Why what? I'll give you 'why?' Eliot Gray. Why have *you* been cheating on me?"

He flinched. He was grateful that he was still in his work suit and tie. It helped him feel less vulnerable. But first, he needed to find out what she knew.

"Who told you I cheated on you, Alicia?" He stuck his hands into his pants pockets and walked to the window opposite her. He stared out into the darkness. He couldn't look at her.

"Your *mistress*. Faith."

He sighed—perhaps too theatrically—and continued to stare out the window into the night. "Faith is a liar. You shouldn't believe anything she says."

"So, you admit knowing her?"

"I do. We met at a firm event two years ago."

"Which event was that?"

He loosened his tie. "It was a day-long, offsite meeting with some senior attorneys and partners. She gave a speech to kick off the meeting."

"Why would she make up a story about having an affair with you? She even showed me a photo of the house you bought for the two of you and a copy of the purchase and sales agreement with your signature on it."

Suddenly, he was so very tired of all this. But he had to stay strong. "Alicia, the woman is demented. I'm not leaving you." He turned to his wife, but she wouldn't meet his gaze, so he turned back to the window. "And I didn't sign any documents. She must have forged my signature."

He sighed again. "All of this nonsense started when she came on to me at the offsite meeting. I politely told her that I was happily married and had no interest in her. But she wouldn't take no for an answer and has been in pursuit ever since."

"And you didn't tell me?"

"I thought I had it handled. I didn't want you worrying, but I didn't realize how sick she was. I never imagined it would reach this stage, with her communicating with you, spewing her lies."

"So that's your story, huh? Are you sure?"

He left the window and slowly approached her, standing directly in front of her so he could read her expression. She had dimmed the bedroom lights. The scent of her favorite bedtime lotion assailed his nostrils, a sweet-smelling cherry almond scent that wafted throughout the room. She wore a purple silk nightgown with lace at the bust and a matching robe. In any other circumstance, he would have taken her to bed. But now, looking at her, he couldn't even muster a flicker of desire.

"It's the truth."

A heavy weight rested on his chest. He couldn't quite name it, but it sent chills all over his body. He wished time could speed up so this awful night would end quickly. But that would make him a coward, running from the muddled chaos of his life. Eliot was no coward. He would face the music.

"Well, you're consistent. I give you points for that," Alicia said coolly.

"What does that mean?"

"It means, Eliot, that I can no longer trust a man who is able to look me straight in the eyes and lie to me with no conscience," she shouted, pointing an accusing finger at him. "That's what it means. I asked you before, and you lied. And I've just given you another chance, but no. Faith is not some random woman who's obsessed with you. It's Kat who's obsessed with you, and you with her."

He gulped. Her words were the equivalent of being throat-punched by a raging bull. He slowly backed away from her to put some distance between them. He yanked his tie off completely and let it slide to the floor.

"Are you going to deny it?" she challenged. She got up from the rocking chair and took a few paces toward him. She shot him a venomous glare.

"Are you going to deny that you aborted my son?" he shot back.

She stumbled backward. Her face went pale, as though someone had just danced on her grave. Her mouth fell open, then drew into a tight line.

"So, we're comparing sins? Is that where we are now, Eliot?" Uncertainty rang in her voice.

"You tell me. My perfect, shy, sweet wife, who had my child butchered by Jack Witherspoon, passed it off as a miscarriage, and then watched me mourn his loss. Now who's diabolical, Alicia?"

"How dare you?" she said between uneven breaths. "You know nothing. I didn't want to come back after it happened. I wanted to die, so I could be with him and tell him how sorry I was. I still miss him, every day."

She collapsed back into the rocking chair. She appeared frail and helpless, her arms wrapped around her body as if holding it together.

Eliot didn't understand his emotions. He was frothing with grief, fury, pain, and yet, he wanted to cradle her in his arms like he had done during those dark days after their loss. How was it possible to feel compassion for someone he hated so much in that moment?

And yet, part of him wanted her punished. She had denied him his son. She had gone behind his back and consulted a divorce lawyer. She'd forced him to confront the harsh reality that his perfect angel was capable of indescribable treachery.

"How convenient that your guilty conscience was absent before you made the decision, before you walked into Jack's office and had him rip our child from your womb."

"Stop it! Stop it!" She covered her ears and rocked back and forth.

His words had hit their mark. He wanted her to suffer, to feel his pain, to feel the weight of what she had done and have it haunt her for the rest of her life. She had put it behind her. He would make sure she never forgot.

"Answer me, Alicia." He took slow steps toward her, once

more. "Why did you get rid of our son and lie about it? We could afford more children. We could have hired an army of nannies if that's what you needed. Lily and Marston were already in their teens. They didn't need constant attention or supervision. You knew how happy it made me that we were having a boy."

Her entire body shook. She wept loudly and noisily. But he would not rest until he got a satisfactory answer. He walked over to the nightstand, grabbed a box of tissues, and thrust them at her. He waited while she wiped her tears, got her breathing under control, and calmed down.

She clutched the box of tissues on her lap. "I was scared of you. You were turning into a jackass. I saw what happened to Joan after she and Kevin divorced. I couldn't go through that."

His head flinched back slightly. He swallowed several times. "I scared you? Joan and Kevin? Kevin moved out of state years ago, and Joan remarried. You're not making any sense, Alicia."

She took a long deep breath, as if gathering the courage and strength to speak. Finally, she said, "During the time leading up to the pregnancy and even afterward, you treated me like a second-class citizen. I could have your babies, cook your meals, and keep an immaculate home for you, but I was not your equal.

"The way you dismissed my opinions when I tried to engage in conversation with you and your friends or colleagues was humiliating. And the way you would answer me when I asked you when you would be returning from a business trip was hurtful. 'I'll get back when I get back' you used to say."

He slipped his hands into his pockets and leaned up against the dresser. He did not like where this was headed. But he'd asked her to explain why she had aborted his son, so he had no choice but to listen to her side of things, no matter how ugly

180

it made him look or feel.

"You had all the power," she continued. "Then I panicked when I heard about Joan and Kevin. You and Kevin were close back then. He used his law degree to exert power and control over Joan. Like me, she had no college education to fall back on, or anything. He convinced a judge to cut child support in half and refused to pay alimony for no other reason than to spite Joan. She had three little kids to take care of. *His children.* He didn't care, though."

She started weeping again. Guilt and remorse were etched all over her face. She shifted about in the rocking chair and then turned away from him. It was too late, however. His son was gone and never coming back. A picture was emerging for him, though. And he was beginning to see Alicia's deepest fear. She didn't want to go back, couldn't go back to the struggles of her childhood and early adulthood. Joan was a symbolic reminder of what could happen.

Eliot had the power to send her back into poverty. At least temporarily. That was the way she'd seen it. She'd interpreted his behavior as signs of things to come. Another baby would have cemented her fate. With the girls off to college, she would have been at his mercy if his unsavory behavior had continued. She didn't have any resources to raise a baby on her own, so in essence, she would have been stuck.

He hadn't realized how much his actions hurt his wife, wasn't even aware of it. A sinking thought occurred to him. Was he partially to blame for what she did? He knew how sensitive she was about her past, her father leaving when she was still a young child, her mother doing the best she could, but never having enough of anything. But that still didn't justify what she'd done. Nothing did.

"Alicia, why didn't you come to me? We could have talked. I would have listened... But what you did—I can't forgive you for it. He was my son, too."

She let out a mirthless laugh and then turned to face him. "Don't pretend you would have listened or taken me seriously. You talked to me like I was beneath you, Eliot. Frankly, you were emotionally abusive."

He shook his head. "Alicia, stop this. Tell me the whole truth. Now!"

CHAPTER 35

S HE ROCKED BACK and forth as the raw, savage agony ripped through her, overwhelming her fury over Eliot and Kat's betrayal.

It all came roaring back. The months leading up to the event. The daily struggle to appear like the happy, contented housewife. Hiding the prescription pills in a vitamin supplement bottle so neither Eliot nor the girls would uncover the truth.

At times, it had been easy to hide. While Eliot and the girls were away at work and school, she had seen a therapist twice a week. On the days when feelings of worthlessness and despair had consumed her and she'd become too fatigued to function, she simply slept. The excessive worrying had been more difficult to control, however—the fear that Eliot's behavior had signaled that he was growing tired of her and would soon kick her to the curb. Whether or not those thoughts had a single grain of truth to them, she had had no way of knowing.

"I scheduled the appointment with Jack to have it done," she said, barely above a whisper. "I didn't think about it much.

I lived on autopilot during that time. An impenetrable fog had swallowed me whole, and I couldn't find my way out. The medication helped most days, but sometimes it didn't work. I couldn't stop feeling awful about myself and worrying that you would leave me."

Eliot plopped down on the sofa across from her as if his legs couldn't support him anymore. "What are you talking about? What medication? Where did you get the idea that I was leaving?" He blinked rapidly, then his gaze swept around the room, as though searching for answers.

"It got worse after I found out I was pregnant. I was struggling, Eliot."

"Struggling with what? Why did you need medication? I don't understand"

She lowered her gaze, and pinned her arms against her stomach again, and said, "At first I tried to brush it off, thought I was being too sensitive—your behavior, the belittling, put downs, making me feel like I wasn't worth much. I'm not saying you were responsible for my feelings. I'm just telling you how it started."

Eliot sat perfectly still, his eyes glued to her face.

She continued, "After a while, I couldn't shake it... Day in and day out, the self-loathing, doubt, fatigue. All I wanted to do was sleep, so I wouldn't feel anything, so I went to see Dr. Randolph. She diagnosed me with depression."

He just stared at her. They both sat still. The revelation hung heavy in the air, unabashed in its ugliness.

Eliot broke the silence. "I don't understand how I missed it. Why didn't you say something? Why didn't you tell me you were suffering so I could help you?" Tears pooled in his eyes.

"Depression doesn't work like that, Eliot. In my mind,

another baby would only make things worse. I didn't think about the consequences until afterward."

"What do you mean by that?"

"After the procedure, Jack drove me to the Four Seasons Hotel in Boston and reserved a suite under his name. He told the staff not to disturb 'Ms. Sarah Thomas', throughout her stay. But when the loneliness, guilt, and pain, both physical and emotional had threatened to completely wreck my existence, I reached out to Kat in desperation."

Eliot continued to stare at Alicia, silent, and as she recounted the story, she was simultaneously taken back into the time and place from the moment she'd opened the door of the suite to let Kat in. Alicia had almost collapsed on the floor, but Kat had caught her in time and had slowly walked her to the bed.

"Alicia, what the hell is going on? You look like you're dying."

"I should be so lucky."

"Are you insane? What happened? Where is Eliot?"

"Eliot's at work. He doesn't know I'm here."

As she lay on the bed, she laid out the whole tragic tale through bouts of inconsolable wailing and hiccups. When she was done, Kat showered Alicia with kindness, brought her water, wiped her face with a warm cloth, and told her to take a nap.

When she awoke, thirty minutes late, Kat was still there, seated in an armchair across the room, looking out the window to views of Boston Common.

"You don't have to tell me if you don't want to," she said, turning to look at Alicia. "But why? I ran every scenario in my head, and I can't think of any reason why you'd want to get rid of your baby."

"I thought that if I had the baby, it would be all over."

"What do you mean?"

185

She described her mental health, Eliot's behavior toward her, and how afraid she was that she would end up like Joan or her mother.

Kat said nothing for a long while. Alicia didn't expect Kat to understand. She had it all—stunning good looks, a thriving and successful business, influence, independence, and family. Why would she comprehend the woes of someone like Alicia?

"I get it," Kat finally said, surprising Alicia. "You don't think he values you, which means you have zero security. You want to do something for yourself, so you can stand on your own two feet. You don't want to struggle to get by like you and your mother did after your father left. But things got out of hand."

Kat's understanding was the lifeline Alicia so desperately needed, and she grabbed it with both hands. "Swear, Kat," she said. "Promise me you will never tell another soul what I have done. It must stay between Jack, you, and me, forever. Swear!"

"I swear," Kat said, holding up her right hand while placing her left on her heart.

As the story tumbled out of Alicia, Eliot continuously shook his head, as he tried to grapple with everything she'd told him.

"I can't believe it," he said repeatedly.

"When I came home, I couldn't live with what I had done," Alicia said, closing the door to the pain that transpired in that hotel room, as another, more horrible, suppressed memory surfaced in her mind.

She took a deep breath, knowing that she had to let it all out before she gave in to the pain and despair. She held Eliot's gaze. "One day, while you and the girls were out, I locked the garage doors, sat in my car with the windows up, turned on the engine, and waited for the carbon monoxide to do its thing."

She ignored Eliot's gasp of horror.

186

"My cell phone rang. I don't know why I'd taken it with me. It was Kat. I ignored the first few calls, but she must have suspected something was wrong, because she kept calling until I answered. She saved my life that day."

A dazed, desperate look formed in his eyes. "Alicia, you could have said something, dropped a hint, some kind of distress signal."

"It's easy to look back and say what I could have or should have said or done. Perhaps you didn't see what was happening because you didn't want to."

He rested his head in his hands. "That's not fair. I may have been a blind idiot—*am* a blind idiot—too caught up in my career to see what was going on in my own house, but we're partners, a team. You should have sounded the alarm, hard and loud."

Maybe he was right. But she couldn't rewind the clock and make different choices. She had worked hard to regain her mental health and strength, and she wouldn't allow herself to fall back into that oblivion.

CHAPTER 36

I CAN'T DO THIS anymore," Alicia said. "I spoke to Eliot, but he lied. Again. I'm going to divorce him, Kat. I spoke to a lawyer already. He said I could easily take Eliot for half of everything he has."

Kat's stiff posture and dazed glare were telltale signs that she wasn't pleased with Alicia's unexpected office visit. Ambush would be a more appropriate description. Kat picked up a pile of papers from her desk and pretended to look busy and important, but the sheets slipped through her fingers and scattered all over the floor.

Alicia wanted to look her soon-to-be former best friend in the face and hear the lies slide effortlessly off her tongue, one last time. She expected Kat's usual phony encouragement, and her pretense to despise "Faith" as much as she did.

"So, what do you think? It's the right thing to do, isn't it?"

Kat haphazardly gathered up the papers from the floor, retreated behind her desk, and sat down, her back ramrod straight, hands clasped—the epitome of poise and control.

But it didn't fool Alicia for one minute. Kat had proven herself to be a talented actress.

She finally found her voice. "What made you finally decide to leave him?"

"I just don't see a way forward for us. I've already given him two chances to tell the truth, but he continued to lie and deny. He claims that Faith came on to him at an offsite meeting, two years ago. Can you believe that bull? Does he really think I'm that stupid?"

In her restlessness last night, as sleep eluded her, Alicia had finally made the connection between Kat and why she'd chosen Faith as her alias.

One afternoon, after Kat had moved into the neighborhood, Alicia had commented on her glamorous style and impeccable tastes when it came to accessorizing, hair, and makeup. Kat had said that she modeled her style after Faith Hernandez, the wife of her next-door neighbor in the Miami suburb where she grew up.

Kat had said that even at twelve years old she had known there was something special about Faith—her beauty and confidence, the way she turned heads and captivated an audience. Kat had admired the way the woman strutted like a queen. Kat had wanted to be just like Faith when she grew up.

But by Kat's own account, she didn't realize that emulating Faith would become a problem as she got older. People only recognized her for her looks and nothing else. The fact had wounded her throughout her teens and early twenties, and soon she had begun to resent her beauty but had learned how to weaponize it when it suited her.

"I'm very busy, Alicia," Kat said, her tone stiff. She shuffled more papers and opened and closed her desk drawers as if searching for something important. "You could have told me all this over wine later. There was no need for you to come into the city and disrupt my workday. I don't have time on my hands like you do."

"That's where you're wrong, *mi amiga*," Alicia said sweetly. "I had to make a special trip. You see, I wanted to be able to take a good look at you when I called you a two-faced, backstabbing tramp. You were never my friend. You were just a cunning predator, who spotted my weakness and moved in for the kill. Yes, I know you were sleeping with my husband, and hid behind your 'Faith' alter ego."

Kat got up from her chair and took deliberate steps toward Alicia, a cruel smile tugging at her lips. She folded her arms and said, "Well, well, well. What do we have here? Mousy little Alicia must have stocked up on some courage this morning. Bravo."

"That's all you have to say to me, after all the lying, conniving, the fake friendship? It was all for nothing."

"You know what your problem is?" Kat asked.

"Please, do tell." Alicia gestured.

"You're too naïve for your own good. You can't win this game. Why do you think Eliot and I fooled you all these years, right under your nose?"

"Give me some credit. You never counted on me finding out, let alone who Faith was. You got away with it for two years."

Kat smirked. "Still pathetic. And naïve."

"Meaning what?"

"Alicia, I don't have the time or inclination to explain this to you. What does it matter, anyway? Eliot and I are the same. That's why we're compatible. You're old news, Alicia."

"Wrong again," she said. "Eliot isn't going anywhere, Katalina. You betrayed me repeatedly for a shot at him. You played your last, desperate card by telling him about the abortion. You thought that would be the last straw, didn't you?"

Kat glared at her. "You have no idea what Eliot and I mean to each other, how deeply connected we are. It's about time that farce you call a marriage is finally over."

Alicia stood up, her eyes glued on Kat's thunderous expression.

"You know what your problem is? You're too arrogant for your own good. Think about it. Your connection with Eliot was so deep that not once during the time you were together did he ask me for a divorce? Instead, he went to great lengths to hide the affair. You were his dirty little secret from the beginning. He continued to lie, even after I found out."

"Can you blame him? He was afraid that weak little Alicia would spiral into another depression. Nobody wants that. It was ugly enough the first time around. By the way, how are you feeling these days? Pretty useless, huh?"

Alicia bit down hard on the inside of her cheeks until the salty, metallic taste of fresh blood invaded her mouth. She never wanted to go back to that place—the darkness, the fatigue, the despair. She'd been fearful that's exactly where she was headed once the truth about her marriage was laid bare. But she had been a fighter all her life, a survivor. Kat would not have her victory lap.

"Eliot never confessed the affair, Kat. I gave him chance after chance to come clean and he denied it, he denied *you* every single time. He never asked for a divorce. He never said he loved you or that he wanted a life with you. He told you the opposite in those emails and, I'm sure, to your face, as well. If I hadn't uncovered the betrayal, Eliot would have continued to see you on the side. And that's all you were, would ever be—the side salad he occasionally picked at. Get this through your head, tramp. Eliot will never be yours. Fake pregnancy or not."

"You've lost, Alicia. Get over it." The vindictive edge to her voice felt like fingernails scraping against a chalkboard. "So why don't you run along, crawl back to the ghetto where you came from."

Fueled by a blinding rage Alicia didn't know she possessed, she reached out and shoved Kat. She crashed into the desk and screamed from the force of the impact, before falling to the ground. Alicia stood, unable to move, paralyzed by the shock of what she had done.

Moments later, the office door flew open and Kat's assistant rushed into the room. "Oh goodness, Kat, are you okay?" he asked.

Kat pointed at Alicia and said, "Get this piece of trash out of here!"

"After you, *mi amiga*," Alicia said with a smile. "You'll get what you deserve. I promise."

CHAPTER 37

WHEN ALICIA ARRIVED home, Richard DeLuca was standing in her driveway. What could he want? Did Kat tell him what happened and he'd come to inform her that they would file assault charges? *Why had she lost control so badly?*

"Richard, what a surprise to see you here," she stammered as she stepped out of the Range Rover and shut the door. "What's going on?" She hoped he couldn't detect the anxiety in her voice.

"May we speak inside?" he asked gravely.

"Yes, of course."

Alicia's hand shook as she unlocked the front door and led Richard into the living room. She gestured to the sofas.

"I would prefer to stand," he told her and began pacing the floor, jangling his keys in his pocket.

"What's on your mind?" she asked.

"Katalina called me, said she went to the hospital to have herself checked out because you shoved her hard and she may have injured herself."

"Richard, I'm so sorry, I—"

He held up his right palm to silence her. "You don't need to apologize. I have an idea what the fight was about."

Her breath snagged on the fear and worry that had filled her chest like a boulder. Richard's face remained expressionless, his amber brown eyes almost vacant.

"Are you sure? I'm not sure she'd tell—"

"I've known for a while, Alicia."

Alicia's eyes widened. "Known what?"

"That my wife was having an affair with your husband."

She rubbed her forehead to ward off a headache. "How?"

"Maxim overheard her on an incriminating phone call a few months back. He realized she was speaking to another man. Then she called Eliot by name."

Alicia gasped. But inwardly she was thinking that Kat had gotten off lightly with just a shove.

"Anyway," Richard continued, "Maxim told me what he'd overheard. I'll save you the details, but needless to say, it confused him. He demanded answers. I couldn't lie to him. I did my best to cushion the blow. Then I hired a private investigator to follow his mother."

Alicia was afraid to ask the next question, but she did. "What did the investigator find out?"

"He confirmed what Maxim had overheard. She and Eliot met regularly at an apartment in Chestnut Hill. She told us she had to work, even on days she was supposed to be home having dinner with us or attending one of Maxim's events."

The enormity of the deception was dawning on Alicia. The affair was so intense; instead of meeting at a hotel, they'd gotten an apartment and met there regularly. Maybe Kat was more than a side salad, after all.

194

"Is that why Maxim is so angry, because he knows?"

"Yes. He asked me why she didn't want to be with us. 'Mr. Gray has his own family,' he'd said. Then he'd asked, 'What if she leaves us for Mr. Gray? Lily and Marston are cool, I guess. But they're my friends, not step-sisters.'"

Alicia wanted to cry. No child should ever be in the middle of an adult situation like that. Maxim was a boy who needed his mother, but she was too busy giving her time and attention to someone else.

"I was tempted to tell him she had already left us," Richard said in a doleful voice. "That our home was just her physical address, a place to put her head down at night. But that would have deepened the wound. I couldn't do that to him. He's struggling as it is."

"If you knew all this time, why didn't you say something to Kat?"

He didn't answer at first. Silence hung between them, raw and awkward. He'd stopped pacing now, and his legs were planted wide, arms crossed, cheeks flushed with anger.

Then he said, "Do you know how humiliating it was sitting at your dinner table the other night, knowing Eliot was screwing my wife?"

Alicia sat quietly, her hands folded in her lap. There was a coldness in his eyes she had never observed before, not once in the four years she had known him. Shame sliced through her. Was his question of condemnation aimed at her, too? He'd spoken as if he thought Alicia was in on their deception and had also caused him pain.

"I had no idea what was going on, Richard. I thought it odd you didn't reprimand Maxim when he mouthed off to his mother. Later on, Kat said you two were struggling in your marriage. I had no way of knowing how bad things really were."

He wrinkled his nose as if he smelled a dead rat. "You had no idea? Not even a sneaking suspicion? You've been married to the man for two decades."

"How could you not know your wife was cheating?" she shot back. "If Maxim hadn't overheard her on the phone, she would have continued to fool you. She would have remained free to carry out her plans to destroy my family, while pretending to be my friend."

Richard collapsed onto the cushion next to her on the sofa. He rubbed his jaw, as if exhausted by the whole sordid mess. "I'm sorry. I didn't mean to imply you were his silent enabler. Maybe this is my fault, too. Perhaps I neglected her."

"No one but Eliot and Kat are responsible for their actions," Alicia said.

"I know that. But if I feel responsible in some small way, it will keep me from having terrible thoughts that consume me day and night."

"What kind of thoughts?" she probed.

His gaze wandered around the room. Then he turned to her and said, as if no one else could hear, "Revenge. It would solve my problem if they were both dead."

Alicia eased away from him as if he carried a contagious disease. Rina had called Richard a long-suffering husband. What other pain besides infidelity had Kat heaped upon him? What had brought him to the point of thinking about vengeance and murder? Or perhaps the answer was simple. Alicia didn't know Richard at all. Sure, their families socialized, and their kids got along, but what did she really know about the man?"

"You don't mean that. The pain of betrayal can drive people to dark places, but it doesn't mean they'll act on those feelings, does it?"

"I suspect Katalina was unfaithful in the past with other men as well," he said, sidestepping her question. "I don't have proof of anything, but a pattern may be emerging. I'm no saint, but there is only so much humiliation a man can take."

Alicia stared at him. His confession left her feeling as though her head was being held underwater and she was about to run out of oxygen. Yet somehow, she could see it clearly now. Kat's callous disregard for how her actions affected others. Her dishonesty, superficial charm, and ability to the break the rules—in this case, her marriage vows—without a sliver of guilt or remorse. *Isn't that the very definition of a sociopath?* Alicia shivered.

"Are you okay?" Richard asked.

"I'm fine." She was anything but.

"I should go," he said, and stood up.

"What are you going to do?" Alicia asked, panicked at the thought that Richard might make her a widow before she had a chance to leave Eliot.

"I'm taking my son and moving on. I'll make sure she never sees him again."

As a woman with children of her own, part of her still wanted to defend her former best friend, but she bit her tongue. Old habits and all that.

"You do what you have to do," she said.

"How about you?" he asked.

"My brain says to divorce him, but—and I know you'll think me foolish—my heart is still holding out for a different resolution. When you've built a life with someone that spans decades, it's not so easy to walk away, no matter the circumstances."

His sad and sullied expression emphatically stated that he did not agree. Kat had broken the man.

"Well, I wish you the best of luck," he said.

A sudden, urgent question pushed its way to the front of her brain. Two questions, actually. "Richard, did you run into an old college friend at Arnie's party back in April, the one whose father is dying of Alzheimer's?"

Richard frowned. "Who told you that bogus story?"

"Never mind. One more thing. Did you buy Kat a diamond-and-gold Cartier bracelet in recent months, the one she wore to the party I threw for her at the country club?"

"The one she flaunted the entire night? No. I did not buy her that bracelet. Maybe Eliot did."

They were desperate questions, she knew. A final attempt to find one shred of redemption in her husband, one glimmer of hope that her marriage might be worth saving.

Kat had wanted everyone to see that bracelet, including Alicia. It was a power play to mess with her head, poke at her insecurities, and it worked like a charm. Knowing Kat, she had probably pressured Eliot to make the purchase, until he caved. The bracelet was part of her devious strategy.

As they made their way to the front door, Alicia asked, "Are you going to confront her about the affair? She didn't deny it when I did. To be honest, she seemed relieved that I found out. That way she didn't have to pretend to be the dutiful friend anymore. It was a bad scene, Richard. It turned ugly—well, as you know by Kat's call. But just to warn you, she's not sorry at all."

He served up a smile that didn't quite reach his eyes. "I

know she's not sorry. She put him first, before Maxim and me. I hinted that I had suspicions of infidelity, but she didn't care, offered no reassurances that I was imagining things. No denials, but she never admitted anything either."

Richard's earlier confession that he entertained thoughts of revenge replayed in her head. Her feelings for Eliot were still complicated, but when it came to Kat, she could no longer say she didn't share Richard's dark outlook.

CHAPTER 38

B Y THE TIME Alicia arrived at Howell House, she had exhausted her brain with excessive rumination on the strange conversation with Richard yesterday. How would Kat react to the news that Richard was leaving her and taking their son with him? Was she too selfish to care? All Kat wanted was Eliot, and she didn't care who got in her way, including her own child. If there was a custody battle, Alicia would support Richard, but would Maxim be better off without her? Alicia only wanted what was best for the boy whom her whole family had grown fond of.

The waiting room was already overflowing with patients as she stepped through the door. The sound of the printer spitting out documents and the door constantly swinging open added to the bustle.

"How's it going?" she asked Monica.

"Crazy. The phone has been ringing off the hook as usual."

She smiled at Monica's mantra. "You're doing a superb job. What would we do without you?" Alicia said as she blew past

Monica and headed down the hallway. Alicia didn't have time for lengthy chit-chat.

She poked her head through Jack's office door. He was looking through a patient's file, but he gestured for her to come in. When Alicia had taken the seat across from him, he closed the file and looked up at her. "You said it was important?"

"It is."

"What's going on?"

"Kat told Eliot about the abortion."

Jack pinched his nose and let out a deep, frustrated sigh. "Alicia, this is bad. You told me she'd keep the procedure confidential. She's your best friend. Why did she do this?"

"*Former* best friend."

"I don't have time for your girlfriend politics. I don't care whether you ended your friendship because she betrayed you to Eliot—"

"It's more complicated than that."

"Look, Alicia—"

She blurted it out. "Kat was having an affair with Eliot. She used an alias to communicate with me, saying some harsh, awful things. She even sent me a sonogram to make me believe that Eliot was leaving me. I don't know whether she's really pregnant or not."

Jack's already pale face turned a grayish, ashen hue that gave him a wax-like appearance.

"Jack, what is it?" she asked.

"I, I gave her the sonogram. It was either that or..." He trailed off, a faraway look taking over his features.

His words took the form of dagger-like icicles dumped into the pit of Alicia's belly. "Why would you do that?" she

201

whispered. She already knew the answer, but she wanted to hear it from him.

"She had me over a barrel."

"How?"

"She said if I didn't provide a sonogram with her name on it, she would tell your husband that I performed the abortion. I'm sorry, Alicia, if that makes me a coward. My private practice can't afford a drawn-out legal battle. I performed the procedure as a favor to you, but I could lose everything if Eliot sues me."

"Eliot has no legal grounds to sue you. I'm not a lawyer, but I don't see what he could sue you for. Abortions are legal in Massachusetts."

"He would find a way to destroy me. That's what scares me. We told him it was a miscarriage. I produced paperwork—falsified paperwork—to back up that narrative. He's not one of the top lawyers in the city for nothing. He would come up with a way to make it a malpractice lawsuit. If that happens, I'm finished. Oh, this is so bad…"

Jack shifted around in his seat, as if the movements allowed him to move his thoughts around to rearrange themselves into any outcome, other than losing his livelihood. The color still hadn't returned to his face.

"Jack, please don't worry. Eliot is not in a position to pass moral judgment on anybody."

"What do you mean?"

Alicia laid out the complete story in truncated bursts. The length of the affair, Eliot's continued denials, and the final confrontation at Kat's office yesterday.

He raked his hair back repeatedly. When his hands landed in his lap, his hair was sticking up.

As she took in his distressed appearance, a terrible thought occurred to her. "Jack, what if Kat asked you to be her gynecologist for a specific reason, other than the obvious? I thought it was strange, but like everything else having to do with her, I dismissed it."

"What do you mean?"

"Of all the doctors she could have picked, why you? If her plan all along was to convince Eliot to leave me by pretending she was pregnant—"

"What better person than a doctor on whom she had leverage," Jack finished.

"Yes. That's what I was thinking."

"She's a user then."

"I didn't see it before, but that's who she turned out to be, a user and an opportunist. Can't you dump her as a patient, make up an excuse, and have one of the other doctors in the practice take her on?"

"Frankly, Alicia, if she's capable of blackmail, not to mention the heinous way she treated you, then I don't want her anywhere near my practice. Period. If she's still determined to lure Eliot away from you, we can't predict what she'll do next."

When they'd finally spoken about his betrayal and about the abortion, Alicia hadn't asked Eliot whether or not he'd ended the affair. She'd been too caught up in the emotional pain of the moment. But when she'd gone to see Kat in her office, she'd made it sound as if the universe had predestined them as a couple and that they were still together.

Eliot hadn't addressed his infidelity. He'd been too busy interrogating Alicia about the abortion. She hoped he didn't think he was off the hook, that he would get away with cheating on her so easily. He had blindsided her that night.

Soon, it would be her turn to ask the tough questions. Why? How often had they met up in their little love nest in Chestnut Hill? What promises had he made to Kat? And the big one… Did he love her? Scratch that. She wouldn't make that mistake. It was an open invitation to more lying, and she couldn't handle any more of Eliot's lies. Two years. That told her everything she needed to know.

"Actions have consequences, Jack. Even for Kat."

"They do," he agreed. "I could be brought before a medical ethics committee. I provided a fake sonogram. Not to mention that I treated a patient and sent her to recover in a hotel suite booked in my name. If Katalina tells all, I'm done. The practice is already struggling financially. Any additional pressure, well…"

"Jack, I had no idea," she said gently. "Is that why you were vague when I asked for a job a while ago?"

"Yes. I wanted to help, but I simply can't afford to hire anyone, not even part-time. Things are tight enough as it is."

Alicia felt her insides deflate like a trapped hot-air balloon. If she ended her marriage, she would need a job to support herself. She'd been counting on Jack to help her out until she finished her degree. Although Wes George had assured her that she could walk away with a huge settlement, she couldn't stake her future on that possibility. She knew Eliot. He had a mean streak. He could make things difficult for her if he wanted to, especially now that he knew she had aborted his son.

She didn't have a vast network of friends or former colleagues she could tap. Jack was it, and he had problems of his own. It was a terrible ordeal for someone like Jack who had made a career out of serving others.

"There's a solution to every problem, Jack. Don't give up. You'll—*we'll*—find a way to come out of the red and make the practice profitable again."

She would take her own advice. There was a solution to her current dilemma. If Eliot caused her more problems, she would reach out to Arnie Tillerson. She didn't care if it made her look vindictive. She was way past that now.

CHAPTER 39

A FEW MINUTES AFTER ten the next morning, Alicia leaned against the kitchen island, popped her earbuds in and scrolled through the audiobook library on her phone. She'd downloaded a book on the art of negotiation, and she wanted to listen to the first few chapters of the book while she had the house to herself.

After she left Jack's office yesterday, she'd realized how inadequately prepared she was for the looming battle with Eliot. Eliot had been a lawyer for twenty-plus years; negotiation was his bread and butter. There was a fair amount of negotiation skills one needed to bring up two strong-minded girls, but it was nothing in comparison to beating a titan at his own game. She needed to do some homework.

She hit the 'play' button, but the author's voice was immediately interrupted by her text-notification tone. She opened her text app.

Rina: Something's up at the DeLucases.

Alicia: What do you mean?

Rina: Police cars everywhere.

What?

Panic and horror licked at Alicia like the greedy, destructive flames of an all-consuming fire. *Chaos.* That was the only way to describe the scene before her as she scrambled down the street. Emergency vehicles were everywhere. Red lights flashed. Neighbors gathered on the lawn, pointing and whispering. Uniformed police officers and EMTs hurried toward the front door. Any lingering thoughts of a good outcome vanished when the officers began applying yellow crime-scene tape around the parameter of the property.

Spurred by pure adrenaline, Alicia marched past several vehicles.

"Ma'am, stop right there." A young, uniformed officer held up his arms to slow her advance.

"My friend lives here. What's going on?" She tried to sound normal—whatever that was anymore—but the questions came out in short, frightened breaths.

"This is officially a crime scene. Please step back."

The donut and coffee she had for breakfast earlier were in danger of making an unwelcome splash all over the officer. She took several steps back and turned around in time to see several news vans screech to a halt. Reporters and camera crews jumped out.

When she looked behind her again, the officer had disappeared. A new scene emerged, one so surreal she wondered if she had conjured it from her overstressed psyche. A black body bag was strapped to the stretcher that two EMTs wheeled out of the house and then loaded onto the ambulance.

Something caught in Alicia's throat and lodged there, making speech impossible. Breathing became laborious. Time slowed to a crawl. More news vans pulled up. Reporters tripped over each other for the perfect spot on the lawn to broadcast the horrifying news. More neighbors arrived.

When Richard appeared at the front door and walked toward the ambulance, Alicia called out to him. It didn't sound like her though. It sounded like someone who had contracted a serious case of laryngitis.

Richard approached her with an unnatural calm, or perhaps it was shock. "She's gone, Alicia."

CHAPTER 40

EVERYONE REMEMBERS WHERE they were when events of stunning historical or personal significance happen. For Eliot, those events included the explosion of the Challenger Space Shuttle, right after take-off, when he was in the eighth grade; the fall of the Berlin Wall; the Boston Marathon bombing; the election of President Barack Obama; and September 11, 2001.

He had booked a flight on United Flight 93, the one that crashed into a field in Somerset County, Pennsylvania. He had overslept, got a late start, and had arrived at the gate too late.

Now, two days later, the effects of the most significant tragedy in his life still lingered. Ice coated his skin. The horror of it whiplashed through his veins. *Katalina was dead.* The finality of it struggled to take root in his mind.

He sat next to Alicia in the family room, under the scrutiny of Detectives James McBride and Bill Sears from the Weston Police Detective Unit, who sat across from them. McBride resembled a college frat boy who had partied hard the night before, just rolled out of bed, and realized he had a major exam in an hour. He wore a short-sleeved polo shirt and rumpled khakis over his gangly frame. *This was the man who'd be investigating her death.*

"Why don't we start with you, Mr. Gray?" McBride asked. "We're interviewing friends, neighbors, and close acquaintances to help us with the investigation. Mrs. DeLuca was a friend of yours?"

"Yes. Richard and Katalina were friends of ours."

"Care to elaborate? Is there anything you can tell us that would be helpful?"

"Such as?"

"Had she been agitated or anxious of late? Did Mrs. DeLuca mention being threatened or afraid?"

"Are you saying this is a homicide?" he asked.

He didn't mean to blurt out the question. From Alicia's account, and from the news reports, Richard had found a non-responsive Katalina on the kitchen floor. He'd checked for a pulse and found none. He'd called 9-1-1 and told the dispatcher that his wife was dead. The fact that detectives were asking these types of questions when the cause of death had not yet been determined seemed odd to Eliot. Then again, his specialty was corporate law, not criminal investigation.

"It's too early in the investigation to make that determination." Sears, with eyes alert, broad shoulders, and thinning hair, spoke for the first time.

"But you're asking if she was threatened or in trouble, which could indicate her death was premeditated," Eliot said.

McBride said, "Let's not get ahead of ourselves. As Detective Sears said, it's too early to tell anything. All we're doing at the moment is gathering information that could point us in the right direction as to how Mrs. DeLuca died."

He knew what would come next. The alibi question. Where was he when Katalina took her last breath? He didn't have a rock-solid alibi. And he couldn't admit where he really was and what he was doing in that timeframe.

Eliot had learned that Brandon Carr, that loser kid who used and discarded his daughter, played Varsity Volleyball for the high school, so Eliot had cornered the boy after practice, that morning.

"Do you know who I am?" he'd asked in his most menacing tone. The bulging eyes and rasping breaths told Eliot that Brandon had no idea who he was but was smart enough to know that he should be afraid of him.

"I'm Eliot Gray, Marston's dad. You disrespected my daughter. That makes me a very unhappy father. I'm only going to say this once. Stay away from my daughter. If you don't, I'll make sure your college career ends before it even begins. Are we clear?"

The little prick had caved like a cheap tent as he'd understood the implications of the threat. "I'm sorry... I promise, I won't bother Marston ever again. I won't go near her. Please, I don't want any trouble," he'd said, as he slowly backed away from Eliot before he turned on his heels and ran like his life depended on it.

Eliot shifted his thoughts back to the present when he caught McBride looking at him strangely. When Alicia had called late Tuesday morning to tell him that Katalina Torres DeLuca, the woman who wanted more than anything to usurp Alicia's position in his life, had left home for the last time in a body bag, Eliot thought his wife had finally snapped, payback for the affair. But deep down, he knew that Alicia, even in her darkest moments over what he and Katalina had done, would never stoop so low. It was not in her nature to be vicious or vengeful. Then again, she'd aborted his child, so he wasn't so sure he knew his wife anymore.

"When was the last time you saw Mrs. DeLuca?" McBride asked.

"A couple of weeks back. She and her family had dinner with us, here. The next day, I went to visit her at her office."

"Why would you do that if you had dinner the night before in your home?" Sears asked.

"The dinner didn't go well. I wanted to check in on her. Besides, it was a tough day for her."

"Why was that?" McBride probed.

Eliot rubbed his wrists. The back of his throat tightened as though an ever-expanding lump had lodged itself there, causing infinite agony.

"She had a difficult relationship with her son. He embarrassed her in front of everyone. It upset her. The next day was the anniversary of her brother's death."

He hoped the detectives didn't pick up on his distress. Alicia hadn't looked at him once since the interview started, but with every word he spoke, he could feel the weight of her presence. The heaviness of the truth that he couldn't reveal.

McBride asked, "Who was present at this dinner?"

Eliot explained what transpired the night Katalina announced her feature on the cover of *Tigress Magazine* and how Maxim had lost it. He glanced at Alicia, hoping she would back him up, since she had taken Katalina out to the patio afterward. But his wife just kept her gaze straight ahead.

McBride forged forward with the interview. He asked how

long they had known the DeLucases, who their friends were, family, associates, and of any known enemies. Eliot easily sailed through those questions.

There wasn't much to tell. Katalina's parents still lived in Miami. She had spent most of her adult life in New York, until she met Richard and they moved to the neighborhood. Eliot told them that Kat spent most of her time building her agency and its reputation, so besides his family, he wasn't aware of any other friends with whom she might have had a close friendship. Richard's family was still in New York, both parents still alive, and his brother was a chef at a downtown Los Angeles restaurant.

"Where were you between the hours of ten fifteen and eleven thirty on Tuesday morning?" Sears lobbed the question at Eliot, before countering. "It's a standard question, Mr. Gray."

"I went jogging around the neighborhood."

"Did anyone see you?"

"I suppose so. I wasn't paying attention to others around me."

"You jog regularly?"

"Three to four times a week when I can squeeze it in. If not, I use the office gym."

"How well do you know Richard DeLuca?" McBride asked.

"He's a family man, good guy. Successful hedge-fund manager. Well-respected. Somewhat reserved. Why? You don't think he had anything to do with her death?"

"We're just trying to form an accurate picture of the DeLucases. Personal information often provides the best insights or clues."

"Have you spoken to Richard, yet?"

"Yes, we have."

By his tone, Eliot inferred that McBride wasn't in the

mood to share information. But Eliot would find out what the police knew. He had access to investigators at Tillerson Brenner. The firm was Katalina's client, and Arnie wouldn't mind using company resources to help find the facts about the case, details the police wouldn't necessarily share with Eliot.

Katalina had been responsible for helping to build their brand image, and Arnie was all about image. If the investigation threatened the firm's reputation, Arnie would insist on getting ahead of potential damage. Eliot would simply neglect to mention that he had a personal stake in staying apprised of the investigation, too.

Eliot had avoided Alicia's questions in the past few days, questions about the affair he wasn't ready to answer. He had cared deeply for Katalina, though her vicious attacks on Alicia had diminished the woman in his eyes. Then there was the forged signature on the purchase and sales agreement for a house he knew nothing about.

It pained him to admit that he'd blown his life apart for a selfish, obsessed, cruel woman who hadn't cared who got in her way, as long as she got what she wanted. He didn't have time to think about how her death would affect his life. Right now, he was worried that if the police found out that he and Katalina had been having an affair that his wife recently uncovered, both Alicia and he would become number-one suspects. Suspects with strong motives for murder.

Prior to the detectives coming over, he'd coached Alicia. "Keep answers short and factual. If they enter dangerous territory, I'll jump in and end the interview. We're both in a tight spot, Alicia. We have to be careful."

It was only a matter of time before McBride would

question Katalina's employees, who would tell him about Alicia's visit, and how it didn't end well. Alicia had listened to his advice without saying a word and then shook her head once to indicate that she had heard him and would follow his instructions.

Eliot speculated that the next obvious question would be centered around the cause of the fight, especially since Alicia and Katalina were close. Then the truth of the affair would come out. There was no avoiding that. But he had already thought of ways they could spin it. Having an affair was not a crime, although it was still a strong motive for murder. He had to determine what information to provide and what to hold back without impeding the investigation or breaking the law.

But Katalina had died on Richard's watch.

They always looked at the husband first. It didn't mean he and Alicia were safe, however. It just meant they had options—someone else on whom investigators could cast suspicion.

CHAPTER 41

WATCHING ELIOT IN action both infuriated and reassured Alicia. He was in lawyer mode. But what was going on inside his head? Was he grieving for Kat? Did he regret the affair? Did her death devastate him?

Alicia was caught up in her own sea of grief and confusion since she'd stood in Kat's driveway and saw her taken away in a body bag. When was it? Forty-eight hours ago? Yes. Alicia hardly knew what day it was. She had eaten little, and sleep had fled. She'd been breaking down in tears at odd times. Her insides were a muddled boiling pot of nervous knots, a sore throat, a shattered heart, and a strange fog that blanketed reality.

She and Kat had exchanged vicious parting shots. What was the saying? *Be nice to those closest to you because you never know when you'll see them for the last time.* Alicia never thought that catchphrase would ever apply to her, but if she'd learned anything lately, it was the unpredictability of life. One minute she was a happily married woman; the next, she'd found out it was all an illusion, a mirage. The two people closest to her were puppeteers and she their unsuspecting puppet.

"Mrs. Gray, did Mrs. Deluca confide in you about any personal problems? For example, was she depressed, scared or nervous?" McBride's question jolted Alicia from her miserable musings.

"Please call me Alicia. You think Kat committed suicide?"

Alicia hated to admit it, but that seemed unlikely. Kat loved living too much. Plus, drawing from Kat's attitude at their last meeting, the woman had thought she was winning, that Eliot was hers. Why would she suddenly throw all that away?

"Just a routine question. As we said, we don't yet have a cause of death, so we can't rule out anything."

"She was having issues with her son, Maxim, as Eliot mentioned. She worked a lot, and he resented the time she spent away from home. He made no secret of it, but Kat was handling it. And no, I've never known her to suffer from depression, nor was she suicidal."

"People are good at hiding the truth, especially from close friends and family."

You're telling me.

"My wife already answered your question to the best of her ability," Eliot cut in. "She was not Katalina's shrink!"

Alicia ignored Eliot's outburst as she recalled her conversation with Richard. Would Richard share the details with the police but omit that he'd thought about killing both Kat and Eliot? Alicia hadn't told Eliot about that when they'd been planning their strategy earlier, which in hindsight, was a mistake. Despite the fact that she loathed him for what he'd done to her, she didn't want him blindsided. As much as it pained her to say it, she might need him.

"You're right, Mr. Gray," McBride said calmly. "But women talk. We were just wondering whether Mrs. DeLuca confided in your wife about her state of mind."

Alicia had as much as she could take, and her eyes brimmed with tears.

The detectives picked up on her distress and assured her that the interview was winding down for now, but that they had a few follow-up questions.

Eliot held her hand. She stiffened. It took a colossal effort not to brush off his touch, especially in front of people trained to observe body language. The feel of his fingers on hers was like holding on to toxic waste.

"Before we go, Alicia, can you answer one last question?" McBride asked. "Where were you at the time of Mrs. DeLuca's death?"

"I was here at home. A friend texted me saying something was going on at Kat's house." She explained the text exchange between her and Rina, emphasizing that it was because of Rina that she ended up at the DeLucases. Alicia made a mental note to warn Rina, especially since Alicia had asked her to hack Faith's email. Detectives had a way of extracting information from people, and the last thing Alicia needed was her friend getting into trouble for doing her a solid. Illegal as it was.

"What time did you receive the text?"

Alicia dug her phone from her pocket, glad for the opportunity to let go of Eliot's hand. She scrolled through her text messages until she found the right one. "Rina texted me around ten twenty, Tuesday morning."

They asked for Rina's full name and address and said they'd be in touch with further questions.

After the detectives left, she got up from the sofa and walked toward the fireplace. The framed photo of her mother, Margaux, sat on the mantle. Alicia stared into her mother's eyes. She needed her mother's strength to see her through this crisis. What would Margaux Thomas do?

Alicia picked up the frame and turned around to face Eliot. "There's something else."

"Okay. What's on your mind?"

"Richard knows."

"What?"

She slid her thumb back and forth over the photo for an extra dose of courage.

"Richard found out you were having an affair with his wife. He's known for a while. Had her followed. He found out about the secret apartment."

Boom! With that damning revelation, his entire body went limp as though his bones were made of Jell-o.

The grandfather clock on the wall, one of the few possessions of her mother's Alicia had left, ticked loudly. The aroma of sweet orange oil drifted from two stone diffusers she'd strategically placed around the room. She welcomed the warm, energizing mist. She'd read somewhere that sweet-orange aromatherapy reduced anxiety.

When he still hadn't said a word, she pushed. "Humiliating, isn't it? Richard sat in this very house not too long ago—he knew then that you were sleeping with his wife. I was the odd one out that night. All three of you were in on your dirty little secret."

"I never meant for it to come to this."

"That's all you have to say in your defense?" She took

one step closer. He was still seated. Standing gave her a psychological advantage. "What did you think would happen, Eliot? That no one would ever find out? Or maybe one day you would just tell me that it's over, abandon me and the girls for Kat? That's what she wanted. She was crystal clear in her emails to me. What did you promise her?"

"Nothing. I made no promises."

"She went through an awful lot of trouble to convince me otherwise. Why would she work so hard to create the impression that we were over?"

"I don't know."

Alicia promised herself she wouldn't ask this next question, but she had to know, *needed* to know. "Did you love her?"

"It was complicated."

"It's not. A simple yes or no will do."

"It's not what you think."

"Meaning what?"

"No one can ever replace you in my heart. In my life."

She folded her arms and glared at him. It took enormous restraint not to bash his head in with the picture frame. But she couldn't do that to her mother's photo. *Lucky him.*

"You're such a weasel. Two freakin' years, Eliot!" Alicia screamed at him.

He jerked back, startled.

"How many nights did you claim to be working late but was cooped up in your sordid love nest instead, huh? You sent her the itinerary for our Paris trip, our anniversary celebration. You made me look ridiculous in front of a woman who was trying to destroy me."

"She had no right to ridicule you. She knew better. It's

obvious that jealousy got the better of her. I'm sorry."

Anger blazed through her, a roaring beast seeking someone to devour. Yet somewhere in the back of her mind, a timid voice reminded her that she was talking about a dead woman.

Her bones ached at the thought. Grief shredded her insides. Unshed tears blurred her vision. She took a seat at the opposite end of the sofa, away from him. The sickening realization was that although she'd lost someone she'd once called a friend, she'd really lost Kat and her friendship two years ago. It was the most cherished friendship Alicia had ever had, outside of her relationship with her mother. The loss was a knife straight through her heart.

Long before she took her last breath, Kat had tossed Alicia aside. She'd perpetrated a cold-blooded deception by pretending to be the dutiful friend until, finally, she'd plunged the knife deep, violently twisting it with her malicious taunts and perverse sense of entitlement.

"No, Eliot. You're sorry you got caught. Something tells me that if Kat were alive, you would have continued your affair. Don't try to deny it. I'm tired of your lies. But tell me one last thing, Eliot. Why did I deserve your contempt? Why wasn't I good enough?"

CHAPTER 42

HURRICANE-FORCE GUILT POUNDED away at Eliot. He lowered his gaze, unable to meet hers. He swallowed repeatedly. He could do with a boatload of antacid right about now.

Alicia reminded him of a delicate, injured bird, broken by his actions, and the unexpected tragic death of a woman who had so savagely betrayed her. He had never counted the cost, naïve in his belief that Alicia was safe, that he could protect her from his affair. He never wanted to hurt her. To be honest, he thought he could have his cake and eat it, too. But now, he had to step up, contain the situation. Alicia must never uncover the whole truth. If she did, it would break her for good.

"Alicia, baby, how could you even think that? You, you're my everything."

"Don't 'baby' me, Eliot. What you did went beyond disrespect. The both of you. The lying, the mockery, the deceit. That's what you do to someone for whom you feel nothing but contempt. She called me 'ghetto trash', did you know that? If that's not contempt, then what is?"

He stood up, walked past her, trudged to the fireplace and leaned up against the mantle for support.

"I was so stupid." Her bottom lip trembled as she spoke. "I thought we were in a good place. Paris meant so much to me because you encouraged me to return to college to finish my degree when I doubted myself. We discussed our future. All the while... All the while, you were... I can't even say it. Who are you, anymore? What kind of person have you become, Eliot?"

"I discussed our future because we have one together."

She snorted. "You can't be serious."

"I am," he whispered. "Alicia, my love for you, what we mean to each other, was never in question."

"And yet you carried on with her. Why? Because I bored you to tears and you craved excitement? She threw herself at you and you couldn't resist her charms? Or maybe you acted on your attraction to her? Which one was it, Eliot?"

He understood her need for answers. But the simple reason was that he'd cheated because he could. He'd taken what Katalina enthusiastically offered without hesitation. He'd acted on his attraction and enjoyed the benefits of a no-strings-attached affair with someone he knew and liked. Because that was what his father had done.

His heart filled with self-loathing as he recalled the day when he was in his teens and had caught his father leaving a hotel with another woman. Later that night, his dad had called Eliot into his study and given him a lecture—his father's way of making sure Eliot kept his mouth shut.

"Your mother is my queen," his father had said. "Nothing and nobody is going to change that. Understood?"

There was no point in upsetting his mother by telling her what he had seen. His father had promised that he wasn't going anywhere.

The statement had confused a young Eliot. It didn't make sense. If his parents' marriage was on solid footing, why was his father cheating? But the adult Eliot finally came around to understanding, and he'd become his father.

"I messed up, Alicia. Let me fix it. I'll do anything."

"Tell me how it started. And don't hold anything back."

Without hesitation, Eliot launched into the story. "It was the anniversary of Katalina's brother's death, two years ago. She was a wreck. She had no close friends besides you and me. I guess the pain of losing Arturo was still raw." Inwardly, he winced. He burned with shame. He looked down at his trembling hands.

"Go on."

He didn't want to. But he owed her. "We had dinner at the Fairmont. Just to share a meal, talk, get her mind off things, distract her, really. But she had too much to drink."

He placed his hands in his pockets. He wanted to sit, but her probing gaze deterred him.

"She couldn't drive like that, so I offered to drive her home. She didn't want to go home. She thought Richard would be ashamed of her for coming home drunk, and she couldn't deal with his disappointment. She would rather sleep it off and go home in the morning, so she booked a room. I escorted her up. She invited me in. I went in just to make sure she was okay. She said she didn't want to be alone and asked me to stay. One thing led to another."

"You just couldn't help yourself, is that it? And at no time in the past two years did you think this was a bad idea?"

He remained quiet, reminding himself he couldn't afford to divulge the full story. He had to hold back, protect Alicia, their family. Her next question, however, left no doubt that she wanted her pound of flesh.

"Were the two of you planning to pass off your child as Richard's?"

He blinked hard. "What do you mean?"

"I received a sonogram."

"She wasn't pregnant," Eliot stated.

"How can you be sure?" Her words dripped with disdain.

"We'd been careful. And I confronted her about it."

"And you believed her? Because she'd been honest to a fault, right?"

"I bought a pregnancy test, forced her to take it. She had no choice but to tell the truth once she discovered I was serious."

"If you say so."

"Meaning what?"

"I'm just wondering how it worked in your relationship, since both of you found telling the truth impossible. In fact, I think you enjoyed your game of deception. Did you two get a rush from how easy it was to dupe me? Did you laugh at my stupidity when you were in bed together? Did that get you all fired up? Is that how it was, Eliot? I want to know."

"I would never mock you."

"You wouldn't, but she did. Tell me, what were you thinking when you bought her the same bracelet you gifted me on our fifteenth wedding anniversary? And the matching earrings."

"What?"

"Think carefully about your answer."

"I didn't buy her that bracelet. I swear."

"But you bought her the earrings. Why?"

In a toneless voice, he said, "She threatened to tell you about us if I didn't."

"Oh. Well, that makes it all okay then?"

"Alicia, I'm—"

"Don't bother explaining anything else," she said harshly. "You're not sorry you cheated. You enjoyed every minute of it. You disgust me. You got off on juggling two women, the sneaking around, the power trip. One woman pressuring you to end your marriage so she could be with you openly. The other, your loyal, clueless wife." The last sentence dripped, no longer with anger, but with total and utter despair.

He opened his mouth to speak but then decided against it. He couldn't dispute the accusation. Though he'd had no intention of giving in to Katalina's demands, he couldn't deny that in the earlier days of their relationship, her pestering had stroked his ego and puffed up his pride.

He prayed this would be the end of the interrogation from Alicia, that she would be satisfied with his answers and leave it at that. He had nothing more to say because he needed to protect her from the truth at all costs.

CHAPTER 43

*E*VEN IN DEATH, *she wears glamor with her trademark confidence and swagger*, Alicia thought.

Exquisite bouquets of white blooms—a blend of hydrangeas, Lily of the Valley, and English roses—filled the sanctuary of St. Julia Catholic Church. Alicia slowly approached the casket. She resolved not to crumble, despite the feeling that her knees could buckle at any moment. She had skipped the viewing at the funeral home. Truth was, she didn't want to be among the scores of people who traipsed through to look at Kat as if she were some object on display. Alicia's emotions were far too complicated to work out as part of a parade of mourners. She needed time. She needed a private goodbye.

Kat appeared to be asleep. Her face was saturated with a serenity that eluded her in life. Finally, she was at peace. Pearl drop earrings clung to her ears. Her raven hair, spread out like a curtain, created a striking contrast against the soft white pillow. She wore a scarlet-red Valentino dress, matching stilettos, and lipstick. Red was not her favorite color; it was purple.

Richard wanted to make a statement.

Alicia heard him loud and clear.

"This isn't goodbye, Kat. You can't leave." She dabbed at her eyes with the crumpled tissue in her hand. "Not yet. I'm still angry." She squeezed the tissue in her fists, nails biting into her palms, as she tried to work through her emotions. She eased over to the top of the casket so she could focus on Kat's face.

"Did you do this on purpose because you felt guilty?" Alicia asked. "No, that's not it. You don't do regrets or apologies. Who did this to you, then?

"Don't think that because you're in this box it excuses anything. I loved you like a sister, and yet you stabbed me in the back, over and over. But I kept coming back for more, didn't I? Oh, how you must have laughed at my stupidity. Every time you touched Eliot, lay next to him, kept him away from me and our girls, it was another stab wound."

She inhaled deeply. "Maxim is heartbroken, you lying tramp. That's how he described you when he heard you were gone. He's inconsolable. Your son still needed you, even if he behaved as if he didn't. But you abandoned him, your only child."

She caught her breath and composed herself. She heard noises and rustling at the back of the church. The mourners would be arriving soon. Time was running out.

"You know, you had a lot in common with my father, Kat. You both wrecked lives and then left others to pick up the pieces. Here I go, clearing up your mess. *Adios, vieja amiga.*"

ELIOT ADJUSTED THE Ray-Ban sunglasses on his face for the third time. His head throbbed, a relentless, exhausting hammering that made him want to cry out in agony. He stood

228

at the back of the funeral tent erected at the garden-like cemetery, maintaining his distance from the clump of mourners.

Loud wailing and sniffling erupted from the sea of black as the priest read from the scriptures. Katalina's parents, in addition to the tragedy of losing their daughter, couldn't take her home to Miami and bury her next to her brother, as they wished. Richard had refused, insisting she would be buried at Linwood Cemetery, the principal burial ground in the town of Weston. A handful of aunts, uncles, and cousins had come up for the funeral. Arnie Tillerson and his wife, Paula, stood stoically at the graveside. Katalina didn't have a lot of friends, but the turnout would have pleased her.

A jaw muscle ticked. Eliot's breath quickened as he placed both hands into his pockets. His chest just about split in half when Alicia placed a protective arm around Maxim. The boy sobbed inconsolably. His daughters flanked them on either side.

He suddenly became aware of someone behind him. He turned to find Detective James McBride's attention anchored on him. Eliot's blood ran cold, but he gave no outward reaction, returning his gaze to the committal service. The priest was wrapping up.

A loud moan escaped Mrs. Torres, Kat's mother, who stood in the family row up front. She placed her hands on top of the coffin and caressed it as though letting her daughter know that she loved her, for the last time. The poor woman had now lost both her children, five years apart. No parent should have to witness the death of a child. It messed with the natural order of things, and it seemed that her agony was felt by everyone present as she wailed.

Eliot didn't need to turn around again to feel the burning

heat of McBride's gaze on him. Eliot bit down hard on his lips. He couldn't stick around any longer. He had no desire to watch Katalina being lowered into the ground. He didn't want that to be the last image he would ever have of her.

"Leaving so soon?" McBride fell into step with Eliot on the winding path that led to the car.

He needed to be alone while he waited for Alicia and the girls. His tone sharp, he said, "Soon?"

"I don't mean to be insensitive. Will you be attending the reception afterward?"

"How is that relevant to your investigation?" Eliot's head continued to throb. McBride's presence exacerbated his irritation.

"Her death was unexpected. I can't imagine how it must be for you, Mr. Gray. You and Mrs. DeLuca were close, yes?"

A strong breeze rustled the leaves of the majestic trees that flanked the cemetery. Eliot removed his sunglasses.

"I have already answered that question during the interview at my home."

He sensed McBride was fishing or looking for confirmation on some piece of information. Eliot had no intention of confirming anything. But then he remembered Alicia's bombshell. Richard knew about the affair. *Had he said something to the detectives?*

"Is Mrs. Gray aware that Mrs. DeLuca made multiple calls to your personal cell phone in the weeks leading up to her death?" McBride asked, casually.

Eliot halted. "I don't appreciate what you're implying, Detective."

"I'm not implying anything. I ask questions. It's part of my job."

"Tillerson Brenner was a client of KTM Creative Edge. I helped her land the account. She called me from time to time to discuss strategy."

"Sounds like you were a friend and ally."

"Sure. If you want to look at it that way. She worked hard to make the agency successful. I lent a helping hand when I could."

"How did Alicia feel about that?"

"Is this an interrogation, Detective McBride? In what capacity are you here? If you wish to express your condolences, that's fine. Otherwise, I will assume that this is official police business, in which case, I have a right to have an attorney present."

McBride held up his arms. "No need for that, Mr. Gray. This is just a friendly conversation. I'm not accusing you of anything. We expect the autopsy results any day now, and it will tell us how Mrs. DeLuca died. That's what we all want, right?"

Eliot's phone pinged. He removed it from his pocket and read the text.

Alicia: Where are you? We're heading back to the car.

Eliot: Will meet up with you. Had an upset stomach.

He placed the phone back into his pocket and said, "This is a tough day for my family and me. We lost a friend unexpectedly and tragically. Please give us some privacy to mourn. At least for the day."

"Sure, sure. No problem. I just have one question. It might be a bit embarrassing considering we're at her funeral, but I must ask."

"Ask away."

231

"Did Mrs. DeLuca ever communicate with you inappropriately? Other than business or friendship, I mean."

"What are you talking about?"

A flush appeared on McBride's cheek. "When we looked at her phone records, there were several text messages to you of an intimate nature. Your responses were terse. I figured she developed feelings for you and that you were trying to let her down easy, seeing that both you and your wife were friends of hers and her husband."

McBride wasn't stupid, and he was now following the trail that would uncover the affair. Eliot was losing control of the situation. He was willing to bet that the issue wasn't if and when Richard would reveal the affair to the investigators, but that he already had.

Richard DeLuca always came across as inscrutable. But the fact that he'd had his wife followed and knew of the affair and had said nothing signaled that he was a man with secrets. What else was he hiding, and what was he capable of?

"Katalina was a big flirt. Maybe I indulged her when I shouldn't have. I think her husband knew about that proclivity. Flirting with other men, that is."

"Oh, yeah?" McBride asked. "He must be a patient and understanding husband. I don't know too many men who would tolerate such behavior."

"I couldn't tell you. Richard can be an enigma."

McBride wrinkled his nose. A pensive look flittered across his face. He nodded slowly, then said, "I don't want to take up any more of your time on such a tough day. Thanks for the chat, Mr. Gray."

"Any time, Detective."

CHAPTER 44

KATALINA TORRES

March 19, 2004

~ DIARY ENTRY ~

I'm not one for fawning all over a man, but today I made an exception. I'm flying higher than a kite as I write this. I snuck out of the closing keynote presentation of the CreativeMax Conference at Boston's Fairmont Copley Plaza Hotel. There was nothing new there. Same old information wrapped up in the latest buzz words to make it sound fresh and exciting. Anyway, in my haste to hit the bar before everyone else did, I forgot I was wearing five-inch-high Manolo Blahniks. It was literally the cliché from every romantic comedy ever (insert dramatic eye roll). Who would have thought I'd have a 'meet-cute'?

I bumped into him and would have had an embarrassing fall to the ground had he not grabbed me. He had strong biceps. The scent of his Clive Christian 1872 cologne tickled my nose. All this happened before we made eye contact.

And when we did, I was smitten. Gob smacked, eyes popped, mouth hanging open, smitten. Couldn't get a word out. If Mamma could have seen me, she would have laughed her butt off. *Hablas demasiado, meja.* She was always telling me I talk too much.

"Easy there," he said. "Don't hurt yourself. I can't drive you to the hospital if you do." Then he winked at me. I mean the kind of wink that would make even the most cynical girl go weak in the knees. Seriously, I wanted to marry him, and I didn't even know his name. A nurturer and protector. He was willing to drive a total stranger to the hospital. He scored major points for that. And by his finely tailored Italian suit that cost at least two thousand dollars, I guessed he was some high-powered lawyer or investment banker.

When blood returned to my brain, I told him he shouldn't say nice things if he couldn't deliver. I thanked him for saving me from an embarrassing fall, and that the least I could do was buy him a drink. He hesitated and then agreed only after I assured him I wasn't recruiting victims for some top-secret pharmaceutical drug experiment.

I ended up at the bar with Eliot Gray, the corporate lawyer. I gave myself points for guessing correctly. I've heard of his firm, Tillerson Brenner. They have an excellent reputation. He said he wasn't much of a drinker but didn't want to be impolite since I went out of my way to thank him. He was charming without even trying, confident, coolness personified.

"Why were you in a hurry to ditch that conference?" he asked, with a big, *I feel you, I've ditched a few boring meetings myself* kind of grin.

I explained that I worked as a junior art director for a B2B

234

creative agency in New York and wanted to learn the latest innovation in visual communication. I took off because I was bored. The speakers presented nothing new that sparked my creative muse. I looked away from him for a moment to chastise myself.

I couldn't believe what happened next. He leaned in and asked me to tell him more. He actually wanted to know more about my work, about me. *He saw me.* Not a pretty face or hot body like most idiots I encountered. Just me. It was so refreshing I almost cried.

"What kind of clients does your agency represent?" he asked. Then he wanted to know about my day-to-day job, what I loved about it and what I hated about it. He asked about my goals and ambition, what was next for me.

He even wanted to know if he'd seen my work anywhere. I promised to send him the portfolio link to our agency's website. I'm as guarded and cynical as they come, two of my superpowers, but something about Eliot compelled me to open up. I should have had myself checked out to make sure I wasn't coming down with something.

Anyway, drinks turned to dinner, and we didn't even notice the bar had filled up around us as we talked about literature, politics, and world travel, the places we've been and still wanted to visit. He didn't want to talk much about his job except to say he was good at it and liked his firm. He was thirty-two and wanted to make partner in ten years or less. Then he turned the spotlight back on me.

Two kids, I thought, as I tried not to stare into his hypnotic face. A boy and a girl. No More. I had my career to think about.

Then all my careful planning came crashing down, rather rudely I might add, when he walked me to my room. The polite thing to do was invite him in, which I did. He stood at the door looking all apologetic and sheepish.

"I'm married, Katalina," he said.

I just stood there, like a mute idiot. He wasn't wearing a wedding ring. I gaped at his empty hand. I called foul. Double foul. He caught me staring and then held up his left palm.

"Allergic reaction to a bite from a not-so-friendly spider. The finger got so swollen I had to remove the ring," he explained.

Then he pulled out his phone, scrolled, and showed me a photo of the most adorable toddlers I had ever seen. He explained that they were his daughters, Marston and Lily, almost two years apart.

Now came the headache. Mrs. Gray. Who the heck was she, and how did she land him? He was only thirty-two, so I'm guessing they married young. Was she a lawyer like him? Perhaps they met at his firm or were they in law school together? A high school sweetheart? A girlfriend who trapped him by getting pregnant? It still happens. He seems like the kind of guy who would step up, do the right thing.

I had to play it cool so I told him how cute they were and I could tell he was a great father. He seemed to like that. I was careful not to bring up his wife. Thankfully, neither did he.

I always get what I want, and I've decided that Eliot Gray is what I want, despite the complication of a family. Sometimes a complication is an opportunity. It comes down to perspective. I've finally met a man who's perfect for me, and nothing is going to stand in my way.

CHAPTER 45

THEY SAT IN the family room. Alicia didn't want to visit the kitchen, the place where Richard had found Kat's body. Alicia had come over to deliver a few days' worth of home-cooked meals for him and Maxim and to keep him company for a while. Maxim was at her house with the girls who were trying their best to keep him occupied.

She glanced at a photo above the fireplace. Ironically, it was taken at Arnie Tillerson's townhouse *that night*. Kat wore a dazzling smile and a stunning Herve Leger mini dress. Richard appeared constipated.

"She was pregnant," he said. "The autopsy report confirmed it."

What? Alicia wasn't sure she'd heard right, but she knew she was kidding herself. She gulped for air. Distressing thoughts paraded across her mind, her brain synapses firing all at once. *Was the baby Richard's or Eliot's?* Had Eliot lied yet again when he claimed Kat wasn't pregnant, or had he been deceived this time, too? Was the sonogram Jack provided real then? But Jack would have confirmed if it was. He hadn't.

Kat had said that she and Richard were in a bad place, but that didn't mean they weren't intimate. Marriage was complicated like that.

"Please don't take this the wrong way, I mean no disrespect—"

"You don't have to walk on eggshells around me, Alicia. You're wondering if I was the father. I can tell you with unshakeable confidence that I was not."

"How can you be so sure?"

"Because my wife wouldn't let me touch her. It felt like we hadn't even been in the same room let alone the same bed in the past year."

Eliot was the father.

She didn't have time to process that depressing tidbit of information before a horrible thought slammed into her brain. *What if Richard killed Kat?* He'd already confided that Eliot might not have been her first affair. Alicia clearly remembered Richard saying he was no saint and that he had a breaking point. What if he'd found out about the pregnancy and knowing he wasn't the father sent him over the edge?

"*I thought if they were both dead it would solve my problem.*"

"Um, Richard, did that push you over the edge? With everything that was going on, and Maxim's struggles, it's a lot for one person to take."

A comical expression spread across his face. His eyes crinkled at the corners. Alicia had trouble recalling the last time she saw Richard laugh.

"What's so funny?" she asked.

"Alicia, I know what you're getting at, and the funny thing is, I wanted to. I wanted to kill her for what she was doing to our son. Our family. But I didn't have the guts to do it."

"I'm sorry. I didn't mean to—"

He waved off her attempt at an apology. "It's always the husband, right? But it would have been a pointless exercise. What would happen to Maxim if they carted me off to prison for killing his mother? The kid's been through enough already. I'm all he has now."

Alicia nodded and said nothing.

"She envied you, you know?" he said.

"W-what?"

"You had Eliot and she didn't. It frustrated her."

She noticed his fingernails biting into his palms. He scrunched up his face and then released the tension, trying to regain his calm, she supposed.

"But after I found proof of the affair, suddenly, it all made sense. She couldn't be with him openly. They had to hide the relationship, constantly lie to our faces, and keep their stories straight. It didn't matter that she had her own husband who always begged her to spend time with him, with our son. I imagine the secrecy was exciting at first, but after a while, it couldn't have been enough."

Sweat appeared on his forehead. He arranged and rearranged the magazines on the coffee table.

"I suggested we move back to New York or even Miami to be closer to her family. She balked, laughed in my face, and asked me if I was high. Then she used her business as an excuse, the connections she'd made in Boston. Her employees. But I knew it was because of Eliot. She couldn't stand to be separated from him."

He dumped it all on her like an exhausted professor who just wanted the lecture to be over with. Impart the information with no feeling or passion. This was his way of dealing with his grief, a cathartic outpouring of his heart. They were kindred spirits, forced to deal with the aftermath of profound spousal betrayal, and death.

When he looked up and made eye contact with her once more, he said, "We're leaving. Once this is over, and the police close the investigation, I'm taking Maxim and leaving this state for good. That was the plan before she died, anyway."

"Where will you go?"

"California. My brother lives in L.A. It will be a fresh start for Maxim and me. Sunshine, palm trees, the ocean. I can work from anywhere, and it's best we're far away from here."

Richard's choice of resting place for Kat suddenly made sense. He wanted to erase her, punish her by leaving her buried in Weston, far away from her family, in a town she had only arrived in four years ago.

"Did you pick her burial clothes?" Alicia asked.

"What do you think?"

"I think you're a devastated husband. You wanted to have your say because you couldn't while she was alive."

The fatigue she'd observed in him the night of the celebratory party returned. The burden of knowing his wife was unfaithful and had been neglecting their son was too much to bear. Looking at Richard now, it seemed like he'd aged ten years in a few short weeks. Sagging skin under his eyes, his hair unkempt, loose-fitting clothes. A shadow of a man.

She stood and picked up her purse from the sofa. "I'll check in on you tomorrow. Maxim is welcome to stay with us as long as he wants."

He got to his feet. "Thank you, Alicia. I'll miss your

kindness and thoughtfulness. Would you mind taking him, just for tonight? I can come get him tomorrow."

"Of course. And Richard?"

"Yeah."

"Eliot's not a bad person. Maybe he and Kat… Perhaps they were both broken, and we just didn't see it."

"But aren't we all broken, though?"

She guessed he was right.

And after this latest revelation, Alicia knew that her marriage to Eliot was now beyond repair.

CHAPTER 46

Unknown: You killed her, didn't you? Got scared she would tell your wife about the affair. Didn't want to lose your shirt in a divorce, so you killed her. Shame on you, Eliot. You're a wicked man.

THE ANONYMOUS TEXT message sent Eliot's brain into a tailspin. He stumbled toward the large glass window with his perfect view of Faneuil Hall Marketplace. He needed to calm down before his thoughts took him down the path of panic and chaos.

The sender obviously used a burner phone. He ticked off possible suspects in his head. Someone from Katalina's office in whom she had confided. A friend, perhaps from back home in Miami, she kept in touch with. The most obvious choice? *Richard.*

It was the only reasonable explanation. Richard had known about the affair for weeks yet had said nothing. Perhaps in his grief, he was lashing out. He and Katalina never got the chance to patch things up or end the marriage. Her untimely death snatched the decision away from him, and now he needed someone to pay. Eliot was an easy target. The only target.

He wouldn't respond right away, if he should respond at all. Such a text was meant to intimidate, inspire panic. The easy response would be to text back, "Who is this?" He would get there eventually, but he wanted to see how far this person was willing to take this game. If it was Richard, additional texts would shed light, provide information about his motive.

The case was still open. Although the coroner had declared the cause of death to be head trauma from the impact of a fall, they still had no clue how it happened. Alcohol could have been a factor, although they were waiting on the blood toxicology report. They had found a half-empty bottle of wine on the kitchen island. She was wearing heels when they found her. Perhaps she had been inebriated and lost her balance, fallen, and hit her head.

A reasonable explanation, but the Weston police detectives were thorough and wouldn't close the case until they were satisfied that it *was* an accident. So far, there was no forced entry, no prints, fibers, DNA of any kind, no sign that another human being had been present at the time of death.

The news media was another nuisance. He could only imagine the stories they would run if news of the affair got out. Alicia's forgiveness was a long way off. His goals were simple: keep his family together and avoid prison.

There was a knock on the door. "Come in," he said.

Delia Evans, his investigator of five years, entered, a file tucked under her arm, a coffee cup in hand, and a pen stuck in between her ears. In her late thirties, Delia was loyal, discreet, and great at her job. She could probably bench-press him, too. She was a fitness nut who took every opportunity to call him a weakling when they worked out in the office gym.

She placed her coffee and file on the table, plopped down on the sofa, and reclined. "Tell me how brilliant I am and how lucky you are to have me in your corner. Then I want a big raise."

"Overconfidence. I like it." He took a seat behind his desk, across from her. "But let's see if the information lives up to the hype."

"Is there ever a question?" she asked.

"Tell me what's in the file," he said. "You can make a root canal sound enthralling."

Delia leaned forward. "Mrs. DeLuca was pregnant at the time of her death."

He gripped the side of his swivel chair. His fingernails dug into the leather. *She was telling the truth all along.* His mouth went dry. He loosened his tie.

"Are you sure you're up for this?" Delia asked. "We can connect later."

"Nonsense. Let's get through it. Katalina was a friend of the firm. Arnie liked her, and so did I. We want to make sure foul play wasn't a factor in her death."

Delia pulled the pen from behind her ear, picked up the file from the table, and scanned the information. She took a sip of her coffee. Eliot wanted to crawl out of his skin, reach over, and snatch the file from her.

"Preliminary toxicology results came back—unofficially. I had to bribe some people to get them. My inside guy wants a pair of Patriots season tickets, by the way."

She continued, "Seems that Mrs. DeLuca was on anti-depressants and Ambien. And to top it off, they found massive amounts of alcohol in her system. Way past the legal limit."

Kat drank a little too much, but anti-depressants? Sleeping pills? Pregnant? She couldn't have known the pregnancy was real when he'd forced her to confess that it was a hoax to pressure him into ending his marriage. Otherwise, she wouldn't drink so much. *Unless she no longer cared.*

"She had a lot going on. It still doesn't give a concrete cause of death, though." His words sounded dead and brittle even to his own ears.

"Maybe. But there's one weird fact that's an outlier. It's been bugging me, and I have no idea if it means anything."

"What's that?"

She flicked through the file again, scanned a couple of pages, and placed it back on the coffee table. "There was a previous injury, prior to the one that killed her."

"What?"

"She suffered a concussion at the back of her head."

"Could they tell how long ago it happened?"

"I hate to say this, Eliot, but it sounds like this was a tragic accident. She got drunk, lost her balance, and fell. Most non-athletic concussions are caused by falls. The latest one proved fatal."

"Both injuries were around the same area then?"

"It appears so."

Was it really that simple? A tragic accident ended the life of the woman with whom he'd betrayed his wife? He still hadn't gotten over Alicia's confession that she suffered from depression years ago and had hidden it from him. Could Kat's death and everything leading up to it cause Alicia to relapse?

"Thanks, Delia. That's all great," he said absentmindedly as he turned toward the window again. He needed to be alone. "Keep me updated on any new developments."

After Delia left his office, he removed his suit jacket, ripped off his tie, and unbuttoned the top two buttons of his dress shirt. His forehead and neck were sweating. Why was it suddenly so hot in here? His eyes lingered on the family photo on his desk.

Everything he had to lose was right there in that image. Katalina's death had blindsided him and continued to do so with these latest revelations. She had never shared with him that she was depressed. Was that why McBride had brought up the subject during the interview at the house? He shook off the thought. No, the autopsy had not yet been completed, so McBride couldn't have known.

People didn't take anti-depressants and sleeping pills and drink excessively when their lives were rosy. She was still the same stubborn, fierce, and proud woman he had come to know. But what if it was all an act for his benefit? Her troubles with Maxim aside, what was she trying to escape, and how did she get that concussion?

He picked up his phone. There were two messages from his anonymous texter.

Unknown: You have nothing to say? I suggest you respond before I tell the police what I know. You should fry for this.

He would poke the bear. The sender had mentioned him by name in the first text. No point in pretending it was a mistake.

Eliot: I have no idea who you are or why you're spewing these outlandish accusations at me. I can only assume you're mentally deranged.

He waited as the three dots bobbed up and down.

Unknown: Tell your wife the truth about you and the deceased Mrs.

246

DeLuca, what you've been hiding from her. That's for starters. You do that, then I'll tell you what I'm after. And do it quickly before the police come sniffing around.

He would ignore the warning for now. Right now, his priority was protecting Alicia and himself. He had a sinking feeling McBride would not accept the findings at face value.

CHAPTER 47

M CBRIDE IS JUST fishing," Eliot told Alicia. "There is
no evidence of foul play, but he wants to be sure. Don't
panic. You have done nothing wrong. Don't answer questions
that aren't asked, and don't elaborate on anything."

Alicia cradled her coffee mug and squeezed her eyes shut.
Her emotions ran amuck. Despite the current crises, they still
continued their morning routine. This time, they sat on the
patio. They couldn't risk the girls sauntering into the kitchen
and catching wind of their conversation.

Detective McBride's call came in fifteen minutes ago,
before she even had a chance to brew fresh coffee. The call
had rattled her. He said an employee from Kat's agency had
reported that the two women had engaged in a vicious falling
out right before Kat died. He wanted to get her statement
about the incident.

They'd scheduled the interview for eleven o'clock. It was
seven forty-five and there was still a lot they needed to get
through. Eliot didn't want to raise unnecessary red flags by

having her walk into an interview room with a lawyer. The goal was to walk in, answer the questions, and put it behind her.

Eliot said, "He'll want to know what the fight with Katalina was about. Her assistant who came forward didn't hear the conversation between you two, so that helps us. He only saw the aftermath, Katalina on the ground after you pushed her, so he can't even prove anything because he didn't witness the incident."

She nodded slowly, then took a sip of her coffee. It was a lot to take in. She cast a glance across their large, scenic backyard, flanked by hundred-year-old oak trees. The only sound that permeated the sunlit morning was the systematic shhh-tik-tik-tik sound of the sprinklers.

The mundane suburban existence she had so cherished as the antithesis of the chaos of her inner-city upbringing now rung hollow. Her life had taken a sharp turn and was now skidding across the highway and heading into a ditch. Who would help her out of it? For all his talk, it was most certainly not going to be the husband who had betrayed her.

He frowned, as if contemplating something life-changing. Then he said, "Tell McBride the truth. That I admitted the affair after you found proof. That would be the emails back and forth when she posed as Faith. You went to her office. Things got heated. You lost your temper. They'll have confiscated her computer and phone and will be going through everything, so there is no point in hiding it. Our goal is to stay consistent with what they know, so we come out looking truthful, with nothing to hide."

There was something else. She could sense it, the way he kept fiddling with his tie, his gaze ping-ponging around the back yard. "What is it?" she asked.

"I received an anonymous text message from someone accusing me of killing Katalina."

"Did you now?" The question popped out of her mouth without permission. She didn't mean to be so flippant about such a serious matter. She knew Eliot wasn't a murderer, but the depth of his deception had shaken her faith in him, made her doubt everything about him. *So, you believe Richard over your own husband?* She no longer knew her husband.

He leveled a blank stare in her direction, then forced his spine upright. He appeared frozen, his eyes wide as though struggling to comprehend what he just heard.

"Is that how low your opinion of me has sunk? You think I'm a killer? I'm trying to help you, protect us."

"I'm sorry, Eliot. I know you're not a killer. It's just that... It's a lot, okay? I have a hard time trusting you now. If you could carry on an affair for two years and hide it so well, it scares me to think what else you could be hiding. I don't want to think like that, but my mind goes there on its own."

His body sagged. "I hurt you badly, and I will spend the rest of my life making it up to you, but let's not pretend you're a saint. You did something pretty horrific that I will never forget." In a strained voice, he added, "Let's just get through this interview with McBride, okay? My other big worry is the media."

He straightened his tie. "If news of the affair gets out, it might affect the firm's reputation and Arnie will have my head. McBride already called me out on text messages Katalina sent to me. Then there's the anonymous texter."

"And Rina."

"What?"

"Rina helped me crack Faith's true identity through her IP

address. That's how I found out Faith was Kat using an alias. Plus, she and David have known about your affair for years. You were spotted together, Eliot."

His shoulders slumped with the weight of his betrayal, the shame of it. Richard, David, Rina, and Maxim, all silent witnesses. Eliot was a proud man, and Alicia knew that the thought that he was now diminished in their eyes would be unbearable to him. As she looked at her husband, she thought of the young, twenty-five-year-old who had swept her off her feet. He'd looked like a boy back then. A sweet, caring, handsome boy who'd wanted to ease her pain and give her the life she could only dream of.

Beyond the material, he'd promised to protect her, which he was doing now. He'd sworn to remain devoted to her and the family they would one day create. But being faithful in a marriage and devoted to one's family weren't necessarily the same thing, were they?

He glanced at the notepad he brought with him. "Let's go over the details one last time, step by step in the order that events unfolded. McBride will be looking to trip you up with inconsistencies or inaccuracies in the timeline of events. You can't walk into that interrogation room until you've mastered every angle. It's the only way to get him off your back."

CHAPTER 48

THEY OCCUPIED INTERVIEW Room 1 of the police department's newly built, state-of-the art headquarters. The room was simple and clean with walls that were painted a grayish blue and furnished with a table and two chairs that were bolted to the floor. A recorder sat on the table.

After declining water and coffee, Alicia told Detective McBride that she was willing to answer all of his questions. She just wanted the interview over with. The shock of Kat's death still haunted her.

"I understand, Mrs. Gray. I'll do my best to make this as painless as possible."

"Alicia, please."

He pulled up a chair across from her and hit the appropriate button on the recorder. He asked Alicia to state her name, address, and occupation for the record before he started his questioning.

"You and the deceased Katalina Torres DeLuca had a violent altercation in her office before her death, is that true?"

"Yes, we had an argument," Alicia replied.

"Tell me what happened."

She did, the way Eliot had coached her. "I found out she was having an affair with my husband. I was devastated, so I went to her office to ask her why, why she had betrayed me so savagely. Things got heated."

"How did she end up on the floor?" McBride lobbed the question with nonchalance.

"I beg your pardon?"

He flipped through a notebook he'd brought with him and read from his notes. "According to the witness, Mrs. DeLuca yelled for help, and when he arrived, she was on the floor. She said you pushed her. Her hospital records showed she suffered mild bruising from her body connecting with the office furniture. Did you have anything to do with her fall?"

It made sense to her now. It wasn't so much about the argument, as it was about the push. Kat fell in her office. She fell at home, which led to her death, though that information was not yet public knowledge. Alicia was no Sherlock Holmes, but she had enough brain cells and had watched enough TV crime dramas to follow the detective's logic, the reason she was here.

"I see where you're going with this detective. Yes, her betrayal left me devastated, but I didn't want her dead. I just wanted her to admit what she'd done. Which she did, with a little extra spice."

"What do you mean by that?"

"The friend I knew and loved was replaced by someone I didn't recognize—vicious, angry, lashing out in a way I had never seen before."

"Are you saying she attacked you first?"

She was about to go off script. She felt it, the idea sprouting in her head, taking root by the millisecond. There were no cameras in Kat's office. No one saw anything. This was a gray area. Not exactly lying, but not the whole truth either. Alicia placed her hands in her lap, afraid McBride might pick up on her anxiety. Yet, she struggled to keep them still.

"I called her ugly names because her actions hurt me and our friendship. She pushed me. I pushed her back. She lost her balance. She always wore high heels. She tripped and fell."

"So, you were angry with each other. Was this the first incidence of violence between the two of you?"

"I don't get your meaning."

"Did you and the deceased have arguments that lead to physical altercations in the past?"

"No."

"Never?"

"Never, Detective."

"When did you find out about the affair between your husband and Mrs. DeLuca?"

"The day before the argument in her office."

"Are you sure about the timeline?"

"I'm sure."

"You had no knowledge of the affair prior to the day before you argued with Mrs. DeLuca in her office?" He looked at Alicia closely. "Just a reminder, lying to the police during an investigation could land you in trouble. Obstruction of justice."

"I'm not lying. I had knowledge of 'an affair'. I had no idea Kat was the other party until the day before I went to her office. She even bragged about how clueless I was."

The admission still hurt even now, but Eliot had been

right. They had gone through Kat's computer with a fine-tooth comb and had discovered the email exchange between her and Faith. Their tech guys must have figured out what Rina had done illegally, that Faith was Kat. Only Eliot knew the truth of how she found out about Kat, and he wasn't about to say anything.

"As your witness explained, Detective," she continued, "he found her on the floor. She was very much alive when I left that office."

He pretended to be engrossed in his notebook. An invisible cloak of silence hung between them. She would wait him out.

Then he threw a fast ball at her. "Did you know Mrs. DeLuca was pregnant with your husband's child?"

He wanted her off balance. His question was a little shock value to cause her to stumble, make a mistake. She was ready. Detective McBride would not trick her, not today.

"Richard DeLuca confided in me that she was pregnant. That's all I know. What proof do you have that she was carrying Eliot's baby?"

His eyes widened, ever so slightly. He obviously hadn't expected that. He straightened the collar of his button-down shirt when it didn't need straightening.

"We've established that she was carrying on an affair with your husband."

"That's correct, Detective, but I don't know who else she was sleeping with. The baby could have been her husband's or a third party that we're unaware of. Anything is possible."

"Right. Is there anyone who can corroborate your whereabouts, that you were home at the time of Mrs. DeLuca's death?"

255

"You have the timestamp of the text message from Rina Stark."

"Yes, but we have no way of proving you were home when you received that text. You could have been at the DeLuca residence prior to receiving the message. You live on the same street. The text would have pinged off the same cell phone tower."

She leaned back in her chair and folded her arms. "Are you accusing me of something, Detective? Do I need to call my husband and have him send an attorney down here?"

"Just trying to solve a mystery, Alicia. The faster we have answers, the faster we can bring the case to a close. We appreciate you coming down. Please take nothing personally. It's all just routine questioning."

She was about to say something snarky but changed her mind. This was neither the time nor place. She just needed to get through this interview and get out of there. She had done nothing wrong. Kat's death was a tragic accident. She fell and hit her head. Case closed. But Detective McBride seemed determined to aim his blinding spotlight directly at Alicia.

"I don't know what else to tell you, Detective. I heard the sirens, like everyone else on our street. It was chaos by the time I got there. You said this was just a routine interview, but it sounds like the interrogation of a suspect. What did I do wrong? There's no law against having a dispute with a friend."

"But there is against assault."

"Well, she didn't file any charges."

She immediately regretted her outburst. Did she just say that? She gulped. Her palms were moist, and the back of her blouse felt like it was sticking to her skin.

"This is difficult, okay. Although Kat hurt me, she was the

closest thing I had to a sister in my entire life. I grew up an only child. And now she's gone, and I'll never see her again. We'll never have the chance to make amends."

He nodded as if he understood. "I'm sorry if this has been difficult for you, Alicia. Believe me, my only objective is to get to the truth. As long as you're being straight with me, you have nothing to worry about."

CHAPTER 49

B Y THE TIME six o'clock rolled around, it was clear the story was far from over. After receiving a text from Rina to turn on the TV, Alicia could only watch in stunned disbelief at the horrendous train wreck that unfolded before her eyes.

"A new twist in the investigation into the death of Weston resident and CEO of KTM Creative Edge, Katalina Torres DeLuca. According to an insider with knowledge of the investigation, Katalina and her best friend Alicia Gray, also of Weston, had a violent confrontation days before Katalina was found unresponsive in her home. The quarrel appeared to be over an alleged affair between Katalina and Alicia's husband, prominent attorney, Eliot Gray, a partner at Tillerson Brenner.

A photo of Alicia and Kat at a gala, dressed to the nines with big grins on their faces and dripping in diamonds, flashed on the screen. Alicia crumpled down onto the sofa as she watched the new nightmare unfold. The reporter tightened the screws.

"Weston police refuse to say whether Alicia Gray is a suspect in the death of her friend."

The broadcast cut to a pack of reporters outside the Weston Police Station and a somber McBride at their mercy. They fired questions at him, but he said nothing as he hustled to his car in the parking lot.

"*Is the case now officially a murder investigation?*"

"*Is an arrest imminent?*"

"*Is Eliot Gray a suspect in the death of his mistress?*"

"*Was Richard DeLuca aware of the affair? Is he a suspect in his wife's death?*"

The damage was done. She picked up the remote control and shut off the television. Someone had exposed them. Perhaps the anonymous texter Eliot had mentioned during their prep for the interview. It didn't matter who it was. Their lives would never be the same. Kat ruined lives and left others to clean up the mess.

But in reality, Alicia didn't care about public opinion of her. She had two daughters to worry about. Kat had ruined their lives, too.

As if communicating via telepathy, Lily and Marston walked into the family room, their footsteps heavy, eyes wet and dull. Marston spoke first, clutching her phone in her hand.

"Is it true, Mom?"

"Girls." Alicia's voice was full of sorrow. "Please sit."

They obeyed. Lily shivered, then rubbed her arms as though trying to keep them warm. Marston, in typical Marston style, held it in, remaining poised and holding herself tall, despite everything. But she wanted answers. There was no point in lying to them. Alicia didn't want the girls to think badly of their father, but it was too late for that. She could no longer protect him. Everything was out in the open.

"We thought Maxim was just upset when he told us,

jumping to conclusions and just acting out," Marston said. "But he was right."

Alicia nodded miserably. "Yes, that poor child. He told the truth."

Lily and Marston exchanged curious glances. "How come Maxim knew about the affair?"

She exhaled and provided an abbreviated version of how Maxim accidentally found out and had been angry at his mother ever since.

Lily stood and raked her hair back, eyes glistening with unshed tears. "What are we going to do, Mom? Are you and Dad getting a divorce?"

"It looks that way."

"Don't tell me you would consider staying with Dad," Marston said. "What he did is unforgiveable."

"Yeah," her sister chimed in. "That's seriously disgusting. They both played you, Mom. I knew something was funny, the way Kat reacted when I showed her pics of you and Dad in Paris. I just shrugged it off at the time."

"What do you mean, funny how?"

"I came back to the house a couple of days after you guys left for the trip. I'd forgotten my curling iron. I ran into Kat. She had just come back from a walk. Anyway, I showed her the pics you guys sent. She was not happy. She gave me a fake smile to cover, but it was too late. I had already caught her reaction."

"Ugh," Marston grimaced. "She sat here that night of the dinner, acting like she was happy you and Dad went away. How dare she?"

Lily said, "And the bracelet she bought."

"Girls, stop it. You're upset, I get it. But it's not nice to speak ill of the dead."

"It doesn't change what she did, Mom," Lily whispered. "I feel terrible she's gone—she was basically like an aunty to us. And I feel awful for Maxim who will never see his mom again and Mr. DeLuca who lost his wife. But as far as I'm concerned, what she did... how she tried to break up our family and steal Dad from you... that doesn't go away. She got her wish. She's just not around to collect her prize."

Alicia reached over and hugged a sniffling Lily. Marston embraced them both. When they pulled apart, Lily said to her sister, "Dad screwed up your big day."

"What?" Marston asked.

"Your graduation. Everyone is going to be gossiping about the latest development. They'll think Mom had something to do with Kat's death. They'll be looking at us sideways the minute we step foot on school property tomorrow. Colby sent me the link to a popular crime blogger website. They're calling it the 'Bestie Murder' if you can believe that. I mean, how unoriginal. It's even trending on Twitter."

Alicia had forgotten all about social media, the digital equivalent of a snake pit in her opinion. She had a Facebook account she accessed once or twice a year. *The Bestie Murder*, she mused with disgust. Now, her daughters were caught up in the melee. The thought of them being targets ripped her heart right out of her chest. She could kill Eliot.

"Girls, it's going to be okay," she said.

"How can you say that?" Marston asked. "It will never be okay again. Don't put on a brave face for our benefit, Mom. We're not little kids. Don't stay married to Dad for our sakes."

Her children were being brave for her, but she could see it

in their eyes that they had been shredded to bits. They adored their father, and the thought of him not coming home every night, not being part of their daily lives, was too much to bear.

"Prom is definitely off." Lily swiped a tear.

Marston concurred, and so did Alicia. It had taken a lot to persuade Marston to give prom a go after the incident with Brandon. Now, with their family crisis out there for everyone to see—and Kat's tragic, untimely death—trying to convince them to attend a party would be pointless.

Silence pricked the air. She had no words of comfort to offer her girls. Whatever she said would sound empty.

"There's just one other thing," Marston said. "I don't want to keep secrets from you anymore. Dad did, and it didn't work out so great for our family."

Alicia braced herself. In the past few weeks, secrets and lies had been popping up like weeds. She wasn't sure she could deal with much more.

"What's going on?" she asked.

"Dad went after Brandon and told him if he ever came near me again, he would destroy him."

Alicia's eyes went wide. "When did this happen?"

"The day Kat died."

So that was what he was up to when he went "jogging". Alicia was partly relieved. At least if he was with Brandon, he couldn't have murdered Kat, right? Alicia hated herself for even contemplating it, but with recent events, she could no longer trust her own instincts.

"Who else knows about this?" she asked.

"Just Brandon and his parents. Brandon started freaking out every time he saw me. I know we've been avoiding each other, but this was just weird. He'd run down the corridor in the other direction the moment he saw me. So, I cornered him at his locker and asked what was going on. He kept looking around all nervous, like he expected someone to appear out of nowhere and beat him up. That's when he told me that Dad threatened him."

Marston scraped back the braids hanging in her face. "Dad promised Brandon if he ever came near me again, he would use his influence to get Brandon's scholarship to Georgetown revoked. The director of admissions and Aunt Dana are close friends. They were roommates at Brown."

Eliot had always been fierce when it came to defending and protecting his children. He'd been enraged when she'd told him what happened with Marston, but Alicia thought he'd been able to control himself. Now he'd just added threatening teenagers to his list of offenses.

Eliot's sister Dana was co-anchor of *The Morning Edge,* a popular network television show. She was well respected in the industry and had won an Edward R. Murrow Award, a prestigious honor that recognized excellence in journalism. Her influence went a long way. Eliot's threat was serious.

"Brandon deserved much worse after the way he treated you, Marston." An unapologetic Lily pulled a face. "Props to Dad for having your back."

"Too bad he didn't do the same for Mom," Marston said. "Cheating is bad enough, but with Kat? What was he thinking?"

"He wasn't," Lily mocked. "Not with his brain, anyway."

"Watch your mouth, Lily," Alicia admonished. "He's still your father."

"Yeah, some father. I can't even look him in the face. I don't think I'll ever forgive him." Then she stood up and walked out of the family room.

Alicia considered going after her but thought better of it. The happy and secure family life her daughters had grown accustomed to had shattered right before their eyes. Each girl would deal with the fallout in her own way. There was little Alicia could do to ease their pain. And that was the worst feeling of all.

She turned to Marston and squeezed her hand. "If I could take away the pain, I would. Just remember your dad loves you very much. That hasn't and will never change."

"So, we're just supposed to forget what he did, act like it never happened?"

"No, Marston. Be true to your feelings. But your dad will never abandon you or your sister."

Marston shook her head slowly. Then she said, "No. I don't believe you, Mom. He *was* going to leave us for Kat. It was only a matter of when. Did you confront either one of them?"

"Now is not the time to discuss this, Marston—"

"You confronted Kat, didn't you? That's what they're talking about on the news. She was mean to you. And Dad lied when you asked him about it."

"Marston—"

"While you guys were away, it became obvious that she had a thing for him. Now we know why. They were already involved, so she got angry that he took you to Paris and not her." Marston continued shaking her head in disbelief. "I can't... I just can't anymore." Her voice cracked. Then, she too stood up and walked out.

CHAPTER 50

THE DOOR FLEW open without warning as Arnie Tillerson stormed into Eliot's office, red-faced and blustering. "We were blindsided. You blundering fool! You put the firm's reputation at risk. Imagine how embarrassing it was to learn this from the news media. Now, we have to put out a statement, all because you couldn't keep it in your pants. What do you have to say for yourself?"

He wouldn't back down or flinch. Arnie was one of the two managing partners of Tillerson Brenner and technically Eliot's boss, but he wouldn't allow the man to treat him like a wayward child in need of scolding. There was always a chance Eliot would lose Arnie's respect and that of his colleagues. He didn't have time to dwell on that possibility, however. More serious matters demanded his attention.

Sitting at the edge of his desk, he said, "It's true. Katalina and I were involved. I regret the decision. I showed poor moral judgement and a lapse in ethics. Alicia and I were working things out privately. We had no reason to believe they would splash our marital problems all over the media and turn us into murder suspects."

Arnie sat down, his face flushed with anxiety. "Talk to me, Eliot. What's going on? It's bad enough we lost Katalina so tragically, now this."

"We were set up, Alicia and I." Eliot explained the confrontation in Katalina's office and McBride's hint at the affair. Eliot chose his next words carefully. He didn't want to appear as though he were placing blame elsewhere to avoid taking responsibility.

"Who set you up?"

"Detective McBride. It's the only explanation that makes sense. He hauled Alicia in for questioning once he uncovered the confrontation and the affair. He insinuated that Alicia caused Katalina's death, but Alicia is innocent and saw through his ruse. That didn't sit well with him, so he leaked information to the media, knowing full well how they would spin it."

"He hoped that the scrutiny and pressure would get to you, force a confession or a stupid move?"

"Precisely. Delia did some digging and came up with some additional information about the case." He provided Arnie with the highlights and included the pregnancy. No point in holding back.

Arnie rubbed the back of his neck, then blew out a long breath. "I'm sorely disappointed in you, Eliot. How could you do something so reckless, jeopardize everything you've worked for, put Alicia and now your daughters through hell? I thought I knew you." His body sagged. "Why didn't you come to me?"

Arnie was more than Eliot's boss. As their relationship blossomed into one of mutual respect and admiration, Arnie had become a father figure of sorts to him. Eliot had shared with Arnie his devastation when Alicia lost the baby. Arnie had consoled him and given him advice, even forced him to take time off from work to grieve and be there for Alicia. In a way, Eliot had betrayed Arnie too.

I thought I knew you.

"It's my mess and I take full responsibility. I'm sorry, Arnie. I'll get it sorted out."

Arnie stood and rocked back and forth on his heels, hands in his pockets. "I've made a decision. You'll work from home until this whole thing blows over. I'll get our PR firm to put out a statement saying you've been put on leave pending the outcome of the investigation, that we have every confidence in your innocence, and that it's a shame the media has besmirched the reputation of such an outstanding man, so on and so on."

"Understood."

"And for goodness sakes, don't say anything to the police without a lawyer present. I can't believe you took the risk."

"I thought Detective McBride was after the truth. It won't happen again. If he wants to speak to Alicia or me, he will have to do it through our attorney."

"Good. Although you might have bigger fish to fry than McBride. Paula is pissed at you."

Paula was Arnie's lovely but formidable wife.

"She likes Alicia. She might try to string you by your nuts the next time she sees you. In the meantime, keep a low profile while I try to reassure our clients that neither you nor Alicia is a murderer."

CHAPTER 51

KATALINA TORRES

August 13, 2015

⁓ DIARY ENTRY ⁓

Eleven long years we have done this dance and now, finally, thanks to my powers of persuasion and a talented real estate broker, Eliot and I live in the same town, on the same street.

Nothing can bring me down from this high. Not even Richard has the power to take away the rush.

"Where did you really go this weekend?" he asked last night after I returned.

I feigned innocence—I could hardly tell him of Eliot and my sweet reunion. A fabulous weekend at Chanler Cliff Walk in Newport, Rhode Island, a nineteenth-century mansion converted into a luxury hotel with rooms that overlooked the Atlantic. Old world elegance combined with modern amenities. My kind of place. The last of our carefully planned weekend trysts, and the beginning of so much more.

But my husband was persistent. Said he hadn't seen me this happy in a long while and he just knew I had a secret lover. I wasn't about to confess, so I ignored him. He followed me into the master suite and shut the door behind him. The more he demanded answers, the more stubborn I became. That infuriated him.

I have never seen him so angry, full of rage. When he grabbed me by the throat and shoved my head into the bedroom wall, I was stunned. But I refused to cry or beg him to stop. That infuriated him further. He then called me a shameless slut, stormed out of the room, and slammed the door behind him. My head hurt, but it didn't matter; I had my sights on a bigger prize.

The next morning, Monday, I was pumped. It was time to meet Mrs. Gray face-to-face, size her up, see what I was up against. I told Eliot I had no intention of being his secret forever. He brushed me off, and then kissed me and then, well... But I wanted out of my marriage to Richard and a future with him, but first, I had to deal with the current wife. And to do that, I needed insight into her personality, her secret fears and insecurities, I needed to learn what made her tick, what brought her joy and pain, learn her backstory. I wanted leverage.

I won't lie. I was disappointed when she opened the front door. Average. Across the board. She didn't possess the beauty, charm, or elegance I expected from the woman who canceled Eliot's bachelor card. I always made it a point to never look at photos of her or learn anything about her prior to this day, as I wanted to imagine myself as the only woman in Eliot's life. Plus, I wanted the in-person meeting to be special, no preconceived ideas to spoil it.

She was barefoot, dressed in a tie-dyed maxi dress, with fringe trim and a fitted bodice. It would have looked better on someone taller with a statuesque figure, but she was around five foot three and far from svelte. I'm not saying she was fat or anything, but she definitely knew her way around a meal or two.

She just stared at me, in wonderment, like she didn't think women who looked like me existed in real life, only on overly air-brushed magazine covers. No air-brushing here. One hundred percent the real deal. I didn't bother introducing myself at that moment. I made some barb about melting in a puddle because she took so long to answer the door and it was hotter than hell that day.

Then I barged into the house like I owned the place. It was best to establish the relationship dynamics right away. I would be in control at all times, and she would be the loyal lackey who would do anything I asked because "desperate for friends" was written all over her face. This was going to be so easy, snatching Eliot away from her. I was almost disappointed as I'd looked forward to a good fight, but it just made my journey to becoming Eliot's one-and-only so much easier.

I listened attentively as she poured out her whole, sad backstory, about how she grew up poor in the hood, her mother dying, how she met Eliot. Ah. So pathetic and desperately in need of affirmation. I can do that. I happen to be a fantastic actress.

CHAPTER 52

Unknown: Did you tell her the truth about you and Katalina? Two years? Ha! Don't make me call Detective McBride, Eliot. Tell Alicia the truth. Tonight. I will text you tomorrow morning to confirm. Then we can move on to my demands.

ELIOT SHOVED BACK his swivel chair and slammed the phone down on the desk. He picked it up again and began composing a response to the text. He stopped midway, deleted the message, and tossed the phone across the room. It ricocheted off the door and landed on the floor near a leather armchair.

He had awakened early with a massive headache hammering away at his skull. After taking two aspirins, he got an early start to his day once the headache subsided. He had yet to tell Alicia that Arnie had, effectively, suspended him, so he'd been holed up in his study since six a.m., unable to concentrate on work.

The story had created a media firestorm, and his phone wouldn't stop ringing, another reason he was on edge. He just yelled at a reporter who had asked him how it felt to turn his wife into a killer. How dare they? And then the text had come in right on the heels of that call. His pulse wouldn't stop racing. Every little sound made him jumpy. Who was he kidding? He was unraveling.

Marston and Lily had slept at their friends' houses so they could get to school without tripping all over reporters who'd staked out their street, waiting to ambush anyone with the last name Gray.

On top of all the chaos swirling around him, Eliot's stomach churned at the thought of how much the anonymous stalker knew. Where was he or she getting the information from? Had Katalina confessed to Richard before she died? But Richard would not accuse Eliot of killing her when Richard was the one who had been home, on the floor above, when she died. Why was McBride casting suspicion on him and Alicia, when he should be worried about that old concussion at the back of Katalina's head and how it got there?

He left the study in desperate search of caffeine. Not a good idea since he was already tense, but he didn't care. He couldn't sit in that room, alone with his thoughts, any longer. As he leaned against the kitchen island, coffee in hand, he observed Alicia whose back was to him at the kitchen table. She hadn't acknowledged him when he entered the room. It was like he wasn't even there. Their home had become a ghost town. His daughters wouldn't look him in the eye, let alone speak to him. The house echoed with the absence of joy. No laughing, teasing, and ribbing during family dinners.

He walked over and pulled out a chair and placed the mug on the table. The move startled Alicia, and she glanced up at him.

"Harry Meyers is coming over later to discuss strategy,"

he announced. "Preliminary findings from the toxicology reports came back. The information will cast significant doubt on McBride's case, if not completely demolish his theory that Katalina's death was a homicide."

He rushed through his words, suddenly feeling nervous around her. Alicia didn't look at him, anymore. She looked through him. She was there, in physical reach, but she was slipping through his fingers. He'd already lost her respect. Her dazzling smile had vanished, the sparkle gone from her eyes.

She no longer took care of him as she had in the past. She didn't compliment him and barely registered his presence when he came home. He recalled the many nights in the past when she'd waited up for him, worried about him. The times she'd picked out his suits, told him how amazing he was, and how proud she was to be his wife. It was all gone.

He had stubbornly refused to move out of their bedroom when she'd asked him to, after she discovered he cheated on her with Katalina.

"You have no shame," she had shouted at him. "I'm not leaving this bedroom, so you can just go. I don't care where."

"I'm not leaving either," he'd countered. "We've hardly slept apart in twenty years except for when I went away on business. I'm not going to start now."

He'd done it to annoy her, get under her skin. He knew moving out would have been the right thing to do, but he wanted to punish her for what she had done to their son. So, they slept with plenty of space between them in the massive, king-sized, albeit cold, marital bed.

Last night, however, he had been at his lowest point since his life imploded. Truth be told, he was feeling sorry for himself. He'd become the villain in this story it seemed. He'd reached for Alicia. She always knew how to comfort him.

But she brushed him off with a harsh, impersonal, "Don't touch me!" Then she'd gotten out of bed and disappeared for an hour, slipping under the covers only after she thought he was asleep.

He wasn't. The humiliation of being rejected by his wife felt like a Mack truck had run him over. *What did you expect, a parade?*

He forced the memory to dissolve and refocused on the present.

Ignoring his comment, as if he hadn't spoken, Alicia said, "The girls are having a hard time at school. It makes them uncomfortable, the not-so-subtle whispers that either of their parents could be a killer. The fallout is huge. The only upside is that the school year is almost over."

This is partially McBride's fault, Eliot thought. The media nightmare was his doing. "McBride's not convinced it was an accident, and he tried the case in the court of public opinion before he had one shred of evidence that this was anything other than an accident. Sloppy detective work. I expected better from him."

He explained the results of the toxicology report that Delia, his investigator, had shared with him, as well as the coroner's report that uncovered the existence of an old concussion Katalina had suffered. He omitted the pregnancy.

She listened without saying a word.

"I must warn you though," he added.

Although she didn't move, he knew he had her attention.

"Warn me about what?" she said, staring into her coffee cup.

"Part of the strategy I want to discuss with our attorney is handing the investigators a potential suspect. Get the spotlight away from us, so we can get back to our normal lives."

"Nothing will ever be normal again," she mumbled in a distant voice.

"But I have a plan, Alicia. We'll give the police Richard—"

She slapped the mug down on the table with a speed that he'd not expected. Coffee splashed across the gleaming cherry-wood table. She blinked at him twice as if he'd just spoken in a foreign language.

"Are you out of your mind?"

"Hear me out. Nobody is looking at the fact that Katalina died while Richard was in the house. That's suspicious. He heard nothing, saw nothing. He said he found her unresponsive and called 9-1-1. There was no forced entry, no evidence of any kind that another person was at the scene. Just the two of them in the house with no eyewitnesses. Then there's the previous concussion."

He stopped to collect his bearings. Pitching this to Alicia was risky, but handing the police another suspect was a popular strategy with defense lawyers. Neither he nor Alicia were officially named as suspects, but McBride had turned their lives upside down when he leaked the affair and the confrontation to the press. Eliot didn't have any proof that McBride had done any such thing. It was just a feeling that someone had, and Eliot's two suspects were the detective and Richard Deluca.

Richard could have leaked the affair to play on public sympathy for the betrayed, grieving husband. It was a straightforward way to deflect suspicion. But if Richard was going to play that game, so would Eliot.

He wanted the nightmare to end, and the best way to do

that was to put the spotlight on someone else. Then he would turn his attention to repairing the damage to his marriage and rebuilding his family.

"I just don't see Richard as a killer." Alicia wrapped her hands around her mug.

"But you see me as one?" he asked bitterly. "You had no problem asking me if I killed Katalina. Richard is the same guy who knew about the affair weeks before you found out; yet, he said absolutely nothing. You think he's a good guy, but I'm not so sure. Consider the previous concussion. Have you ever thought of that? And the injury that caused her death. What if he snapped and, in a rage, pushed her so hard that the impact of the blow to her head killed her? The report concluded the two wounds were in the same area at the back of her head."

Eliot was aware that his declaration betrayed a raw emotion, a desperate tone to convince his wife that this was a good idea.

Instead, her eyebrows pinched together in disgust. "I thought you were a lawyer, Eliot. Even I know this theory won't stand without evidence."

"True. But it's not my job to find evidence. It's my job to create reasonable doubt, and it's available in spades. McBride unfairly targeted us. It's an easy narrative. Cheating husband, wife finds out, mistress ends up dead. But why, if I wanted her dead, would I wait until after my wife found out?"

She drew her lips into a thin line. "If he thinks you killed Kat, what better way to deflect suspicion than the argument you just made?"

"Are you sure you don't want to go to law school after you get you bachelor's?" The joke fell flat.

"Don't mock me." She stared at him blankly.

The threatening text clattered around in his head. This would be the time to tell her, just get everything out in the open so they could plan their strategy together. But he could not do what the stalker had asked. He would try to uncover what the blackmailer truly wanted. He had to keep a lid on the truth of the affair.

He cleared his throat, then said, "Anyway, I don't want to think that Richard killed her either, but you must admit that the circumstances are strange. Besides, we have no idea what he said to McBride."

Alicia sighed. "I'll go along with whatever you and Harry come up with. I don't really have a choice. But I just can't swallow the idea that Richard did this."

"But what if he did? He had motive and opportunity. No witnesses. No evidence that points to him. The perfect crime."

CHAPTER 53

A LICIA SAT IN silence the entire time their attorney was
there. She was merely a fly on the wall while Harry and
Eliot discussed ways to get McBride to back off. They'd even
floated the idea of threatening to sue. Although they had no
proof that McBride or someone within the department leaked
information to the press, the lawyers argued that they could
claim the department was careless in their handling of the
investigation so far. She and Eliot were being tried in the court
of public opinion because McBride did sloppy police work.

As she watched the men plot their strategy, Alicia felt
like she was collapsing in on herself. Her world failed to make
sense. She had no idea what the future held for her. But one
thing was crystal clear, her marriage was over. Period. She could
no longer remain married to this man.

Although superficially unsure, Alicia knew she'd made the
decision a while ago. The moment she'd found out that Kat was
the other woman, something inside her had broken. But then
again, it could have been the bold-face denial when she'd asked

Eliot about an affair that pushed her over the edge. Was it the disgusting and humiliating words Kat hurled at her during their final confrontation? Or the final betrayal: Kat's revelation to Eliot that Alicia had an abortion?

A gathering of papers suggested the end of the meeting. A strategy had been agreed. Eliot would own up to the fact that he was on the receiving end of anonymous text messages accusing him of killing Kat. The two lawyers agreed that Richard was the most likely suspect. Alicia didn't argue.

"We need to talk," she called out at Eliot, who was on his way out of the living room after showing Harry out the door.

He returned quietly and sat down opposite her. "What's wrong, baby? You seem tense."

Really? "I want a divorce."

His hands dropped to his sides, and his fists clenched and unclenched with tension. He looked down at the floor and responded with an emphatic, "No!"

She leaned forward. "Listen to me. I don't want to fight about this. Our marriage is over."

"Over? Every marriage goes through rough times. We can't give up because it's hard."

"Hard? There's hard, and then there's impossible. I was willing to work things out, but you didn't take me up on my offer. For two years you lied. To my face. To our children! Too much has happened. We can't fix this, Eliot."

"What I did was beyond reprehensible. I let you down, and our girls. I let myself down. I will spend the rest of my life making it up to you, but I can't lose my family, Alicia." His shoulders slouched. "Everyone makes mistakes. I didn't ask you for a divorce when you admitted to aborting our son, a son you knew I desperately wanted. A son we mourned together. All the while, you knew what you had done, and lied about it for three years."

Despite the fact that she knew he would have drawn this card, his words still packed a powerful punch, reminding her that she wasn't so perfect. She, too, had messed up badly. He was calling her a hypocrite.

He continued, "I cheated on you. You killed our son. There's no escaping those facts. We're both flawed people. My world makes little sense without you in it. I love you and always will. So, no divorce."

She drew in a long breath. *Why does he want to hold on to a dead marriage? Is he in denial?* She smoothed down the hem of her dress. Despair gnawed at her, stinging, painful bites. Yet, she was determined to have her way. She chose her words carefully.

"What I did was horrific. But it doesn't change the fact that we're broken beyond repair. You would have kept the affair going had I not found out. You claim to love me, but I wonder if that was ever true. So, why did you marry me, Eliot?"

He frowned. "What kind of question is that, Alicia?"

"A simple one. Maybe Kat wasn't the only woman you cheated with. Were there others? Perhaps plain, dull Alicia wasn't exciting enough to hold your interest."

He stood up and began pacing back and forth. "You're talking nonsense."

"Did you think you could mold me into the perfect housewife while you had your fun with other women who excited you? It was easy enough. When we met, I was alone in the world, no family, no friends, no financial security, low self-esteem, no hope."

"Alicia, because I messed up, you're suddenly acting as though the past twenty-two years meant nothing? Questioning my motive at every turn? I married you because I couldn't imagine my life without you in it. You and our daughters are the only thing that makes my world okay."

"Yet, you put it all on the line. You were willing to betray us, me and our daughters, for *her*. We weren't enough to keep you content. And we won't ever be enough. If you and I stay married, we'll destroy each other because Kat will always be the ghost between us. I won't live like that."

He placed his head in his hands. His shoulders heaved. Sniffling sounds emanated from him.

"Where do you expect me to go? What do you expect me to do? You and our daughters are my entire life; it's how I exist in the world. It's what gives my life meaning. You're asking me to give up my existence. I won't do it. We're a family. Families hold on to each other, no matter what."

"You forfeited that support the day you betrayed our family."

He stood, dried his tears with a determined swipe of his hand, and walked over to her. His expression hard and cold, he said, "If you keep pushing for a divorce, I will make damn sure you leave this marriage the same way you came in. With nothing."

CHAPTER 54

KATALINA TORRES

May 16, 2019

~ DIARY ENTRY ~

Enough already. It's exhausting, and I've been more than patient. The excuses made sense in the early years of our relationship. But not anymore. His daughters are grown now. Yet he still won't budge. It's time to take matters into my own hands. When we were together yesterday afternoon, I told him what I expected from him.

"You need to tell Alicia about us," I told him.

His answer was the same. He wouldn't leave her.

In that instant, I made the decision to lay all my cards on the table, especially my ace, but never got the chance to do so. Something took over the man I love, something evil. In the fifteen years we've been together, I had never seen him so angry. He grabbed me and dug his fingers into my face. The move knocked the breath out of me. My legs could barely support me, they trembled so badly.

He said if I told Alicia about us, he would kill me. Eliot Gray threatened to kill me. I know when people are angry, they say that they want to kill someone, but they don't really mean it. But I believed him. I believed he would kill me if his wife found out about us. I've never been afraid of him until now.

CHAPTER 55

Unknown: Have you told Alicia the truth yet?

ELIOT WAS IN no mood for this stalker nonsense. He let the phone drop from his hands, disgusted and furious. With himself, mostly. After he'd threatened to leave Alicia destitute if she divorced him, she ceased communicating with him altogether.

She moved out of the master suite and took up residence in a guest bedroom. He'd tried to apologize, tell her he didn't mean it. She'd looked at him as though he was Satan incarnate. He'd begged, cajoled, and pleaded. Nothing worked.

His daughters also avoided him. He was a stranger in his own home, no longer welcome. Marston spent most of her time in her room, writing. Lily, when she wasn't avoiding him, was out with Jeff or at Colby's house.

He had no idea what his next move should be. There was a possibility that he wouldn't return to Tillerson Brenner. If he lost his family, it didn't matter. He had to salvage his reputation, the damage caused by the media story. Their attorney, Harry

Meyers, was supposed to call McBride today and inform him that from now on he and Alicia would communicate with the authorities only through their lawyer. They had nothing left to say to investigators after the way they had been treated.

He picked up his phone and responded to the text.

Eliot: This is growing tiresome. Speak to my attorney from now on.

Eliot was in his home office when the new message appeared on his phone.

Unknown: I'll take that as a no, that you chickened out, the coward that you are, and did not tell Alicia the truth. Bad move, Eliot. Terrible move.

He contemplated his response.

Eliot: What do you want? Stop with the sanctimonious garbage. You're using a tragedy for your own personal gain.

Unknown: Okay, tough guy. I'm done playing games with you. I do want something in exchange for my silence. One million dollars. You have 24 hours to make it happen.

Sweat percolated on his lips. Richard couldn't be behind the texts. Panic rose from the pit of Eliot's stomach, snaking its way through his insides like a trail of deadly poison. Richard was a founding partner of York Capital Investments, a hedge fund that managed over ten billion dollars in assets. He wasn't exactly hurting for cash.

This texter was another player hiding in the shadows. Inside knowledge of the affair was an opportunity to exploit him for cash. But who would have such information? Who would have the guts and cunning to run an extortion scheme like this, without fear of retribution? Though his thoughts raced, searching every corner of his mind for an answer, none came.

Eliot: I don't think so.

He knew a response was inevitable. When it came, it sent him reeling. His legs felt like overcooked noodles, and he reached out to stabilize himself but smacked his toe into the metal base of his swivel chair. Pain shot up his leg like fiery darts. But not even that pain could quell the shock of what he saw on the screen.

It was a photograph of a hand-written page. A diary entry. Katalina's diary, but one line caused his stomach to plummet. *"I believed he would kill me if his wife found out about us."*

Unknown: one million wired into my account tomorrow by 5 pm, or McBride receives this anonymous gift from me.

CHAPTER 56

ALICIA LOOKED AT the TV screen, dumfounded for the second time in less than a week. A mid-morning press conference was in progress. McBride stood before the cameras and announced the official findings of the investigation into the death of Katalina Torres DeLuca.

"Our investigation concluded that cause of death was blunt-force trauma to the head, a tragic accident. Mrs. DeLuca had alcohol in her system, four times the legal limit. She lost her balance and fell, hitting her head on the marble floor of her kitchen. The impact was severe enough to cause instant death. This concludes our investigation."

She flopped down on the couch, her legs unable to support her.

As soon as McBride finished, overeager reporters pelted him with questions.

"Are Eliot and Alicia Gray no longer suspects?" A reporter from channel seven asked.

McBride said, "I want to be clear. Mr. and Mrs. Gray were never suspects in Mrs. DeLuca's death. The Grays cooperated from the beginning. In fact, the Weston Police Department wishes to extend our sincerest apologies to the Grays for any damage to their reputation this investigation may have caused. Unfortunately, the media jumped to its own conclusions without the facts."

"Are the Grays going to sue the department, Detective?" an off-camera reporter asked.

He didn't answer, his expression somber. He wrapped up his brief statement and walked off.

It was over. Eliot's legal strategy had worked out. Eliot, the man she no longer recognized. It was a new low when he'd threatened to leave her with nothing if she insisted on a divorce; so low, in fact, that long after he made the pronouncement and stormed out of the living room, she'd stood rooted to the spot, hanging on by a thread, afraid that if she even so much as sneezed she would shatter into tiny pieces. She didn't think she had the strength to put the pieces back together again if that happened.

However, it didn't take long for her to remember that she was a survivor. She had survived childhood tragedy and poverty, depression, betrayal, abandonment, and an abortion that would haunt her into eternity. She would also survive Eliot Gray!

Her cell phone chirped. She extracted it from her pocket. A text message from an unknown sender, an image, someone's handwriting. She tapped the screen and read the contents and then wished the floor would open up and swallow her whole. On shaking legs, she stood up and barged toward Eliot's study. She didn't bother knocking. He was on the phone, and his eyes popped in surprise at her intrusion.

"Hey, Phil, I'll call you ba—"

"I just received this," she said, handing him her phone. "What is that about?"

"It's that anonymous texter I told you about." He handed her the phone back.

"It's in Kat's handwriting. And she's accusing you of wanting to kill her."

"It would appear so."

"*Did* you threaten her, Eliot?"

"What do you think?"

"I don't know what to think anymore."

"Well, that's better than accusing me of killing her."

"Don't put words into my mouth. I never said that."

"The entry may be a forgery," he stated, with the wariness of someone who had little fight left.

"Is that a denial? You never threatened to kill her?"

"I have to get back to work. We can talk about all this later—"

"I don't care. You know what. I don't want to talk about it later because I've had enough." Her tipping point was way past gone. Quiet, naïve, insecure Alicia went with it. This would be her last stand. "Let's discuss terms."

"Alic—"

"We bow out gracefully. It was a great run. Twenty years. Few people can say they had a twenty-year marriage. That's one thing we can be proud of, and our daughters."

"I told you I'm not giving you a divorce."

"No, you listen. I want you to pay off the mortgage and put the deed to the house in my name, only," she began. "Lily has one year left of high school. We can't uproot her, so we'll stay here until she graduates. I want full college tuition for both girls put aside in a special account. You are to continue to provide their medical insurance until they both graduate from college and are employed in a company that offers them coverage. I want a monthly allowance and money set aside to provide them a good start in life. Call it a trust fund or whatever." The cool detachment in her voice as she doled out her demands surprised her. Alicia Gray was all sunshine and goodness. What had that gotten her?

Eliot sat like a block of ice, not flinching, not moving a muscle.

His befuddled state gave her the courage to continue. "You will continue to pay the insurance on Marston's car. When Lily gets her license, you will buy her a brand-new car, and you will pay the insurance until she graduates from college, or for as long as she has the car."

She didn't want her girls to depend on anybody, and especially not before they were established and successful in their own careers. Their mother had made that mistake that lasted twenty years, and now she was about to walk out of a marriage that she put her heart and soul into, with nothing.

"What about you?" he asked.

"I'll be fine. It's time I stood on my own. Twenty years depending on someone else for my survival has left a bitter taste in my mouth."

His chin dropped to his chest. He muttered something. She barely made out the words, "What have I done?"

It was too late for regrets, though. She had to accept her new reality. Starting over at forty-two. It was a scary thought that made her want to crawl into a hole and stay there for the rest of her life. But it would be her life, not beholden to a lying cheat.

Alicia had spent more than half her life with Eliot. Prior

to meeting him, she'd never dated. She didn't have a group of close friends to lean on and socialize with. After they married, her life was their family, her volunteer work, and supporting Eliot's career.

"What if I don't agree to the terms?" he asked.

"Then you'll leave me no choice but to barge into McBride's office and show him the text. I'll let him take it from there."

He froze, eyes wide. In a dazed whisper, he asked, "You wouldn't do that."

"Would you have left me with nothing after I devoted twenty years of my life to you?"

Silence enveloped the room.

"We need to tell the girls. Tonight," she insisted.

CHAPTER 57

KATALINA TORRES
May 18, 2019

~ DIARY ENTRY ~

Having never seen Eliot so angry, I stood, dumbstruck for a moment, and I am never at a loss for words. But I knew what I had to do, so I pulled out the heavy artillery, the pièce de résistance. "I'm pregnant," I said. Of course, he didn't believe me. If I was in his position, I wouldn't either. But it was the seed that needed to be planted. I know that because after we had a cooling-off period of a few days, all he cared about was getting me to confess that I made up the pregnancy. So, I told him what he wanted to hear. I said I wasn't.

I know, it makes no sense, but I need him to be calm and rational when I tell him the truth. That I'm carrying his child. There is no doubt in my mind the baby is his. Richard and I have not slept together in a year.

But that's not the biggest news. I can't wait to see his face when I tell him we already have a child. I'm willing to risk it all by telling him the truth.

Richard and I got married shortly after Eliot and I met, but when Maxim was born, I knew in my heart that he was Eliot's. When Maxim turned five, I wanted proof as an insurance policy. And the paternity test confirmed what I knew all along.

Now is the time for that insurance policy to work its magic. When I let Eliot know about my condition, I'm going to present him with the lab results, too. After that, his marriage to Alicia will crumble. How couldn't it? I'm the mother to his boy. Maxim is his son. I will divorce Richard; then the three of us and the new baby will begin our new life together. I win again.

CHAPTER 58

B EAUTIFUL DAY, ISN'T it?"
Alicia took a seat next to the despondent man on the park bench. His dark hair had more than a few extra gray strands than the last time she saw him. His eyes were wary, punctuated by a deep, penetrating sadness that manifested itself in his physical being. His shoulders sagged. He looked down at his feet, not her.

It was the first week of June. There was not a cloud in the sky. Lush trees and shrubbery surrounded them, along with winding paths, trails, and clean air. A young mother pushed her baby in the stroller. A dad and his son kicked around a soccer ball. A family ran with their dog. But from the way Richard looked, it might have been deepest winter.

"Maxim and I are leaving. Tonight." He still didn't look up at her. "I put the house up for sale. Not sure it will sell quickly, given what happened, but we can't stay."

"I'm sure it will."

He sighed, then looked across at her without lifting his

head. "You've always been so upbeat, full of enthusiasm for life. I'll miss that."

"It didn't do me any good," she said, and they both smiled. "I'm afraid to start over," she confessed.

"Don't be. You'll do fine." He reached down and picked up a briefcase. He snapped it open and pulled out an envelope.

Handing it to her, he said, "Please don't thank me. It's the least I can do. I can't erase the pain she caused you, but perhaps this small gesture can help you get a fresh start."

She opened the envelope and read the contents. The small gesture in question was an official offer letter, working as executive assistant to Todd Hayes, the new Chief Compliance Officer of York Capital Investments. The salary? A whopping one hundred thousand dollars annually with the potential for bonuses.

"Richard, this is too generous." She knew the starting salary for an executive assistant with little experience was substantially less. "I don't know what to say."

"Say you'll accept the offer. Officially, you have a week to think about it, sign, and return the letter to Human Resources."

He had paid attention to that conversation, a year ago, that she had all but forgotten. She and Eliot had just returned from visiting colleges with Marston. The DeLucases had come over later that afternoon for a casual get-together. Alicia had confided in Richard that her dream was to finish the degree she'd abandoned, due to her mother's illness, and even pursue graduate studies afterward. They'd briefly discussed her classes and major as an undergraduate student at Suffolk University

Richard had nodded throughout the conversation. She thought he was merely being polite with his encouragement and suggestions, but he'd obviously meant every word. Look at what he had done. He'd given her a shot at pursuing her dream. The offer letter also mentioned that she would be eligible to take part in the career development program at the firm, which meant she could continue to take classes without upfront costs, in some cases.

"I wish there was a way to return your generosity," she said.

"There is. Be happy."

"I'll try. Thank you again, Richard."

"It's the least I can do."

They sat in the quiet afternoon air for a moment.

"How does Maxim feel about the move?" Alicia asked, after a while.

"Neutral. But I think he recognizes that we need each other. Just me and my boy from here on out."

His voice held such sorrow that Alicia almost hugged him. "You and your boy will be just fine. Cherish the time you have together. Soon, he'll be leaving for college, too."

"That's right. Marston graduates soon."

"In a couple of days."

"That must be tough for her. One of the happiest days of her life turned into so much pain. Her parents splitting up. The scandal. Tell her that I'm sorry, and that I wish her the best at college next fall."

"I will."

They both stood at the same time and hugged each other tightly.

When they separated, he said, "Goodbye, Alicia. If you ever have any issues at work or you need help of any kind, please call me. Day or night. Okay?"

And with that, he left.

ALICIA REMAINED ON the park bench and sent a text to an unknown number.

Richard just left.

Moments later, Dr. Jack Witherspoon joined her. It was strange seeing him without his white lab coat and stethoscope dangling from his neck. Instead, he sported jeans, a navy-blue polo shirt and sneakers.

"How did it go?" he asked.

"Better than expected. Richard gave me a most valuable parting gift."

"What's that?"

"Freedom. A way to make it on my own, through hard work and dedication." She told him about the offer letter and the provision for career development.

"That's wonderful news, Alicia. No one deserves a fresh start more than you do."

"You deserve one too, Jack."

"Thanks to you, I get a do-over. The practice will be out of debt and profitable again. I'm even thinking of expanding, taking on a couple of new doctors and appropriate support staff."

She beamed at him. She couldn't have pulled this off without Jack. Richard's gift was an unexpected blessing. *Maybe God doesn't hate me after all*, she thought. She had taken desperate measures to clean up the mess her life had become.

Alicia had concocted the scheme after Eliot had threatened to leave her destitute. Something primal had risen up in her after that. Call it pushback, vengeance, finally growing a backbone, whatever. She'd had enough. She'd refused to be pushed around anymore. Jack had been reluctant at first when she'd approached him with the idea.

"It's the perfect plan," she had told him. "You get the practice back on solid financial footing, and I get to start over on my own terms, free of Eliot's manipulation and lies. It's a win-win."

She wouldn't have gone to such lengths if Eliot hadn't been a grade-A jerk to her. Kat's diary had proven to be a powerful weapon. Alicia would never have noticed it if Kat hadn't quickly moved it out of her line of vision the day Alicia had gone to Kat's office after the crotch-grabbing incident. Alicia had thought it strange that Kat would hide a simple notebook, and then Alicia had forgotten all about it.

But after their blow-up fight, the one that ended their friendship, Alicia had been determined to find out what was in that notebook, why Kat was so protective of it. Later that same evening, she'd returned to the office and told the employee at the desk that she wanted to leave an apology letter for Kat, but because it was so personal, she didn't want to leave it with the staff to pass it on.

"Even best friends have big fights. Our friendship means everything to me. I need to make sure she gets it." She was sure that everyone in the office had been gossiping about their fight, and just as she hoped, the employee had easily swallowed her story.

Kat had not locked the drawer. Alicia had been surprised at the ease by which she was able to scoop up the diary, place it in her purse, and walk out of the office. She would not have given the journal a second thought had Kat not died. That was the irony of the situation.

With the information Alicia had gleaned from the diary, she'd seen a way to exit her marriage with financial security, and a way to help Jack. She'd purchased a burner phone, asked Jack to find a way to set up a special account and sent Eliot those anonymous text messages. A million dollars was a lot to demand, and truth be told, she wasn't sure he would have acquiesced. *Go big or go home*, she thought. She'd made plans to split the money evenly with Jack.

"Any regrets?" Jack asked, pulling her into the present.

She cocked her head to one side, contemplating the question. "No. If there were any other way..." She trailed off. Flushed with Eliot's cash and a great job offer from Richard, she now had the means to a new beginning that had initially petrified her. But no more. She was done with fear. "I played the cards I was dealt, Jack. Even though it terrified me at the time. I think it turned out okay."

"Do you think you'll ever forgive him? Eliot, I mean."

"Only time will tell."

"We'll miss you at Howell House. Come see us any time."

"Are you giving me the boot?" She laughed.

"Come on, Alicia. You're moving on, and I'm happy for you. With a new job, school, your daughters, you'll have plenty to keep you busy. But we'll always have a volunteer spot for you if you ever find time in your schedule."

"Of course I will. You've been a great friend to me. Maybe we can meet up for coffee sometimes, catch up. I'm not leaving the state any time soon."

"You'll stay in the house in Weston?"

"Until Lily graduates high school. Then I'll sell it and find something smaller, closer to Boston."

She stood and so did Jack.

"I'm taking some time off once I get the business of the

practice squared away," he said. "Leanne invited me to go to Hawaii with her, Dan, and the kids. I can't wait to spend time with my grandkids."

"I'm sure they'll love it. They don't get to see their grandpa enough. See you around?"

"You sure will," he said, with a last wave before he left.

Alicia left the park. She had one last piece of important business to wrap up.

CHAPTER 59

WHEN ALICIA RETURNED home, the girls were still out. They'd been spending more time with friends than with family lately, which broke her heart, but she understood their need for space. She was still sorting out her own thoughts, so she couldn't imagine how the girls were still processing their lives turning upside down in the last few weeks.

She lit the fireplace in the family room, even though it was June. She used the poker to stoke the flames. She needed it nice and hot. She returned to the sofa and opened her bag. She pulled out Kat's diary.

Fifteen years. Alicia shook her head as she walked to the fireplace. For fifteen years her husband had been betraying her, lying to her, manipulating her. But she had fought back. It might have come too late, but it still counted. She had given Eliot a dose of his own medicine.

Terrified that Kat's diary entry could fall into the wrong hands, Eliot had wired the funds into the account Jack had set up. She had earned every penny. She would use those resources to reinvent herself and become the woman she was meant to be.

She tossed the diary into the fireplace and watched the flames consume the pages. As for Maxim being Eliot's son, the secret had died with Kat. Alicia had been overcome with a fresh avalanche of grief and anger when she read that tidbit. Kat had given Eliot what Alicia wouldn't. Kat hadn't aborted his son like Alicia had. And Kat was about to give him another child, until a tragic accident claimed her life. Alicia never allowed herself to think about how things might have played out if Kat was still alive. Alicia had enough pain and disillusionment to last several lifetimes.

She, too, would take the secret of Maxim's paternity to the grave. Along with the fact that she, Alicia, had leaked the story of Eliot and Kat's affair to the media. She wanted Eliot to know what it felt like to be vulnerable, backed into a corner. For the first time in her life, she had the power.

"What are you doing?"

She whirled around and came face-to-face with a frowning Eliot. She swallowed, calmed herself and said, "Just burning some trash."

He came closer and peeked over the fireplace. "Is that a notebook?"

"It's an old journal I used to keep. All the hopes and dreams I had written down have turned to dust. No point in keeping it around as a reminder of my failures."

"I don't remember you ever having a diary."

"We all have our secrets, Eliot. You of all people should know that."

Eliot said nothing. She changed the subject. "Marston doesn't want a fuss over her graduation. She's headed to Veliane's house after the ceremony."

"She's avoiding me, you mean."

Alicia rolled her eyes. Something she would never have considered doing in the past. "What do you expect? She's hurting."

"Right. Because I'm the bad guy."

"It's not that simple, Eliot. The girls used to admire and respect Kat. They considered her an honorary aunt. All the while, she was scheming to take their father from them, destroy their family. Marston already doesn't trust men because of how Brandon treated her."

She stopped to catch her breath, to stop the tears from falling. "Now, the man she loves most in the world betrayed her, too. Our daughters, no matter how much they claim to be okay, are not. They will carry this pain with them for the rest of their lives."

Eliot leaned on the mantle. After a long, calming breath, he said, "I spoke to an attorney today. I will grant you the divorce. I won't contest it."

"Thank you. You know it's for the best."

"You don't have to worry. I will take care of our daughters. And you get the house, as you requested."

"Good."

She turned to leave the room but didn't get far.

Eliot said, "Are you sure you won't change your mind, give me a shot at redemption? We don't have to stay in this town, in this state. I can be a lawyer anywhere, maybe open my own practice. Please, Alicia, won't you reconsider?"

She turned around. "You know I can't." It was time to confess that she now fully understood the gravity of his betrayal. "Fifteen years, that's how long you were with her—almost the entire length of our marriage. I never expected to spend most of my married life sharing my husband with another woman. That's not what I signed up for. That's not what you promised."

Her body shook with the grief of it. She stared blindly at the fireplace and the burning diary, wiping away errant tears. He took a seat on the sofa and stared into space.

"I think it's best if you move out as soon as possible," she said.

He nodded. His voice cracked when he said, "This is not the ending I envisioned for us."

"Think of it as a new beginning, a new chapter for us both."

"How did you find out the truth..." His voice trailed off.

"It's a moot point. She mattered to you more than our family. That much I know."

"That's not true."

"Remember what you said to me when you proposed? That you couldn't let me go?"

"Yeah."

"That was the first time you ever lied to me. It was she you couldn't let go of. From the moment you met her, she became your obsession."

Her heart stuttered, and there was a feeling of free-falling with nowhere to land.

"I didn't have much to offer you when we got married. But I loved you fiercely, without condition. You had my loyalty, and it still wasn't enough. I hope you find what you're searching for, Eliot. I'm sorry that I denied you the son you always wanted but thank you for our beautiful daughters. Goodnight, Eliot."

With that, she exited the room without looking back.

CHAPTER 60

Lily – How it Really Happened

EVERYBODY GOT IT wrong. The police, my parents, the media. The only thing they were right about was the cause: it *was* a tragic accident.

How do I know? I was there.

It ate away at me, hiding the truth. All I wanted was to talk to her, beg her not to take Dad from us, not to break up our family. It didn't work. She destroyed it. And she got away with it. Dying didn't count.

We said our goodbyes to our father last night. His bags were packed, waiting by the door like the ending from some sappy family drama. Marston and I cried all night, and so did Mom, even though she was pretending to be strong. I heard her in the guest bathroom, just wailing, like some wounded animal on its last breath.

But I couldn't let it end like this. I had to confess before Dad walked out of our lives. This was all his fault. He didn't get to walk away without having to deal with the final blow. Face the consequences of his actions. Finally, my parents and my sister would learn the truth of how it really happened, every last detail. Because I will never forget as long as I live.

We all gathered in the family room, Dad, who would be leaving in a few short minutes, had been sobbing again, his eyes red and puffy. He wouldn't look at us.

I gathered everyone's attention. They were going to need to be sitting down for this. "Since this is the last time we'll be together under the same roof as a family, I have something important to say."

"What's going on, Lily?" Mom asked. She looked unnerved. She'd gone through so much already. I wish I could spare her what came next.

I wasn't sure where to begin, so I started with the most obvious thing. "It's about the day Kat died."

Everyone looked at each other, confused. I had practiced in front of my bedroom mirror exactly what I was going to say, but now, it felt like I was about to wreck our family all over again.

"What about the day Kat died?" Mom asked.

"I was there."

They were silent for a moment before Dad whispered, "What?"

I was sandwiched between our parents on the sofa. Marston stood. She does that when she is afraid of bad news. It helps her keep it together. I took a deep, long, I'm-not-scared breath and just told it like it was.

"It all started when Colby told me that Dad was cheating on Mom. I thought she was just being mean to say something like that. I cursed her out. But then she showed me the pictures."

"What pictures?" Marston asked.

I took another deep breath and delved in. "Colby and her family were attending her cousin's wedding at the Chanler Cliff Walk Hotel in Newport, Rhode Island, back in April. Colby spotted Kat in the lobby. A hotel employee passed by and called her Mrs. Gray, like she was a regular guest and that was her name."

"I need to sit down." Marston took a seat across from us.

Mom and Dad sat stone-faced. I wasn't sure they wanted me to continue. Then Marston said I should.

"Colby took photos of Dad and Kat all over each other. They were kissing, making out. Heavy stuff. It was obvious they were sleeping together."

Marston breathed hard and fast. "Do you want me to get you some water?" I asked her.

"No. I'm fine," she said. "Are you saying that there are photos floating around of our father getting it on with Kat?"

Marston was apparently the adult in the room because our parents still hadn't said anything. Dad wouldn't look at me or Mom. Mom was trying to catch her breath so she wouldn't break down sobbing.

"I deleted them. So did Colby."

"Okay. That's good. What does it have to do with Kat's death, then?"

"I started paying attention to how she acted around us. I didn't trust her anymore."

"I still don't see what this has to do with her death," Marston said.

"I'm getting to it. This isn't easy for me, okay?"

"Sorry," she mumbled.

I glared at Dad, but he just looked down at his feet, unable to look me in the face.

Mom looked frail, like she was about to fall off the sofa and just pass out.

"I can only do this once," I said. "I don't ever want to go back to this day ever again, so I need all of you to just listen, okay? Don't interrupt me. Please."

Marston nodded. Mom and Dad remained in their zombie-like states.

I cleared my throat. "Maxim confirmed what Colby had seen, so I decided to confront Kat—I thought an honest conversation would convince her to back off."

I swallowed. "As you know, she died the Tuesday after Memorial Day. I took the trail behind the conservation land, so no one would see me, and went around the back of the house. The door was open, and she gestured for me to come in."

I closed my eyes as I recounted the events of that awful day. They unfolded in my mind in real time as if I was watching a movie starring me and Kat.

"What's up, Lily?" Kat said as I walked into the kitchen.

She had a glass of wine in hand. The bottle was on the center island. It was only a few minutes after ten in the morning, but she kept swaying back and forth, like she was already drunk.

"Stop seeing my dad," I blurted out.

She smiled and said, "I always knew you were a clever girl. And a Daddy's girl, too."

I knew she was trying to confuse me by changing the subject. "How could you do that to our family, to my mom? You're her best friend. Her also-married best friend. What did she ever do to you to deserve to be stabbed in the back?"

She laughed and said, "Oh Lily, you'll be a woman soon

enough, and then you'll understand. Your mother is too weak for a man like your dad. We didn't mean to fall in love; we just did."

"I saw how you reacted to the photos from my parents' trip to France. You were pissed, like Dad belonged to you. Well, he doesn't, Kat!"

"Is that so, little girl?" She took a sip of her wine and stumbled against the counter. "Run along and tell your mommy that your daddy and I are together, and there's nothing she can do about it."

Kat took another sip from her wine glass and then laughed out loud again. It sounded like a witch's cackle in one of those kids' films.

"Wait, but you won't tell her, will you, Lily? Because you're a loyal daughter who would do anything to protect your fragile mommy. You wouldn't break her heart now, would you?"

"If you don't stop seeing my dad, I will show the photos of the two of you at the Chanler Cliff to Richard.

"Go ahead," she said in a vicious voice. "You'll be doing me a big favor. Hurry up. The sooner you show Richard the pics, the sooner your father and I can be together." She drained the glass of wine, reached for the bottle, and poured another.

I got more desperate by the minute. I had to get through to her, make her understand she was wrong. I didn't want to cry in front of her, but it hurt, the things she was saying about my parents. I covered my ears with my hand so I couldn't hear her anymore, but it was no use.

"Get over it, Lily," she said loudly. "Your parent's marriage is over. Sometimes marriages don't work out. Your mother is weak and stupid. Your father is way out of her league, always has been. And now, finally, he's going to be with someone better suited for him. But don't worry, you and Marston are welcome to visit us any time you want."

I dropped my hands and glared at her. I saw a side of her I had never seen before, and it scared me, but I couldn't just stand there and let her talk about my mother like that.

"You are mean and vindictive," I cried. "My mom is not weak or stupid. She's a good, decent human being; something you obviously know nothing about."

Kat sneered. "Your mother is just some ghetto trash who got lucky and married up."

"Take it back!" I took desperate steps toward her. She backed up slightly, almost stumbling. "Take it back!" My hands clenched into fists.

She just smiled at me instead, and I swear she had fangs.

"I mean it Kat, take it back."

She drained the second glass of wine. "Or else what, little girl?"

I got up in her face. "You better take it back right now."

She laughed and kept on laughing, mocking me. Mocking Mom. She wouldn't stop. "What are you going to do, little Lily? Your mother is ugly and stupid. She doesn't deserve your father. He's too good for her..."

As the insults kept coming, something deep inside me shifted. I didn't feel like myself. It was as if a raging tiger that had been sleeping inside me for a long time suddenly woke up. I edged even closer to her, got right up in her face. She kept backing up, as though she wanted to get away from me. I kept begging her to take it all back. She refused.

Then it happened, as if in slow motion but it only took seconds. I pushed her. She was wearing one of those five-inch stiletto-heel sandals she likes, you know, the ones with the ankle straps and open toe. She was drunk and couldn't balance herself in time. She fell backward, landing with a thud on the marble floor.

I heard the crack of bone on stone. I stood there paralyzed with shock even as my whole body shivered.

I opened my eyes as I heard a loud gasp.

Marston was sitting with her hand clasped over her mouth.

Mom jerked upright.

Dad's stiff body was glued to the sofa. He looked like he'd been frozen in time.

My family stared at me in stone-faced silence.

I hid my face in my hands in shame. I felt like my chest had split wide open. I hadn't meant for any of it to happen. But a woman was dead, and she was never coming back, all because of me.

Mom reached for my hand and gave it a comforting squeeze. I could tell she didn't have the strength to speak just yet, but I could feel the love she couldn't express in words.

Marston leaned over, clutching her mid-section as if she was about to throw up. "What happened next?"

Through hiccups and tears, I got the rest of the story out. "I went over to see if she was okay. She wasn't moving, but she tried to talk. I told her I would call for help; she just needed to hold on. But I couldn't. I didn't have my phone with me.

"Then I heard someone coming down the stairs. I panicked and left the way I came in. I ran all the way back to school. She was alive when I left. I swear."

Dad suddenly snapped to attention like a robot coming to life. "Did anybody see you on the way back to school? Did anyone ask where you'd been?"

"No."

"Good."

I wiped my face with my hands and looked at both of my parents, desperate for answers.

Mom finally spoke, her expression grave. "Never repeat what you just told us to another living soul. Ever. Do you understand? We'll find a way to help you deal with the trauma, but no one can ever know."

I nodded.

"Katalina died tragically," Dad said. "Her blood alcohol level was four times the legal limit. She lost her balance and fell. The fall proved fatal. The Weston police thoroughly investigated the case. Those are their official findings. Case closed." He shot each of us one of his stern, lawyerly looks.

His eyes zeroed in on me, and his voice cracked as he spoke. "I'm so sorry, Lily. I never intended for any of this to happen to our family. You should never have been placed in the position that you felt you had to go out and fight for your mother, your family. I hope that you will find it in your heart to forgive me, one day."

Before I could respond, he added, "This is our last stance as a family unit, so before we go our separate ways, I need us all to make a solemn promise to be forever silent on the truth surrounding the death of Katalina Torres DeLuca."

We all nodded in solidarity.

EPILOGUE

SEVEN YEARS LATER

OVER FOUR-HUNDRED GUESTS gathered in the opulent grand ballroom of the Plaza Hotel in New York City for the reception. As mother of the bride, Alicia had a front row seat to the festivities. She smiled, laughed, and joked effortlessly, as she made her way to the family seating. She radiated joy from the inside out, and others noticed as she received many admiring glances and well wishes from everyone she passed.

It wasn't because at almost fifty years old she looked incredible in a sapphire-blue evening gown with a belted waist and halter design, a bold choice for her. Nor was it her position as executive director of a well-known non-profit organization. Or that her girls were now happy, thriving adults.

The answer was much simpler. She, Alicia Gray—mother, ex-wife, executive, survivor, soon-to-be grandmother—was finally at peace.

Eliot had spared no expense for his daughter's wedding

to Peter Marks, her literary agent. The success of Marston's psychological thriller, *The Accidental Liars*, the novel she started writing before everything fell apart seven years ago, was published after she graduated from Hamilton College. It had become a global phenomenon, selling over fifteen million copies, and had dominated every bestseller list. Film rights were snapped up right away with the film company commissioning her to write the screenplay.

Lily approached, looking lovely in a lavender Maid of Honor gown and flowers in her hair. The wedding planner had practically imported an entire island's worth of flowers for the ceremony and reception.

"What's going on with you and Dad?" Lily asked, sidling up next to her mother.

"What do you mean?"

"Marston and I caught you two flirting. Dad was all over you. You giggled like a teenager and laughed at his lame jokes."

"Both you and your sister have wild imaginations. Your father and I were being friendly, not flirting. We're in a good place now, after the pain and sorrow of the past. Today is a big day for us. We're gaining a son-in-law and soon a grandbaby."

"Sure, Mom. Whatever you say. That's why Dad was practically drooling when you walked into the church for the ceremony, and why you both showed up without dates. Does he know Marston is pregnant?"

"I haven't told him, yet. I think it's best if he hears it from her."

After the demise of their marriage and their life together, she and Eliot didn't speak for years. It was too painful. He'd moved to DC to work as a lobbyist, then eventually returned to his hometown of Atlanta to take over the sports agency his father had founded. He now represented some of the biggest athletes on the planet.

Alicia had focused on her job with York Capital Investments. She'd worked during the day and had attended classes at night and online until she'd earned her bachelor's. After that, she'd quit her job and enrolled as a full-time graduate student at Northeastern University. She'd earned that master's degree in public administration like she always talked about. Pursuing her dreams and making sure her daughters were happy had kept her busy.

"Have you seen Maxim?" Lily asked. "Marston invited him. He said he'd be here."

"No, I haven't seen him. Is everything all right?"

"Yes, why wouldn't it be?"

"You're fidgeting, all nervous like it's important to you that he's here."

Her daughter looked her square in the eyes and said, "It is important. To Marston and me."

Alicia blinked rapidly. "Oh. I didn't know you guys were still close."

"We kept in touch. He's doing great. He'll be a senior at UCLA this fall."

"Glad to hear he's doing well." She meant it. That boy had been through a lot in his young life.

Lily inched in closer. "Mom, it's okay. I won't date him or anything."

"Oh, don't be silly." She dismissed her daughter with a wave and a smile. Hopefully she'd convinced her. "I wasn't thinking about that."

"Yes, you were," Lily whispered.

Alicia tried to put on her bravest face. But if the girls were ever to find out...

"Marston and I know Maxim is our brother, Mom."

She let out a quick, high-pitched laugh. The ballroom was air-conditioned, yet the air failed to cool her warm, tingling skin. She lowered her head and whispered back to Lily, "Where did you get that idea from?"

"The fire didn't burn all the pages of Kat's diary. Marston found a few scraps in the fireplace. There wasn't much, but enough for us to take a guess. Then Maxim called me three years ago."

"What did he say?"

"He was going through the last of his mother's documents for some reason. I guess it took him that long to gather the courage to do it. You know he still has guilt about Kat. When she died, they weren't on the best of terms." Lily cast a glance at the ballroom entrance, as if scanning for Maxim. "Anyway, he came across the results of a DNA test. He said he asked Richard if he'd known all along. Richard said he suspected Maxim wasn't his biological son, but he didn't have any proof."

They both fell silent as Marston and Peter took to the dance floor for a romantic spin to Etta James' "At Last".

Guests mingled, laughed, drank champagne. Eliot's sister Summer, who was instrumental in Marston landing Peter as her agent, wiped wedding cake from her son's mouth and hands. Eliot's parents, now in their seventies, joined Marston and Peter on the dance floor. Rina and David Stark waved from their table. Alicia's friendship with Rina had grown to a tight bond since the tragedy.

"Hi, Lily. Mrs. Gray. I mean, Alicia."

They both whipped their heads around to see Maxim standing before them, rubbing his palms together with a lopsided, nervous grin tugging at his mouth.

"You made it." Lily stood up and hugged him.

"Of course, I wouldn't miss it."

"It's good to see you, Maxim." Alicia stood and looked at the boy—now very much a man—up and down. "Look at you, all grown up. And as handsome as ever. Women must fall at your feet."

He smiled, big and wide.

Her heart stopped for a moment. His smile was Eliot's, who would have been only a few years older than Maxim, who was dressed in a tailored suit, when she and Eliot first met. She saw Kat in him, too.

"Mom, are you okay?" Lily asked.

She sniffled. "Sure. I'm good. This is the best day. Why wouldn't I be fine? Maxim, please sit with us."

Marston glided over, the epitome of the stunning bride in a Monique Lhuillier Duchess Satin Ball gown and a tiara-adorned floor-length wedding veil. She hugged Maxim and expressed how happy she was to see him. She sat next to him, with Lily on the opposite side.

The Gray siblings. It was a lot to take in.

Now that Maxim, Richard, and her daughters knew the truth, it was only a matter of time before Eliot found out. But was it her place to tell him?

Alicia was a different woman from the one who'd vowed to take the secret of Maxim's paternity to her grave. Back then, she'd wanted to hurt Eliot, a parting shot for cheating on her for fifteen years and for destroying their family. And yet, what purpose would hiding the truth serve now?

"When's your next book coming out?" Maxim asked Marston.

"Next year. My publisher has me on a tight deadline. They want to capitalize on the marketing when the movie for *Accidental Liars* comes out."

"You are one busy lady. I told my friends that I know you. That we grew up on the same street. They don't believe me."

"We can remedy that," Marston said. "Let's take a selfie with me, you, and Lily."

And so they did.

The three siblings chatted with familiarity and warmth. They talked about Lily's progress at NYU School of Law and her plans for after she passed the bar exam, Maxim's hopes for a career in architecture, and a variety of other topics. All conversation ceased, however, when Eliot appeared.

Nervous tension replaced the easy, free-flowing banter of a few moments ago.

"Hello, Maxim," he said.

They exchanged an awkward handshake, before Maxim averted his gaze, staring at the tall centerpiece bouquet flanked by candlelight.

Marston said, "Um, there are some people I'd like Maxim to meet. Come with me, Maxim. Catch you guys later."

She pulled her brother by the arm, and they disappeared into the crowd.

Lily said, "Yeah, well, there are a lot of hot guys at this reception. One of them was checking me out earlier, so I need to investigate. Haven't had time to date with all this studying." She followed her siblings in the hurried march away from the table.

"Way to clear a room, Eliot," Alicia joked, after the kids left.

"What was that all about?" He watched them disappear into the crowd of guests before sitting down next to her.

"It's about the past. And the future."

"Care to enlighten me?"

At fifty-three, he still looked like the boy she'd married, sans the sprinkling of gray hair. She inhaled the scent of him and prayed he couldn't detect her quickening breath or signs of her light-headedness. Even after all these years, she still reacted to him. If she focused on the issue at hand, then she wouldn't embarrass herself.

"Look, this is not easy, so I'm just going to come out and say it. Maxim is not Richard's son. He's yours."

He opened his mouth, but nothing came out. He turned away briefly—to gather his thoughts, she supposed—before facing her again with a, "What?"

"Years ago, when he was a kid, Kat ran a DNA test on Maxim. He found the documented results when he went through her things. He's your son."

He cast a glance across the ballroom toward Maxim, Marston, and Peter, who were deep in conversation. When he returned his gaze to the table, his eyes glistened.

She reached out and stroked his arm until he gained control of himself.

"Do you think he'll hate me?"

"No, I don't think so. He adores Lily and Marston. Just remember he's an adult, not a child. Richard raised him. That's his dad. But it doesn't mean the two of you can't build your own unique relationship. If that's what you both want."

"I'd like that. Perhaps you can help me out, put in a kind word?"

"You want me to be your reference?"

"Ha, if you put it like that. Yes, please. Maxim always liked you."

"Let me think about it."

"That's all I ask." He picked up a table decoration and turned it over in his hands. "I'm proud of you, you know."

"What for?"

"The woman you've become."

"And what woman would that be?"

He looked up at her and smiled. "Confident. Assertive. An exceptional leader. Sexy."

"I have you to thank for that," she admitted.

"How so?"

She carefully considered her response. Then she said, "You forced me to evolve, Eliot. I had no idea what I was capable of until you shattered our life together. Had you not done so, I wouldn't be the woman sitting before you now. A woman you admire."

With his mouth set in a grim line, he said, "I had the rarest of diamonds and didn't know it. I'll always regret that I treated you like glass, Alicia."

"As you should. But remember, diamonds are forever, eternally strong and brilliant."

DON'T MISS THESE GRIPPING READS FROM GLEDÉ BROWNE KABONGO

AWARD-WINNING FEARLESS SERIES

STANDALONES
CONSPIRACY OF SILENCE

SWAN DECEPTION

AVAILABLE IN AUDIO

ABOUT THE AUTHOR

Gledé Browne Kabongo writes gripping, unputdownable psychological thrillers—unflinching tales of deception, secrecy, danger and family. She is the Eric Hoffer, Next Generation Indie and IPPY Award-winning author of the Fearless Series, *Our Wicked Lies, Swan Deception,* and *Conspiracy of Silence.* Her novel *Winds of Fear* was voted one of 24 Books to Read During the Coronavirus pandemic by *Rhode Island Monthly Magazine.*

Gledé holds a master's degree in communications, and has spoken at multiple industry events including the Boston Book Festival. She lives outside Boston with her husband and two sons.

CONNECT ONLINE

🌐 www.gledekabongo.com

✉ glede@gledekabongo.com

f gledekabongoauthor

🐦 twitter.com/gkabongo

📷 @authorgledekabongo

CPSIA information can be obtained
at www.ICGtesting.com
Printed in the USA
LVHW091736210321
682028LV00036B/963